ANY GIVEN DOOMSDAY

"Handeland launches the intriguing Phoenix Chronicles urban fantasy series with a strong story . . . the demons' evil plans and vividly described handiwork create immense suspense for the final battle."
—*Publishers Weekly*

"Fascinating. A fast-paced thriller that will have readers looking for book two."   —Kelley Armstrong

"A fresh, fascinating, gripping tale that hits urban fantasy dead-on. Don't miss this one."   —L.L. Foster

"Sexy, dangerous, and a hot-as-hell page-turner! Lori Handeland world-builds with authority."
—L. A. Banks

"Handeland is back with a striking new series, narrated by a heroine thrown headfirst into a fairly apocalyptic scenario . . . With sex and power intertwined, Handeland looks to have another winner of a series on her hands!"
—*Romantic Times BOOKreviews*

APOCALYPSE HAPPENS

Lori Handeland

St. Martin's Paperbacks

This is a work of fiction. All of the characters, organizations, and events portrayed in this novel are either products of the author's imagination or are used fictitiously.

APOCALYPSE HAPPENS

Copyright © 2009 by Lori Handeland.
Excerpt from *Chaos Bites* copyright © 2009 by Lori Handeland.

All rights reserved.

For information address St. Martin's Press, 175 Fifth Avenue, New York, NY 10010.

ISBN: 978-0-312-36602-5

Printed in the United States of America

St. Martin's Paperbacks edition / November 2009

St. Martin's Paperbacks are published by St. Martin's Press, 175 Fifth Avenue, New York, NY 10010.

10 9 8 7 6 5 4 3 2 1

CHAPTER 1

They are free.

Those words had whispered through my head only a few weeks ago. Taken out of context, the phrase should be uplifting.

Freedom's good. Right?

Unless you're talking about demons.

The earth is full of them. They're called the Nephilim. They're the offspring of the fallen angels—or Grigori—and the daughters of men.

Yes, the angels really fell. Hard. Their story is a perfect illustration of why everyone should toe the proverbial line. Piss off God, wind up in Tartarus—a fiery pit in the lowest level of hell.

Word is God sent the Grigori to keep an eye on the humans. In the end, the angels were the ones who needed watching. So God banished them from the earth—bam, you're legend—but he left their progeny behind to test us. Eden was a memory. We'd proved we didn't deserve it. But I don't think we deserved the Nephilim either.

Fast-forward a million millennia. The prophecies of Revelation are bearing down on us like runaway horses. Perhaps four of them? No matter what the forces of good do to prevent the end of the world, nothing's working.

And that's where I come in.

Elizabeth Phoenix, Liz to my friends. They call me the leader of the light. I got dropped into the middle of this whole Doomsday mess, and I'm having a helluva time getting back out.

For reasons beyond mine or anyone else's comprehension, Tartarus opened; the Grigori flew free, and now all hell has broken loose. Literally.

"Dammit, Lizzy! Duck!"

I ducked. Razor-sharp claws swooshed through the air right where my face had been. Not only did I duck, but I rolled also. Good thing too, since seconds later something sliced into the ground right next to me.

I'd come to Los Angeles with Jimmy Sanducci, head demon killer and my second in command, to ferret out a nest of varcolacs. Eclipse demons. Kind of rare considering they hail from Romania, but I'd seen stranger things.

Sure, the smog in LA could be blamed for the dark splotches that kept appearing over the moon and the sun, which is what everyone around here believed. But I knew better.

The varcolac tugged on his arm, trying to free the needlelike appendages he used for fingers from the desert dust. Part human, part dragon, varcolacs are rumored to eat the sun and the moon, thus causing said eclipses. And if they ever succeed in actually devouring those celestial bodies, the end of the world is nigh. Since I've been trying to prevent that, I dragged Jimmy to LA and we started hunting.

Before the varcolac could use his other arm to kill me, Sanducci sliced through his neck. When you're dealing with Nephilim, head slicing usually worked. At the least, being without a head slowed down even the most determined demon.

Jimmy's dark gaze met mine. "Get up," he ordered, before turning away to dispatch more bad guys.

I tried not to let the chill in his eyes bother me. Sanducci would never allow anything to hurt me; he'd loved me once. Right now, however, love was no longer on the table, and I had no one to blame for that but myself.

I did a kip, from my back to my feet in one quick movement—the skills that had garnered me a state champion medal in high school gymnastics had been coming in very handy lately—then retrieved my own sword and went back to hacking.

Once Jimmy and I were in LA it hadn't taken us long to find the varcolacs in the desert. Most days they appeared human. They lived their lives; they blended in, only going dragon beneath an eclipse.

Which came first, the chicken or the egg? The dragon eating the moon or the moon going dark and bringing out the dragon? Hard to say.

What I did know was that as soon as the Grigori flew free, all the Nephilim stopped hiding. Their time had come. And things, for me and my kind, had become a bit dicey.

Previously, each demon killer had worked with a seer—someone who possessed a psychic gift to see past the Nephilim's human disguise to the demon that lay within.

I'd been a seer once myself, but things had changed.

Oh, I was still psychic—always had been. Since I was old enough to talk, maybe before, I could touch animate and inanimate objects and I'd know things— what people had done, where they'd gone, what they thought.

But later, when I'd become the leader of the light, I'd inherited the ability of the woman who'd raised me. As Ruthie Kane died in my arms, all her power transferred to me. I'd wound up not only psychometric, but suddenly I could channel too. Ruthie might be dead, but that didn't mean I couldn't hear her, talk to her, sometimes even see her. She became my conduit. Whenever a Nephilim was near, I heard about it in Ruthie's whisper on the wind, and when they were up to something major—they always were—I received a vision that told me all about it. At least until recently.

"Too many," Jimmy muttered.

We were covered in varcolac blood. We'd hacked up a dozen, but a dozen more had appeared. We needed help, but there wasn't any to spare.

The federation—that group of demon killers, or DKs, and seers who'd been charged with fighting this supernatural war—had been seriously depleted after Ruthie's death, and we couldn't just pick up a few new demon killers at the demon-killer superstore. They had to be trained. New seers had to be discovered. I hadn't had time to do much recruiting, even before the whole Tartarus-opening, Grigori-escaping incident. And now . . .

Now I wasn't going to have time to do much but ride the runaway train to Armageddon. Basically, we were fucked. But that didn't mean we were going to quit. Besides, I had a secret weapon. What I liked to call a vampire in a box.

I lifted my arm, traced my fingers along the magic jeweled dog collar that circled my neck. As long as I wore the thing, I was me. But if I took it off—

"No, Lizzy."

I glanced at Jimmy. He'd seen me fingering the necklace. Even if he didn't know me better than just about anyone, it didn't take a genius to figure out what I'd been contemplating.

One of the varcolacs charged, dragon wings flapping, talons outstretched. Jimmy hacked off his head with only a token glance in that direction. Jimmy was good. I still needed to put a bit more effort into killing things.

I let go of the collar, faced the next varcolac with both hands around my sword and did what needed to be done. I lost track of Jimmy for a while. The damn demons seemed to be multiplying. For every one we killed, two more came out of the darkness. Their wings flickered against the silvery light of the gibbous moon, reminding me of the night the Grigori had flown free, their spirits darkening what had then been a perfectly round orb.

Jimmy cried out, the sound making my heart jolt, my head turn. One of the varcolacs had speared him through the shoulder with a talon, lifting him clear off the ground. Blood dripped into the sand, turning the moon-pale grains black. Jimmy's sword lay at his feet.

There appeared to be an army of dragon men behind them. Their scaly wings flapped in syncopation, filling the sky with a morbid ticktock. Dragon heads and arms, human legs and torsos that sprouted dragon's wings.

"Surrender, seer." The varcolac snorted fire from his nose. Jimmy hissed when the flames started his pants on fire.

"No." I lopped off the nearest varcolac head, which hit the ground with a dull thud, rolled a few feet and disintegrated into ashes along with the still-upright body. If you killed a Nephilim correctly, cleanups weren't any problem at all.

"You can't win," the varcolac said. "We are legion."

He was probably right, but giving up . . .

Just wasn't my style.

CHAPTER 2

"Nice job," Jimmy muttered.

We were tied with golden chains, staked into the desert ground, naked. Man, I hated when that happened.

"This is my fault?"

I turned my head. The moon sparkled in his dark eyes, sparked off his hair, threading the black strands with silver. The sheen glistened off the supple, bronzed skin of his chest. Sanducci had always been too damn pretty for anyone's good. Especially mine.

"Had to come to LA," he continued. "Had to find out what was creeping around in the desert."

"Isn't that what we do?"

He sighed. "Yeah. But I don't think it's going to go as well as it used to."

He was right. Where before the federation had been stemming the demon tide, the tide had become a flood, and the dam had a shitload of holes.

"You okay?" I asked.

"Does it look like I'm okay?"

Jimmy and I had always had a volatile relationship. Hell, the first time I'd met him he'd put a snake in my bed; then I'd loosened his teeth. We were twelve.

At seventeen he'd relieved me of my virginity; a year later he'd broken my heart. Same old tune, heard a thousand times before.

Except Jimmy and I weren't like a thousand other couples. I was psychic and Jimmy—

Jimmy was a dhampir.

My gaze lowered from his face to his gored shoulder, which wasn't gored anymore. The gaping wound had almost healed.

Most demon killers were breeds—offspring of a Nephilim and a human. With less demon to contend with, they could choose to fight for the forces of good, and because they had demon blood, breeds had supernatural powers. To fight demons of biblical proportions, they needed them.

Jimmy was the son of a vampire and a woman. He was very good at finding and killing bloodsuckers of any type. As a dhampir, Jimmy had mythical strength and speed; he could heal just about anything—although wounds made with a weapon of pure gold took longer, and they stung like a bitch.

My gaze went to the approaching cadre of varcolacs. Each of them now carried a weapon that glinted golden beneath the moon. Hell.

"What do you want to know?" I asked.

"Lizzy," Jimmy snapped. He was the only one who called me that, the only one who dared.

"Doesn't cost anything to ask," I said, but I was just stalling. I wasn't going to tell them jack. Jimmy wouldn't either.

Just because he could heal didn't mean he couldn't hurt. Though I'd spent the past seven years hating Sanducci's guts, lulled myself to sleep many a long, lonely night imagining ways to make him cry and scream, beg and bleed, times had changed. Now I just wanted him to forgive me, but I didn't think he was going to.

"Sanducci and Phoenix, what a prize we have won."

The varcolacs had returned to their human forms.

I'm sure it was difficult to perform torture with claws where your fingers should be.

"You know killing us won't change anything," I said.

"Killing you will change everything, seer. You are the leader of the light. If you die without passing on your power, all that power is lost."

Well, there was that. What they didn't know was that I was even harder to kill than Jimmy.

The head varcolac—a guy who resembled some minor pretty-boy actor on a stupid show with numbers for a title—crouched at my side. Another one— big guy, wide shoulders and teeth that reminded me a lot of the Governator before he'd had them fixed— hovered over Jimmy. They both carried sharp, golden weapons, and they appeared as if they knew what to do with them.

But really, how hard was it? Pointy end goes into flesh, rip and tear. The only difficulty was if hurting someone bothered you. These were demons. It didn't.

"I'm going to give you one chance, seer. You answer my question, I will kill you . . ." He took the flat of the blade and ran it over my hip. Wherever it touched, I burned. "Quickly."

In the depths of his eyes, yellow flames flickered. He wasn't going to kill me quickly no matter what he promised. I wasn't capable of dying quickly anyway.

The point of the knife, which was big enough to have been fashioned by Bowie himself, pressed to the throbbing vein in my neck. "Where is the key?"

"To what?"

He nicked my skin, and blood trickled. "What do you think, fool? To your house? Your car? Your heart?" His eyes twinkled yellow again as he lowered the knife.

"Ah, your heart. I always wanted to see what one looked like."

He sliced me across the left breast. The blade grated along bone, and I gritted my teeth to keep from reacting to both the pain and that annoying noise. Wouldn't do any good.

"She doesn't know anything about the key," Jimmy said.

I blinked. That sounded like *he* did.

The varcolacs exchanged glances. Pretty Boy lifted his chin, a signal to the other, and Jimmy grunted. I caught the scent of fresh blood.

"Leave him alone."

The varcolac at my side snorted. "I don't take orders from you."

"Who do you take orders from?"

A few weeks back I'd torn their leader limb from limb, literally, so the forces of darkness should be in chaos. That they weren't was more disturbing than I wanted to admit. Because if hell had flown open and all the demonic fallen angels were now free, that meant the one who'd instigated the rebellion in the first place was free too. And we all know who that is.

"Samyaza," I said. Another name for Satan. There were quite a few of them. "Beelzebub is pulling your strings?"

His eyes flared. He was pissed about something. But what?

I shifted. I was tied pretty tightly, and any movement caused the golden chains to scrape my skin. The burn was excruciating, but I managed to brush my finger against his knee, and suddenly I understood. "Whoever has the key can command the demons. And you want it to be you."

Dissension in the ranks. Gotta love it.

The varcolac shrugged. "I don't take orders well."

Most Nephilim didn't. Which made me wonder how Satan planned to rule this rock. Simple answer— he was going to need the key too.

What I'm referring to is the *Key of Solomon*, a grimoire or book of spells, supposedly composed by King Solomon. In it are incantations used to summon, release and command demons—for starters. Over the years several translations had been made, but none of them were complete. What we were looking for was the original copy, which held everything.

Unfortunately, no one knew where that was. The last person to see it had been a rabbi by the name of Turnblat. Wild dogs—code for shape-shifters—had killed him, and the key hadn't been found in his personal effects.

I'd figured the Nephilim had it. How else had the damn demons flown free? But if they were asking *us* where it was . . . Well, that threw things into a whole new light.

"Where is the key?" the varcolac demanded again.

"Seriously, pal, we thought you had it."

"Lizzy!"

My name ended in a curse as the other varcolac cut Jimmy again. He'd heal; hell, so would I, although I kinda hoped they wouldn't notice. So far the Nephilim didn't know all the things I could do, and I'd like to keep it that way.

"Why would we have it?" the varcolac asked.

"You killed Rabbi Turnblat."

He grinned. "Not me personally."

"Then you took the key." He shook his head; I managed to shrug without moving my chains. "Someone did. You'd better start slapping around the minions."

For an instant, doubt flickered along with the yellow flames in the varcolac's eyes; then he scowled. "We know you have it. The key is with the Phoenix. That is what the rabbi said."

I had a feeling the rabbi would have said just about anything when confronted with whatever Nephilim had been sent to kill him, maybe even the truth, but—

"I don't have it. Swear to God."

The varcolac hissed, and I rolled my eyes. The name of God didn't hurt them. If it did I'd be singing hymns 24–7.

"You will tell us. I will make you." He lifted the golden knife and tried to slice my neck, but the dog collar prevented it. With a sound of annoyance, he reached for the latch.

"I wouldn't do that if I were you," I murmured.

He ignored me.

"Don't!" Jimmy shouted. "She needs to have that collar on. Shit!"

I shifted my gaze. The muscle-bound varcolac had begun to hack at Jimmy in earnest. "Knock that off!" I ordered.

The varcolac nearest to me grinned. "And who will make us?"

"I might."

He leaned closer, put his face right next to mine. "You are bound, seer. You will never be free again. You will tell us everything we want to know. You will watch us kill your 'minion.'" His lip pulled back in a snarl. "Then we will satisfy ourselves on your body—all of us, and we are legion. If you are still in one piece, and this I doubt, then we will make you beg to die." He licked my cheek, and his breath smelled of rot. "Where is the key?"

"Fuck you."

He tried to nick my throat again—exactly what I was after. When his knife encountered my jeweled collar once more, he returned his attention to the clasp, fussed and fiddled, but eventually released it.

The breeze stilled. Jimmy murmured, "Uh-oh."

The change came over me like a flash flood, a forest fire, a tornado—natural but deadly. The collar kept my inner nature contained. Without it, I became the new and improved me.

Not really a problem when I was killing demons. The trouble came when it was time to put the vampire *back* into the box. There were very few beings on this earth that were capable of it, and right now one of them was chained to the ground.

When Jimmy said, "Uh-oh" the varcolac had glanced at him; now the demon glanced back and his eyes widened. Mine must be bright red.

He tried to scramble away. Before he could, I ate his nose. He wasn't going to need it anymore. Then I sank my fangs into his neck and drank. Nephilim blood tastes like candy, and the rush . . . pure sugar.

I tossed the varcolac aside with a flick of my head. He wasn't dead, but he wasn't moving either. I yanked my arms upward, my legs too. The stakes came out of the ground with a sifty, sandy shift, and I was free.

"Free." What a fantastic word.

The chains flapped about—striking me here and there, making me burn. I slid my fingers between the cuffs and skin, broke them off and tossed them aside. Sure, that stung a little, but it didn't last long enough to matter.

The varcolac leader wasn't dead yet, an easy fix. I picked him up and yanked his head free of the rest of him. He was ashes before the two halves hit the ground.

"Who's next?" I asked.

"You-you-you're a vampire," Jimmy's captor stuttered.

"What was your first clue?"

I breathed in, relishing the fear and uncertainty. When I was like this colors were brighter, smells so much smellier, sounds reached me from miles away as if they were right next to me. I could hear blood coursing through veins, the increase in the swish-swash signaling terror. Anticipating the flavor, I licked my lips.

I was so strong I could do anything. Kill anyone. I had no conscience, no morality, not a worry in this world or any other.

"I-I-I'll kill him." The varcolac had the knife to Jimmy's throat. I reached out and snatched the fool by his Adam's apple—in this form I was so fast my movements became a blur—and tore it out with one sharp yank. The blood washed over Jimmy like a warm spring rain.

"Sheesh, Lizzy."

I licked my fingers. "You're welcome."

As I turned away, what remained of the varcolac burst into ashes, the remnants sticking to Jimmy's glistening skin like feathers on tar.

I'll give the varcolacs credit. They didn't run. They came at me like an army.

But they didn't stand a chance.

CHAPTER 3

When the only things left alive were Jimmy and me, I lifted my glistening arms to the moon and shrieked my triumph. Then I looked around for something else to kill.

My gaze fell on Sanducci still chained to the ground. Though Jimmy had given me this power, that didn't matter to me when my demon was driving.

All those old wives' tales about vampires making other vampires . . . not entirely true. Vampires are Nephilim, but they were created from the mating of a Grigori and a human. You can't become one just by being bitten. You had to be born.

Unless you were me.

As far as I know, I'm the only sexual empath on the planet. In layman's terms, I absorb supernatural powers through sex. In other words, because Jimmy is a dhampir, I'm one too, and dhampirs become vampires by sharing blood with them.

Jimmy hadn't wanted to make me like him. He'd done everything to prevent it. He'd run away. He'd tried to hide. He'd even locked himself up in an enchanted Irish cottage, complete with a golden door and golden bars on the window. Didn't matter. I'd found him, and I'd seduced him.

Jimmy was strong. He kept his vampire nature contained. But once a month—beneath the full moon—it got free. And when it had, I'd been there waiting. Long before the sun rose, I was just like him.

Why had I done it? Because the only way to win this war was to be as ruthless as they were. The supernatural powers and extraordinary strength didn't hurt either.

I inched closer to Jimmy, who lay naked beneath the moon. He was so damn pretty. My tongue darted out to wet my lips, snagging on my fangs, which cut the tender flesh. I tasted my own blood and paused for just an instant to enjoy.

For a vampire, sex and violence, blood and lust, are all rolled together. It's hard to differentiate between them, and we don't really want to.

My body tingled from the adrenaline, from the change, from the food. My skin cool, the blood beneath coursed so hot. Every sway of the breeze lifted the hairs on my arms, my neck, creating a delicious shiver. My shadow fell over Sanducci like a thundercloud.

His gaze met mine. "No, Lizzy."

"Not Lizzy."

He winced. "I know."

I ran my hand over his perfect chest, his taut belly.

"Let me go," he said. "You need your collar back on."

"No."

His sigh, full of pain, drew me in. I wanted to drink his agony slowly like a fine, expensive wine.

"So sad," I whispered. "Broken inside."

Jimmy's mouth tightened; his eyes narrowed. "Not as broken as you think."

I lowered my body onto his. Naked hip to naked hip, breasts to chest, his penis hot against my belly. "I can fix that."

I kissed him. He might pretend to be human, but he wasn't. He never had been. The violence called to him. He couldn't deny its allure.

The thought of taking him on the blood-drenched ground, while he was tied, he was helpless, made me so aroused I writhed. In seconds, his penis was not only hot but also hard. He was unable to keep himself from kissing me back.

My hands glided over him. Down his arms to the manacles at his wrists, down his thighs to the restraints, then back up to the soft, tender flesh where his leg melded into his hip. I became fascinated with the skin there, the vein that blared blue beneath the silvery moon.

I licked it, and his breath caught. I gazed up his body. His face tense, torn, he wanted this, he wanted me, and then again he didn't.

My teeth grazed the vein, my tongue pressed against it; the blood pulsed beneath, and I couldn't resist. I drank from him.

He tasted both tart and sweet. His groan wasn't pain or fear but lust. I lifted my head.

"Not yet," I whispered, my breath brushing across him, making him shudder. "Wait for me." Then I licked his tip, tested it with my tongue, traced it with just a hint of fang until he cursed and pulled against the chains.

"Take them off. Let me—" His head thrashed. I found myself intrigued.

"Let you what?"

He gave one final jerk against his bonds, and the stakes jiggled, but they held. The scent of burning flesh permeated the air. It reminded me of . . . hell. Not that I'd been there, but I could relate.

"Let me touch those breasts. They've been in my mind for a decade."

I lifted my eyebrows. "I'm twenty-five."

"What do you think a fifteen-year-old boy has in his head? You've had those breasts since you were twelve, even though you did your best to hide them."

I'd been mortified to develop early. I'd worn loose clothes and hunched my shoulders. Not only because of my mortification, but also because I knew all too well that a girl in the foster-care system needed to slide through life unnoticed.

But I didn't want to think about the past now. Maybe never again. I was strong. Invincible. How did that song go?

"I am woman," I murmured.

"Not really," Jimmy said.

I gave his thigh a final lick—the wound had already healed—then straddled him, allowing his erection to slide exactly where I needed it to. "Tell me more of what you'll do if I release you."

His lips curved, though the smile never reached his eyes. "Grab those hips, pull you down, push myself up so deep you'll remember me for days."

"Mmm, and then?"

"Sink my fangs into your breast, drink from you as you come. The usual."

"Yesss." I took him in, rode him beneath the moon; he lasted a long, long time.

The chains rattled. "Let me go."

I was so close to an orgasm, I listened, sliding my palms down his legs, up his arms, snapping his restraints into pieces. Then I waited, breathless, for him to touch me. And he did.

His hands at my hips, he pulled me close; then he arched and filled me up. He rose from the sand, his lips took my breast as promised, and he suckled, the rasp of his teeth almost, but not quite, enough to send me over.

He put his hands around my throat, squeezed just a little. They were rough. I liked how they made me feel. Breathless, on the edge of life and death, blood in the air, on the ground, on me. It didn't get much better than this.

"Mmm." I let my head fall back, my eyes slide closed. "Harder."

He wouldn't kill me. I wasn't sure anyone could.

"No problem," Jimmy muttered, and in his voice I heard something disturbing.

My eyes snapped open just as the catch of my jeweled collar snapped closed. I let out one furious shriek at the moon, and then I was me again.

As always, once the vampire was back in the box, I cringed at what I'd said and done and been. My breath caught, a sound very like a sob, except I didn't cry, had learned long ago that crying did no one any good.

Jimmy and I were still wrapped together; he was still deep inside me. He was hard; I was wet. Despite the change in my mind and my heart, my body still trembled on the edge of orgasm, and so did his.

His hands slid from the collar to my shoulders, clenching for an instant. I thought he meant to push me away. I didn't blame him. What I'd done to him, what I'd forced him to do to me . . .

I tensed, prepared to move before he made me. I tried to see his eyes, but he pulled me close, buried his face against my breasts.

"Jimmy—"

"Don't talk." He traced his hands from my shoulders to my hips and cupped them. "Just . . . don't."

I swallowed, tasting things I didn't want to think about. But an instant later I forgot everything else as his body moved against mine.

We'd always had this. No matter how much time

passed, when we came together we couldn't help but touch each other, and when we touched . . . sex happened.

I rocked against him, his hands showed me the rhythm, his breath against my skin, my cheek against his hair; only a few slick movements and I came. As I clenched around him, he did too, shuddering in my arms as the silence twirled around us like mist.

When it was over, I lifted my head; he lifted his. We disentangled ourselves. Our eyes did not meet. Would it be like this between us forever from now on?

Our clothes were nearby—a little torn, a lot bloody. We'd left the car on the road maybe a quarter of a mile east. In the trunk we kept clean jeans and shirts, a jug of water, some towels.

We'd done this before; we knew what would happen. If we lived, we'd look like the lone survivors of a mass murder. We'd need to clean up before we could find a hotel and then . . . clean up some more.

Jimmy snatched our things, and I followed him to the car. He still wouldn't meet my eyes.

"Are you going to be like this forever?" I asked.

Jimmy dug the key out of his pants, hit the button for the trunk, tossed everything in. "Forever? Doubtful."

"A week, a month, a year?"

"I don't know," he said quietly.

"Nice job, by the way."

He frowned, but he didn't glance up. "Glad you enjoyed it."

"I *meant* pretending to be into it, then snapping the collar on."

"Someone had to."

And that someone was usually him.

In the past we'd always had love, shared memories,

Jimmy and me against the world. Now, I wasn't so sure what we had and it bothered me.

"You hurt me too," I murmured.

A few months ago, Jimmy had been possessed by his demon of a vampire father. Jimmy had kept me as a sex slave, drunk from me until I nearly died, until I wanted to.

"You think I don't remember?" Jimmy's fingers clenched on the open trunk of the car. "You think I don't hate myself still? But you of all people should know what it's like to be forced to do things you don't want to. To have your body betray you while your mind screams, 'No.'"

I did know. I also knew I'd had no choice.

I took a step forward, and he took a step back. "Let it be," he said. "You got over it; I will too."

I wasn't sure I'd gotten over it. But I'd gotten past it. I understood that when he'd done those things, Jimmy hadn't been Jimmy. Unfortunately, when I'd seduced him I'd been more me than I was now.

We washed up as best we could with the water and the towels. Basically cleaning our faces, necks, hands and arms, leaving the rest for later.

Jimmy tossed me some clothes. I put them on without looking at them, but Jimmy's made me smile. He wore one of his T-shirts.

Jimmy's "cover" for his globe-trotting demon killing was portrait photographer to the stars. Someday—if we weren't all dead—he'd be able to collect his greatest hits into a few coffee-table books. He was a genius with a camera. Almost as good as he was with a silver knife.

His pictures had graced magazine covers, book covers, posters, CD cases, once even Times Square. Up-

and-coming rock bands, country western wannabes, fresh-faced tween queens and steroid-puffed future action stars knew that if Sanducci took their photograph, they had arrived.

Jimmy liked T-shirts. He wore them with jeans, dress pants, sports coats, tuxedos and sometimes nothing at all. The true sign of becoming the "it" guy or girl or the band of the century was when Sanducci was photographed in your shirt.

Dozens arrived at his postbox every month. He donated them all to charity. He only wore the shirts of those he'd actually photographed. But that never stopped anyone from sending the garments.

Tonight his shirt read: *NY Yankees.* I hated the Yankees. The reason I smiled? Jimmy knew it. Needling me about the Yankees was another of Jimmy's favorite things.

I was a Brewers fan. Milwaukee was my hometown. Had been since Ruthie brought me there at twelve. It was the only place I'd ever been happy, and right now I missed home like a piece of my heart.

"When did you do a shoot with the Yankees?" I asked.

Jimmy cast me a surprised glance, then glanced down with a puzzled frown. The expression made my heart hurt worse. He hadn't known what shirt he'd put on. He hadn't been needling me at all.

"When they won the division." Jimmy shrugged. "Last year?"

"Or the year before or two before that. It ain't hard to win if you buy every damn prospect."

"I'm not gonna argue baseball with you tonight." He sounded so tired.

I turned away, watched the remaining mounds of

varcolac ash shiver and shift, then drift off into the night. "I shouldn't have killed them all. I should have kept one alive to question about the key."

"You think you've got any restraint when you're like that?"

I didn't, no, but—

"Some do." I turned back. "Your . . . father for instance."

Jimmy's mouth thinned. He was understandably touchy on the subject of dear old dad—a strega (definition: medieval vampire witch). He'd done things to Jimmy that rivaled what had been done to him on the streets, and that was saying quite a bit.

I was so glad I'd put a stake through the miserable bastard's black heart.

"The strega had centuries to work on his control," Jimmy said. "And he never confined his nature like we have. When you do that and then you let it out, bad things happen."

I returned to watching the varcolac ash swirl, the moon shimmering through each particle as if the heavens were spilling silver-tinged snow. Pretty if you didn't know what those flakes had once been.

"Or good," I said. "Depending on your point of view."

Jimmy remained silent. I knew his point of view. Going vamp was never good. On the one hand, I agreed. On the other, fighting extreme evil called for extreme measures. I'd pledged myself to saving the world. I wasn't going to go about it half-assed.

"By restricting our vampire nature, we only make it stronger, more volatile, if possible more violent," he continued. "The monster can't wait to get out and kill."

I wanted to disagree, except I knew he was right. Sometimes when I was sleeping and I awoke into that twilight time between states, I heard my demon scream-ing. A few times when I was alone and wide awake, I heard a murmur in my head enticing me to do terrible things. When the collar came off, I did them.

"We need to find a way to release your demon more than once a month," I said.

"Not." He slammed the trunk and headed for the driver's seat.

I stood there for a few seconds, then scrambled around to my side and jumped in just as he hit the gas.

"You know that we do." Jimmy didn't answer. "Ruthie said."

"'Ruthie said,'" he mocked. "I don't give a flying fuck."

"Don't let her hear you say that."

Ruthie wasn't above smacking someone in the mouth for "smart talk," "back talk," "blasphemy" or pretty much anything she didn't like. Her being dead hadn't stopped the back of her hand from connecting with my face. It had hurt even if it had been in a vi-sion. However, since Jimmy wasn't able to channel the dead, he was probably safe.

"You need to convince Summer to reverse the spell," I said.

Jimmy's vampire had been pushed beneath the moon. In other words, he became a monster only when the moon was full. The other twenty-odd days, he was just Jimmy. Dangerous as hell, but not damn near un-stoppable. Like me.

"She won't." His hands clenched on the steering wheel. "I don't think she can."

Summer Bartholomew was a fairy. Think life-sized Tinkerbell without the wings; add cowboy boots, a white hat and slutty clothes with a lot of fringe.

Summer and I hadn't bonded well, mainly because

she was head-over-heels, do-anything-and-everything in love with Jimmy. It hadn't helped that when he'd left me the first time, he'd gone to her.

She was also the one responsible for the dog collar around my neck. Not that I didn't need it, but couldn't she have bespelled a nice silver chain, a diamond ear stud? Even a leather bracelet would have been better than what I had. But Summer had seen a way to infuriate me, and she'd taken it.

That I'd have done the exact same thing were I capable of performing magic didn't lessen my irritation with her one bit. To make matters worse, Summer had performed a sex spell to confine Jimmy's demon.

I know. I shouldn't throw stones—sexual empath and all that—but the fairy annoyed me. Probably because several times when I'd touched her, or touched Jimmy, I'd seen them. Made me want to scrub out my brain with a gallon of scalding water and a whole lot of bleach.

"What's so hard about it?" I asked. "Can't she just . . . do you backward?"

"Apparently not," Jimmy said.

"She's refusing to reverse the spell because she knows that you don't want her to."

"I don't, but that doesn't mean I won't. I think we need a bigger fairy."

I'd been taking a sip from a tepid bottle of water I'd left in the car earlier. That sip sprayed all over the windshield. "What?"

His lips twitched. "A more powerful fairy."

"There are grades of fairyness?"

"So Summer says."

"Repeat *that* five times fast," I muttered. "Where do we find a grade-A, top-of-the-line, more-powerful-than-Summer fairy?"

"You're gonna have to ask her."

"You didn't?"

"I don't *want* to go back to the way that I was."

"You said you would."

"I didn't say I'd help."

"Fine," I snapped. I hated asking Summer for anything, but I was the leader of this merry band of demon killers, and Summer knew it. She'd tell me.

Or I'd make her. I kind of hoped she didn't want to tell me.

"I really thought the Nephilim had the key," I murmured. How else had they released the Grigori?

"It's probably a good thing if they don't."

It was on the tip of my tongue to say, *No shit*, but I refrained.

"Do you know anything about the *Book of Samyaza*?" I asked.

Jimmy cast me a quick glance, his dark eyes unreadable in the eerie glow from the dash. We were headed toward LA; the press of the lights against the night made the sky luminescent and really kind of creepy.

"That's a myth."

"So are we."

Every legendary tale of monsters from the dawn of time was true. They were Nephilim or breeds, but they were very, very real.

Remember Goliath—that giant of antiquity? Nephilim.

Vampires. Werewolves. Evil, dark scary things. Nephilim. Or, in some cases, breeds.

Witch hunts? They probably had the right idea but the wrong execution. Pardon the pun. You can't kill witches just by drowning them. Most of them won't even burn.

"Samyaza was the leader of the earthly angels," I said.

"Satan," Jimmy agreed. "Thrown into the pit. I don't think he had time to write a book."

"I think he had plenty of time to do a lot of things. According to Ruthie, he's been whispering to the Nephilim from the beginning."

"What's he been whispering?"

"Revelatory prophecies for the other side." I shrugged. "Instructions for winning this war."

"And you're saying someone wrote them down in the *Book of Samyaza*?"

"Yes."

"Bullshit."

"We got the Bible in pretty much the same way," I pointed out.

"God whispering. Satan whispering." Jimmy's mouth twisted. "I don't think that's quite the same."

"I suppose not." I took a deep breath. "And there is one big difference."

"What's that?"

"According to legend, whoever possesses the *Book of Samyaza* is invincible."

Jimmy chewed on his lower lip for a minute as he contemplated the steadily lightening night sky. "Then we'd damn straight better find it first."

CHAPTER 4

I had a lot on my plate. Find the *Book of Samyaza*, even though no one had ever seen it.

Find the *Key of Solomon*—everyone who'd ever seen that was dead.

Find an über-fairy to release Jimmy's demon vampire.

Deal with the Grigori somehow—either discover what they looked like, how to kill them, and then do it or get our hands on the key and command them back into Tartarus.

Attempt to keep the chaos that was overtaking the world from ending the world with a seriously depleted cadre of seers and demon killers.

Discover who was jockeying to become the new leader of the demon horde—code name the Antichrist—and, what the hell, kill him too.

"I need a drink," I muttered, wishing like crazy I was back at work in Milwaukee, where I made ends meet by tending bar at Murphy's—a cop bar on the East Side of town.

The job had begun as a form of penance. I'd once been a cop. Then my psychic gift had led my partner and me into a situation where only one of us had emerged alive. I still wished it hadn't been me.

Max Murphy had been a great guy, a good cop, a wonderful husband and a caring father. He'd been the best partner an officer could hope for. He'd believed in me, and his belief had gotten him killed.

I hadn't been able to remain a cop after that—no one trusted me; hell, I didn't trust myself—so I'd quit the force. I could find no better way to be punished for my sins than to work for the widow of the man I'd destroyed.

To my amazement, Megan didn't hate me. She didn't blame me. The crazy woman loved me.

While I wanted nothing more than to head into Murphy's and draw a Miller Lite, then sit down and drink it with Megan, I couldn't go back there and risk her life and the lives of her three kids the way I'd risked Max's.

Jimmy drove toward LAX. Even at this time of night, make that morning, the traffic was obscene. How did people live here?

He found a decent hotel, went inside to book a room. He was less bloody than I was. When he came out he handed me a key. I stared at it dumbly. Separate rooms? That was . . . different.

I didn't comment. Jimmy was in charge of the bills; he could do what he liked. This saving-the-world gig didn't pay well. Hell, it didn't pay anything. Once "recruited" into the federation, DKs and seers obtained "cover" jobs that allowed them to easily do their secret jobs while providing them with enough cash to live on and fund their clandestine activities. Ruthie had run a foster-care facility, which allowed her to take care of her duties as both a seer and the leader of the light while also recruiting for the federation.

The most troubled kids are usually the most powerful kids in terms of supernatural gifts. They're different, big-time, and they end up getting kicked out of home after home because around them weird stuff happens.

And when they try to explain it, they can't. Or what's the truth sounds very much like a lie: *I don't know how the family dog ended up in pieces. I can't remember how I got out of the house, or what I did for the past three hours. I can't explain why my clothes are always torn and bloody yet I'm not.*

Ruthie had been the first person to tell me it was okay that I "knew" stuff about people just by touching them. That I wasn't evil or crazy. That I didn't have to hide it—at least from her.

Jimmy and I each grabbed our own duffel and went into the hotel. The two rooms were located right next to each other. I guess I should be glad he hadn't asked for separate floors.

"Night." Jimmy disappeared inside.

I went in, saw the connecting door, felt a little better, until I opened it and discovered the one to his side remained closed. I left mine open and got into the shower.

The blood had dried; it took a while to get it all off. I let my hair air-dry—there wasn't much of it; I'd learned the hard way when I'd been a cop that long hair was an invitation for morons to pull it out or spit gum in. I'd hacked off my dark brown tresses a few weeks into my rookie year, and I kept them short now by snipping at them with any sharp implement available. For some reason the choppy, messy style suited my face.

It was an exotic face, or so I'd been told. Skin darker than the average Caucasian, hinting at a mixed heritage, my bright blue eyes as much a mystery as the rest of me.

The hotel was more upscale than I'd been staying

in lately. There was a mini-bar, and I pulled out that beer I'd been craving. Ten bucks. I twisted off the cap. Jimmy could afford it.

My finances were in flux. Cop to bartender was considered by most a downward trend, although on a busy night, tending bar was definitely more lucrative. But since I'd had to go on the road as the leader of the light, my cash flow had dwindled.

The only money coming in was from a rental property I'd bought when I left the force—a combination storefront, occupied by a knickknack shop, and a second-floor apartment, where I'd lived until everyone and their demon sister found out about it.

Not too long ago a seer had been murdered right on my doorstep. That she'd been torn in two had caused no small amount of consternation to the tiny police force in Friedenberg—population around three thousand. They'd called in the FBI. As far as I knew, the case was still open. Probably always would be.

I could rent out the apartment to increase my income—if I could find anyone willing to get past the whole murdered-woman-on-the-doorstep issue—but the idea of having no home, like Jimmy, was more than I could stomach. Brought back too many memories of the years before Ruthie. I might be a rough, tough demon-killing psychic, but being homeless scared me.

Finishing the beer, I glanced at the clock. Three A.M. and the connecting door was still closed. Silence pulsed from Jimmy's room. Nothing to do but sleep. But I wasn't sure I could.

I guess I did because the next thing I knew the clock read four thirty and the dark wasn't so dark anymore. I went still, listening. Jimmy was moving around on the other side of the wall.

Since Sanducci had been known to sneak off and

leave me behind, I got up, threw on some clothes and headed toward the connecting door.

One quick flick of my wrist and the lock snapped. The superior strength I'd absorbed empathically when I'd become a dhampir definitely didn't suck. Unfortunately, when the door was grabbed from the other side and yanked open I was too surprised to use my superior speed to duck and just stood there as cool sparkling mist dampened my cheeks and stuck to my eyelids.

Fairy dust. I hated that stuff.

"Why do you do that?" I scrubbed my palms over my face. "You know it doesn't work on me."

Summer Bartholomew scowled, hands clenching into fists before she spun on the heels of her cowboy boots and stalked away, the fringe on her white leather halter top swaying. "I didn't know it was you."

"Who else would it be?" I followed her into the room.

"Since when do you two sleep alone?"

I wasn't going to discuss Sanducci's sleeping arrangements with the woman—make that fairy—who loved him.

My gaze went to the bed, as I wondered why Jimmy wasn't waking up and telling us to clam up, but it was empty. Hell, not only empty, but also never been slept in. He'd pulled a Houdini again.

"What did you do to him?" Summer asked.

My mind flashed to last night in the desert. Jimmy staked to the ground, naked skin on naked skin. The scent of the blood, the feel of his body in mine when it hadn't really been mine.

Mmm, the demon whispered. *Wanna do it again.*

"Shut up," I muttered.

Summer shot me a glare, and her hand lifted, as if she'd shoot her sparkling "make me" dust one more time. It wouldn't function any better than the last time. Because fairy magic doesn't work on those on errands of mercy, and that would be my new life in a nutshell. That she couldn't make me do whatever she wished drove Summer batty.

"You don't need to be so bitchy," she said. "I didn't break him. You did."

"He isn't a toy."

Toy, my demon whispered. *Yessss.*

I smacked myself in the forehead. All that got me was the beginnings of another headache.

"What is wrong with you?" Summer asked.

I wasn't going to inform her that I'd started to hear the vampire in my head even when it wasn't loose. No telling what she'd do to me then. Maybe lock me in the golden-barred room of her Irish cottage back in New Mexico.

I couldn't let that happen. I had too much to do.

"Los Angeles is kind of a hike for a booty call," I observed. "Not that Sanducci isn't worth it, but have some pride."

Her blue eyes narrowed in her perfect little face. Long blond hair, body that fit into size zero jeans as if they'd been invented for her, dewy pink lips that matched the hue of her fingernails. Hell, she drove *me* batty just by breathing.

Sure, fairies practiced glamour—magic that made them appear more attractive—but since Summer's magic didn't work on me, I figured she'd been stunning from the day of her birth. Although I don't think fairies are born.

They aren't Nephilim or breeds. Back when the angels were sent to earth to watch the humans, some of them actually watched instead of chasing us around like satyrs after wood nymphs.

When God slammed closed the pearly gates on the Grigori and dropped them into Tartarus, those angels trapped on earth that were too good to go to hell but not angelic enough to return to heaven—earth was no longer paradise, and it appears that just being here tarnished even the most crystalline soul—became fairies.

Some of them work for us and some of them have gone to the dark side—or so I hear. I'd yet to meet any other fairies but Summer. Which reminded me. "I need the name and location of an über-fairy."

Summer snorted. "Yeah, that'll happen."

"You seem to forget who's the boss of you."

"Since you're no longer the conduit to Ruthie, I'm not sure how in charge you are."

I frowned. "I'm the leader of the light."

"Big fat hairy deal."

"You have to listen to me."

"I'm not compelled to follow orders; I choose to. Right now I choose to say—" She gave me the finger.

I jumped her. Couldn't help myself. Summer had been begging for an ass-kicking from the moment I'd first seen her in Jimmy's head. That I'd refrained this long was downright saintly.

Summer had supernatural powers. She could do magic, cast spells; she could fly without wings. She was one of the federation's top DKs, with countless kills to her credit. But she'd never had to fight me in a bad mood.

We hit the ground hard. I got a pointy elbow in the throat. Coughing, I rolled free; as she started to get up, I decked her. She flew into the wall. Didn't seem to hurt her any. She was on her feet again as quickly as I.

Blood trickled from her lip, which had started to swell. Fairies were pretty hard to kill—had to use cold steel or rowan—but they didn't appear to heal as fast as a dhampir. Lucky me.

"I suppose you usually throw your damn fairy dust, order the Nephilim to stand still, and then you skewer them," I said. "Must be nice."

"It is." She threw two knives at me with a quick flick of her slim wrists. Where they had come from I had no idea.

I caught one, but the other stuck in my chest with a sick thunk. I glanced from the knife to Summer's face. "Are you kidding me with this?"

She lifted one shoulder. "Slowed you down."

I yanked it out; the wound healed in seconds. I tossed both weapons over my shoulder. "Not really."

"Freak," she muttered.

"Jealous?"

Summer snarled, and for the first time I caught a glimpse of something *other* beneath the pretty face. Fairies could shape-shift, or so the legends said. Maybe Summer's beauty wasn't her true form.

She came at me like an animal—roaring in fury, pink-tipped claws outstretched, pearly white teeth bared. I grabbed her by the throat and smacked her head against the wall.

One tap and she stopped fighting. I had no more time to mess around—we were getting pretty loud. I was surprised someone hadn't called the cops already. Not that Summer couldn't toss magic dust into their faces and tell them to go away; she'd done it before. But police would bring attention, interruption. I didn't want that. I wanted this done. I still had to find Sanducci.

I let her go. She slumped to the floor. For an instant I allowed her to think we were through; then I knelt. She looked up, her eyes dazed, pupils dilated.

"Who can reverse your spell?" I asked, and then I touched her.

Dagda.

"Where—," I began, but the door flew open.

I spun around; it was Jimmy. For an instant joy bloomed. He hadn't left me behind this time. He'd come back for me. Then he stepped inside, and the lamplight fell across his face.

Someone had beaten the crap out of him.

CHAPTER 5

Summer let out a little cry. I threw out an arm and said, "Wait."

For us to still be able to see his injuries meant a Nephilim had made them—those took longer to heal than any wound made by a human—and not long ago. Whatever had hurt Jimmy could very well be right behind him.

I moved forward, yanked him in, glanced into the corridor—empty—then locked the door. A thud had me spinning around.

Jimmy had gone to his knees. Summer caught him before his face kissed carpet. She began to fuss over him, gentle touches, soothing murmurs. He laid his head in her lap; the bruises flared dark purple against his olive-toned skin, but even as I cataloged them, they began to fade.

"Back off," I ordered Summer "He needs to talk."

She ignored me, whispering into his hair, petting him like a child.

I shoved his leg with my foot. He didn't open his eyes. Passed out. Fantastic.

Reaching down, I patted him myself—once, hard on the cheek.

"Don't," Summer ordered in a voice I'd never heard

from her before—low, deadly, that of the demon killer she'd become and not the fairy she pretended to be.

I might have been scared, if I wasn't already terrified. Something that could kick Sanducci's ass like this was something we really needed to be prepared for.

"He can't take a nap," I snapped. "I need to know how many, of what and how soon they're going to get here."

"They're all dead, or he wouldn't be back."

"What *are* they?"

"Doesn't matter."

"I think it does. Why didn't he wake me? Why didn't they call me too?"

"He didn't get a call. He just went hunting."

"Excuse me?"

"He does that sometimes. When he's . . ." She lifted one bare, perfect, white shoulder. "Upset."

"Upset," I repeated, and something shifted in my chest. For an instant I felt like crying; then I remembered I didn't cry.

"When he feels out of control." Summer threaded her fingers through Jimmy's shaggy black hair. "Like when he was a child and—" She looked up. "You know."

I did. When we were kids, on the street, we'd been prey and not predator. Things were different now.

Unless you were staked to the ground being tortured by Nephilim. Or being raped by someone you trusted.

"This is your fault," Summer said. I didn't argue.

Once I'd known Jimmy better than anyone on this earth. Sure, there were things he hadn't shared—he was a dhampir, a demon killer, a bastard; I'd had to find all that out for myself. I'd thought I was the only one—besides Ruthie—who knew about his past. Guess not.

Jimmy moved, groaned; his eyes fluttered, then opened and stared directly into mine. For an instant, his lips curved, and the expression in his eyes was one I remembered. He loved me. But memory returned, and the smile died along with the love.

His gaze slid away. He peered at Summer. "What are you doing here?"

"I knew you'd need me."

Fairies supposedly have the sight, though I hadn't observed any evidence of that myself. If Summer was so damn psychic, why was she a DK and not a seer? Maybe she wasn't that good at it.

Summer had told me I'd meet my mother one day, and that I wouldn't like it. So far that hadn't happened, and I wasn't holding my breath. My mother had dumped me, probably because I'd done something weird. No one had ever mentioned my father.

"What the hell, Jimmy?" I demanded. "You just take off? You could have gotten killed, and I'd have no idea what happened."

"I wasn't going to get killed."

"How did you know where to find any Nephilim?"

He snorted, then winced and lifted a bloody hand to his nose, which was crooked. He twitched it back into place, and the thing knit together with a sickening slurch. "They're everywhere, Elizabeth."

Usually he called me Lizzy; sometimes, to my ever-lasting annoyance, he called me baby. But apparently not anymore.

"The way this works," I said, "is that your seer has a vision, contacts you and tells you where to go, what to kill."

Jimmy sat up, shrugging off Summer's helping hands. "I know how it works."

"Then explain what you just did."

"I sense vampires. It's what I do. What I am."

"So you went out and staked a nest by yourself?"

"Yes," he said simply.

"Why do you think that's okay? We get our orders from—" I stopped. I'd never been quite sure where those orders came from. Ruthie said God, and who was I to argue? I did know that the orders came; we obeyed. We didn't just go hunting. Or at least I didn't.

I glanced at Summer. "You ever go out on your own?"

"Sure," she said.

"And how do you know what's a Nephilim and what's a human with an overdeveloped asshole gene?"

"Experience," she answered. "I can sense them too."

In theory, I understood what she meant. When evil came near there was a certain buzzing in the air. But still—

"What if you're wrong? What if you cut the head off of a . . ." I paused, uncertain where to go with that.

"A serial killer?" she supplied. "A child molester? A gang-banging, drive-by-shooting, drug-dealing prick?" Summer flipped her palms upward. "Bummer."

I blinked. "Bummer?"

"You know as well as I do that most of the psychotic killers in this world are just Nephilim begging to be dusted."

"Most?"

"All. They're *all* Nephilim."

Somehow I doubted that.

"You don't think the world is a better place without them, be they half demons or not a demon at all?" Summer asked.

"I didn't say that." But I'd been a cop. I'd believed in what I'd done, loved it, thrived on it. That I'd had to give it up didn't make me believe in it any less.

"We let the law handle the human bad guys."

"Because they've done such a great job so far," Summer muttered.

"They're doing the best that they can."

"We can do better."

"Everyone thinks that."

"But we actually can."

Jimmy got to his feet, lips tightening in pain even though most of the bruises and cuts had disappeared. "Let it go," he said. "Hunters hunt. We can't help ourselves. Evil is evil, and it has to be stopped."

I knew when I was beaten. I could tell them not to go out and fight the Nephilim, but they were going to do it anyway, and who was I to change the way things were, the way they'd always been? The federation had been around a lot longer than I had. Than we all had.

I narrowed my gaze on the fairy. Except for her.

Jimmy took a step toward the bathroom and stumbled. Both Summer and I lunged forward, each grabbing an arm; then we froze and glared at each other.

"You can fly away now," I said.

"Eat shit and die," she returned.

"Um, you mind?" Jimmy tugged on his arms. "You make me feel like you're going to split me down the middle like a wishbone."

I started; so did Jimmy. We'd both made use of that practice to kill when we were vamps. The spray of blood was like a Las Vegas fountain.

Do it again, whispered the demon.

Jimmy licked his lips. I knew what he was thinking. Same thing I was. Or same thing my demon was.

He shifted his arm. I let him go. Summer didn't, so I grabbed him again and he sighed. "You can go back to your room, Elizabeth. Get some sleep. I'll be fine."

As if I could sleep—

"What about her?" I asked. My voice sounded childish, petulant, which worked out because that was how I felt. I wanted to kick Summer, and Jimmy, in the shins. "Is she going back to her room?"

Jimmy didn't answer. Instead he limped into the bathroom, and he took Summer along.

Which, I guess, was answer enough.

At least his damn Yankee shirt was toast.

My cell phone was ringing when I got back to my room. The connecting door was busted, so I left it hanging open and snatched the phone from the dresser.

"Phoenix," I answered.

"Yes, hello."

The voice was familiar, but not one I immediately recognized. Not surprising since the remaining members of the federation all had my number, yet most of them I'd never met.

"This is Xander Whitelaw."

Not federation, but he at least knew the score. Alexander Whitelaw was a professor at Brownport Bible College in southern Indiana. Specialty: revelatory prophecy. However, before he'd gotten his doctorate in that, he'd studied obscure supernatural legends, particularly those of the Navajo. He'd been a great help last month when I'd needed to find a way to destroy the Naye'i, a particularly nasty Navajo witch with an Antichrist complex.

"Dr. Whitelaw, what can I do for you?"

"I found something," he said.

I'd sent Whitelaw to look for the *Book of Samyaza* and the *Key of Solomon*, or at least a clue about the location of either one. He was a fantastic researcher, but I hadn't figured he was this fantastic. He'd only been at it for a few weeks, and those books had been lost for . . . hard to say, since one of them had never been seen and the other was mostly a rumor.

"You need to come to Brownport."

"You can't just tell me?" I asked.

"Not a good idea."

He didn't elaborate, but I could hear what he wasn't saying even without touching him.

Cell phones aren't secure, and the information he had for me wasn't information that we wanted in the wrong hands, for obvious reasons.

"I'll be there tomorrow," I said, and hung up.

The eastern horizon was turning a murky peach when I strode back through the broken door. I hadn't heard anyone come out of the bathroom. The bedroom, the bed, was empty—thank God—but . . .

Outside the closed bathroom door, I hesitated, biting my lip; then I knocked once and walked in.

Jimmy lay in the bathtub, the water tinged rusty with blood, his skin paler than usual, ghostly white against the blue-black length of his hair.

For an instant I thought he was dead, and my gaze went to his hands as I imagined the horizontal slashes on his wrists. Of course they weren't there. Jimmy couldn't kill himself that easily.

Nevertheless, I gasped, and he opened his eyes. "What's the matter?"

The image of Jimmy dead in the water fled and

another took its place—the real one, the one in front of me now.

Sanducci sprawled naked in the tub, one leg hanging over the rim, his hair curling from the heat, the ends floating on the surface, tickling his shoulders, his chest muscles, his abdomen slick and moist.

I couldn't help it. I licked my lips, and the curiosity in his eyes turned to disgust.

"No," he said, and sat up, twitching the curtain across the rod with a shriek that nearly made me jump out of my shivering skin.

No. That was new. Since the first time he'd touched me the answer—at least to that particular question—had always been yes. Of course we were no longer the people we'd been at seventeen. We weren't really people at all.

"Don't you knock?" Jimmy asked.

"I knocked."

"I didn't hear you or I'd have said, 'Go away.' "

I was getting pissed, probably because I understood his disgust, felt it myself. I hated the vampire inside of me almost as much as I hated the one inside of him.

The demon began to laugh.

"Shut up," I muttered.

Jimmy cast me a quick, sharp glance around the edge of the curtain. I wondered how much his vampire whispered to him—and how often he listened.

"We've gotta go."

The water sloshed as Jimmy sat up. "What and where?"

He thought we'd gotten a call. We had—or at least I had—but not that kind of call. "Not Nephilim," I said. "A lead on the key." Or maybe the book.

"All right." Water sloshed again. "Can you—uh—get out?"

I blinked. "What?"

"I'm naked."

I laughed. "Right."

"I'm serious."

"I've seen it all before, Sanducci." And it was good.

"Then you don't need to see it again. Get out." His voice shook, broke.

I got out.

Our roles had reversed. Not very long ago I'd been the one saying, *Don't look. Don't touch. I despise you.*

It hurt more than I'd thought it could. How had he stood it when I'd hated him more than I'd loved him?

I took a deep breath and forced myself to stop shaking.

"Big, bad demon hunter," I muttered.

I needed to hit something. Summer would do. Beating the location of a dagda out of her was next on my list anyway. I glanced around the room. Empty.

I walked into mine and found it the same way. By the time I returned, Jimmy was coming out of the bathroom fully dressed and scrubbing a towel through his hair.

The scent of him wafted over me—sweet water, tart soap and cinnamon aftershave. Jimmy always smelled like he'd just stepped out of the shower. Usually because he had. When we were kids he'd hog the bathroom two or three times a day. It had taken me a few years to figure out that his time on the streets without the luxury of cleanliness had made Sanducci a tad obsessed with it.

"Where's the fairy?" I asked.

"Gone."

"Where?"

He shrugged.

"Sanducci, you knew I wanted to talk to her."

"Is that what you call it?"

"Talk to. Beat on. Whatever. I need to know where to find a dagda."

"She wasn't going to tell you."

"You told her to fly away," I accused.

"*You* told her to fly away."

Shit. I had.

"I can ask Sawyer."

Jimmy's lips curved. "Not right now you can't."

Sawyer was a Navajo medicine man. He was also a skinwalker—both witch and shape-shifter—one of the most powerful beings on earth. And he didn't have a telephone.

"It's only a matter of time until I find out what I want to know. You could tell me and save everyone some trouble."

"I don't know where to find a dagda."

I crossed the room and put my hand on his arm. He shoved me so hard I flew onto the bed, bounced once and tumbled off.

"My thoughts are my own," he said. "Stay out of them."

I got to my feet. Before he'd shoved me, I'd seen the truth. He didn't know.

"You can't just go around touching everyone, invading their minds, stealing their secrets."

"Actually, I can."

Jimmy narrowed his eyes. "Oh, really?"

In the past I couldn't read everyone all the time, couldn't see everything. I still couldn't, but I was getting better at it.

I picked up my duffel bag and walked toward the door. Jimmy followed.

"Maybe you're more dangerous than the things we're fighting," he muttered.

I looked up at the hazy morning sky. "Maybe I am."

CHAPTER 6

We hopped a flight from LAX to Indianapolis. The security level was up. The news on television and radio was all bad. A sudden and significant increase in assaults, murders, rapes. The psychiatric hospitals—hell, all the hospitals—were packed.

The powers that be were at a loss. They were prepared for terrorism, natural disasters, wars. But when the world ran amok, when the citizens you were trying to protect were suddenly the ones everyone needed protecting from, no one knew what to do.

During the several hours it took to fly halfway across the country, Jimmy and I didn't talk, which was fine with me. I listened to the people around me. They were scared. I didn't blame them.

"It's a terrorist plot," the woman to my right whispered. "They've put something in the water to make people go insane."

"No, it's an epidemic," the man behind me insisted. "We aren't going to be wiped out by AIDS but by a brain-eating bacteria that makes everyone believe their neighbor wants to kill them."

"The end of the world." An elderly woman near the front nodded slowly. "Thought it was nine-eleven. But that was only the beginning."

The damn Grigori were having a field day. Mating with humans, repopulating the world with Nephilim, just as the prophecies stated. The end was definitely at hand. I wondered how long we had before complete panic set in and what we would do once it did.

The pilot announced touchdown in ten minutes. Jimmy, who'd been pretending to sleep, sat up. I could tell by the tightness around his mouth that he'd been listening too and he didn't like what he'd heard any more than I did.

I probably should have sent Sanducci on his way. I didn't need him to come to Brownport; I could handle Xander Whitelaw myself—but I didn't trust Sanducci not to disappear the instant my back was turned. I'd wasted a lot of valuable time lately looking for him. I didn't want to waste any more, so I let him think I needed help.

Once on the ground, we picked up our checked bags—couldn't carry knives on the plane, but we never went anywhere without them—then I headed for the rental-car area. However, Jimmy walked right out the front door, and in the interest of not losing him, I followed. He headed straight for a black Lincoln Navigator idling at the curb. Jimmy liked big cars. His last had been an obnoxiously huge Hummer—also black.

The man who climbed out of the driver's seat was also obnoxiously huge, but white. I held my breath, waiting for the whisper that, in the past, would signal a Nephilim, before I remembered that Ruthie no longer spoke to me. Harboring this demon was proving to be an even bigger pain in the ass one might think.

Though I'd allowed the transformation—allowed? Hell, I'd chased Jimmy down and stolen it—for the sake of the world, the consequences of embracing evil had been more painful than I had anticipated. Where before I'd heard Ruthie's voice on the wind, I'd seen her in my dreams and she'd felt so much less gone, now she spoke through someone else and I was on my own.

I watched Jimmy for a clue. He smiled and strode toward the guy with his hand outstretched, and I relaxed a bit. Sanducci had been doing this long enough to feel the vibe from a Nephilim. He might not know exactly what type of demon they were or exactly how to kill them, but I doubted he'd smack one of Satan's henchmen on the back and say, "Good to see you, Thane."

Since Thane didn't grow another head, or sprout claws and tear out Jimmy's eyes, I joined them.

Only to scramble back when the guy went down on one knee and bowed his head. "Mistress," he murmured in a burr so Scottish I smelled heather.

"What the hell?" I glanced at Jimmy. Taking my eyes off the giant Scotsman proved a mistake. He grabbed my hand, and I beaned him with my duffel bag.

He didn't fall down, but he didn't wrap his huge arms around me and bear-hug me to death either. Instead, he peered up at me with eyes so blue they mimicked my own and rubbed at his strawberry blond head.

"Ach, I jest wanted to kiss yer ring."

"I don't have a ring."

"Ye should. It's good for smackin' folk with, right about here." He made a jab toward his own eye. "A nice piece of silver about yer finger can split the skin to the bone."

"What is wrong with you?" I demanded.

"Yer the leader of the light, aren't ye now? I'm t' swear my allegiance."

Ruthie had said that the members of the federation would come to me and pledge fealty. So far none had for several reasons.

One—most of them were dead following an infiltration of our secret society. Two—I wasn't exactly staying in one place or broadcasting my whereabouts. Three—I'd sent word through all the grapevines I had for everyone to continue doing their jobs and skip the swearing-allegiance portion of the program. But I supposed some might feel compelled upon meeting me to drop to their knees and kiss my ring.

I glanced around. In LA, no one would have noticed any of this. In Indianapolis, people were staring.

"Fine," I said. "You're sworn. Get up."

"Not until I've kissed yer hand."

"Sheesh, let him kiss you and be done," Jimmy ordered, so I did.

Thane's lips were warm but his breath so cold my skin ached as if I'd been walking in the snow without gloves for hours.

"What are you?" I asked.

He lifted his head and smiled, revealing slightly pointy teeth. I snatched my hand away as he got to his feet, towering over me by at least ten inches. Considering I was five-ten in my casual flip-flops, giant wasn't out of the question.

"Nuckelavee," he said, and tossed Jimmy the keys to the Lincoln.

Then, with a wink, he jumped into a Jeep parked right behind the Navigator. The young woman at the wheel held her crucifix in my direction as she drove past. The sun sparked off of it and gave me a helluva headache. I fingered my collar. When I wore this, I could touch a blessed cross. When I didn't, the icon gave me second-degree burns.

Once I'd worn Ruthie's crucifix—a connection to her as dear to me as her voice in my head and her presence in my dreams. But I'd chosen to embrace the darkness, to become it and to let it become a part of me. So, for now, perhaps forever, wearing Ruthie's necklace was no longer possible.

Jimmy was stowing his duffel in the cargo area, so I joined him, tossing mine in too. He reached up to shut the door, and I stayed his hand. There was more to this car than what met the eye. I could smell it.

"Federation vehicle?"

Instead of answering, Jimmy yanked up the false bottom. Beneath the carpeted base rested weapons of every imaginable metal. Guns with silver bullets. Golden knives. Bronze swords. Crossbows. Gallons of accelerant—gasoline, kerosene. Probably dynamite.

"A rolling bomb," I murmured. "Fabulous."

We got in, and Jimmy headed south toward Brownport.

"What's a nuckelavee?" I asked.

"Thane is part Scottish Fuath fairy."

"Keep going."

"The Fuath are evil Gaelic water spirits."

"He's evil?" I remembered the icy touch of his breath.

"No. He's a breed like me. His father was a Fuath, his mother human."

"His powers?"

"Vampire breath that causes people, plants and animals to wither and die."

No wonder my skin had ached, but it took more than vampire breath to kill me.

"He can also shape-shift," Jimmy continued. "Half man, half horse."

"So a nuckelavee is a vampire, a shifter and a fairy?"

"Pretty much."

"How do we kill one?"

Jimmy blinked. "Why would we want to kill him? He's on our side."

"So were you once, and then—shazaam—you weren't."

Jimmy scowled and didn't answer.

To be fair, his disloyalty hadn't been voluntary or permanent. He'd been captured, tortured and turned into a vampire against his will. But Jimmy had found his way back. He was as loyal now as I was.

I hoped.

"I need to know how to kill supernatural beings," I continued. "What if I encounter a nuckelavee who chose the other side?"

Jimmy sighed. "Freshwater repels them."

"Water repels a water spirit?"

"*Half* water spirit. If you cross a stream, they can't follow."

"I'll remember that if one's ever chasing me and I'm lucky enough to discover a stream nearby. But wait!" I put up one finger to signal a brilliant idea. "What if I just kill it? If only I knew *how*."

"Steel."

"Fairy. Right. Shit!" I smacked my fist against the dashboard.

"What?" Jimmy looked around, one hand tightening on the steering wheel, the other going for the silver switchblade he took everywhere he went.

"If I'd known he was a fairy," I said, "I could have asked him where to find a dagda."

Jimmy relaxed. "Oops."

"Any other way to kill a nuckelavee?"

"Not that I know of."

"How about a Fuath fairy?"

"Sunlight."

"Really? Yet their offspring walks in the day-time."

"So do we," Jimmy said.

"Your father was a day walker."

Certain vampires—considered inferior by the rest of the vampire legion—couldn't go out in the sun. Others—like Jimmy, me, his daddy—were day walkers. We could go out whenever the hell we wanted to.

"There's no rhyme or reason to this stuff," Jimmy said. "You know that."

For the rest of the trip, Jimmy kept the radio turned up so high there could be no possibility of a conversation, and I let him. Whenever we talked lately someone got hurt. Usually me.

Brownport appeared on the horizon. The highway bled into Main Street, lined by the usual businesses necessary for a small college town.

The school, bordered by fields, stood at the far end of Brownport. We pulled into the only parking lot, and I pointed to the administration building, which housed all the faculty offices.

Stalks of corn swayed in the heated afternoon breeze. Jimmy followed me to the door. It was locked. A note said the campus was closed until the fall semester, still a few weeks away. The last time I'd been here, summer school had been in session. Not a lot of kids, but some. The place hadn't felt so—

"Dead," Jimmy murmured.

I frowned. I was getting a really bad feeling. I used my cell to call Xander, but he didn't answer.

"Open it," I ordered.

Jimmy punched his fist through the glass. By the time he'd reached in and flipped the lock, the cuts had already healed.

Inside, the building hadn't changed a bit. The walls needed painting. There were water stains and cracks. I still didn't know where they kept the elevator, but even if I had, I wouldn't have bothered. I ran up the three flights of stairs with Jimmy right behind me.

Whitelaw's door stood open; light spilled into the hallway. "Xander!" I shouted as I skidded on the ancient yellowed tile.

He didn't answer, but he liked to listen to his iPod while working. Guns N' Roses. Despite his button-down shirts and khaki trousers, or maybe because of them, Whitelaw badly wanted to be a rebel.

I slipped as I neared the office, thought for an instant the roof was leaking again, though from the crackly state of the grass outside there'd been no rain for several weeks.

I glanced down. A trickle of crimson spread over the threshold like a tiny creek running south. I palmed my knife and went in.

The walls were decorated with blood, as was the floor, the desk, the books, the papers and what was left of Xander Whitelaw.

Jimmy, coming up fast to the rear, bumped into me. I threw an elbow. Couldn't help myself. When someone came at me from behind, I reacted.

Blame it on the foster-care system. I did.

"Oof," Jimmy said, his breath stirring my hair. "That him?"

"Yeah."

Jimmy stepped around me, checked for a pulse,

even though the slice across Xander's throat told the tale before Jimmy shook his head. "They trashed everything." He flicked his finger, stained with Whitelaw's blood, at the books and papers. "Even if there was info for us, we wouldn't find it now."

"I doubt he wrote anything down."

"Whoever—whatever—got here before us did their best to torture something out of him."

Jimmy turned the professor's arm over to reveal burn marks on the skin. Bruises made his face nearly unrecognizable. I thought I might be sick.

"Do you think they got it?" Jimmy asked.

Xander wasn't a DK. He was just a guy. He might look like a blond Indiana Jones, but he wasn't Indy. No one was.

"Yes," I whispered. "They got it."

"We need to go through his stuff anyway; then we'll burn the place."

I nodded. I knew the drill. Leave behind nothing to arouse suspicion, and this—

I traced my fingertips over Whitelaw's shoulder. This was suspicious as hell.

"You take that side." Jimmy jerked his head to the right. "I'll take this one."

We found nothing. I wasn't surprised. If there'd been any information—written or otherwise—the Nephilim had it now.

We checked every room in the place; then we started a fire in Xander's office, setting it up to appear as if he'd fallen asleep working and dropped a cigarette onto a pile of ancient books. We'd call 911 once we were on the road. They might save the building, but the office and Xander himself would be gone.

As we walked out, I snatched Xander's hat—a replica

of a familiar battered brown fedora—off the coat rack and took it along.

"What was he?" Jimmy asked as we drove north again.

"Professor of prophecy."

"I meant breed, fairy, psychic, what?"

"Just a guy."

Jimmy's hands jerked, and we nearly drove off the road. "He was human?"

"Yeah."

"You recruited a human into the federation."

"He wasn't in the federation; he was doing research."

"Are you nuts?" Jimmy shouted. I jumped. He rarely shouted, but when he did, it was always at me. "You can't let just plain people in on this."

"I didn't let him in on anything. He already knew." Kind of.

Xander had been studying the legends for years. He understood more about revelatory prophecy than just about anyone else. He'd put two and two together. He'd only needed me to come along and agree that it made four.

"Just look where knowing got him," Jimmy said through his teeth.

"Ruthie was watching him," I blurted. "She said he was good at his job."

"But she didn't ask him to put his neck on the line." I flinched, remembering the huge hole that had been sliced into Xander's throat because of me. "She knew better. Only beings with supernatural powers have any chance of living through a meeting with a Nephilim, and not even some of them. Who else have you told about this that isn't one of us?"

"Nobod—" I froze, my lips still forming the word, but all the breath had left my body.

"Who?" Jimmy demanded.

My horrified gaze met his. I closed my mouth, swallowed, then managed to whisper, "Megan."

CHAPTER 7

My best friend didn't answer the phone—not at home and not at the bar.

Since it was around happy hour at Murphy's, she could easily be snowed with customers. She wouldn't answer until things settled down. Even if she did, I wouldn't have been able to accept her assurances that everything was all right. I'm sure there were Nephilim that could mimic a person's voice and their appearance. The only way I'd know if Megan was okay would be to go to Milwaukee and touch her.

Jimmy pointed Thane's Navigator toward Wisconsin without my having to ask. "Anyone else in on the secret?"

"No."

"You're sure."

"Yes."

"You understand what a secret is, don't you?"

I gave him a glare.

"What were you thinking?" he demanded.

"Megan saw a Nephilim. What was I supposed to do?"

"Lie."

"That's what you're good at. Me, not so much." Especially to Megan. She was a mom. She could smell a lie before it even took form in my head, let alone came out of my mouth.

"You can't put human beings in danger like this. Even if they're aware of the Nephilim, they have no means of defending themselves against them."

"I had a guard sent to watch over her."

His forehead creased. "Who?"

"I'm—uh—not sure."

"Do you know the meaning of 'sent'?"

I narrowed my eyes and managed to keep my temper. "I asked Summer to send a DK, and she did." Or so she'd said. I'd been a little too busy to follow up on that.

Jimmy gave me a quick glance, then returned his gaze to the road.

"She wouldn't say she was going to do something and then not do it just to mess with me." I grabbed his arm. "This is Megan's life we're talking about."

Jimmy shifted, removing himself from my grasp. "You should've thought of that before you told her the truth."

The Bradley Clock loomed up next to the freeway, behind it the skyline of Milwaukee, behind that the navy blue expanse of Lake Michigan. Another ten minutes and we'd be at Murphy's.

We'd tried to reach Summer. I wasn't shocked when she didn't pick up for me, but she ignored Jimmy's summons too. Of course if she was flying without wings it might be a little hard to answer a cell phone while avoiding low-cruising planes.

The Navigator had blown a tire outside of Gary, and Thane didn't appear to believe in spares—or perhaps he'd had to toss it out in order to fit in all the ammunition beneath the rear panel.

Though both Jimmy and I were extremely strong and equally fast, we weren't magic and we couldn't manufacture a new tire from thin air like some people who weren't really people. At any rate, the tire fiasco slowed us down, and we didn't pull up outside of Murphy's until long after closing.

Located on the East Side of Milwaukee, Murphy's was a throwback to the time when every neighborhood had its own personal pub. Thus, houses surrounded Murphy's. One of those was Megan's—an aluminum-sided two-story where she lived with her three children: Anna, Aaron and Ben. I'd come to the house a thousand times before—but only one other time in the middle of the night. A night I never wanted to revisit—the night Max had died. I swallowed thickly as the memory loomed large.

She'd been waiting on the steps. She'd already known—and they called me psychic. But I guess when Max didn't arrive home on time, when it was all over the news that there'd been a shooting in the city and an officer had died, she really hadn't needed to be psychic, she hadn't needed to look at my face or wait for me to open my mouth, to know her world had just changed.

I got out of the car and hurried the short distance to the house with Jimmy right behind me. He'd never been here before, never met Megan or Max, though I'm sure he'd heard about them from Ruthie.

Jimmy had been out of my life so completely for the past seven years that having him in it now still felt like a dream. Hell, my whole damn life felt like a dream these days—and not a very good one.

I paused on the porch steps. The night was clear and warm—exactly like the night Max had died. But the moon was different. Then it had been just a sliver; tonight it was headed toward full.

I glanced at Jimmy. When it became full, his demon would break free of its bond. I wasn't sure what we were going to do about that. Jimmy reached for the doorbell.

"No," I said quietly. "The kids."

I didn't want to scare them, and a doorbell in the middle of the night would. Hell, it would probably scare Megan. If she was still alive.

I reached for the knob, planning to break the lock. There wasn't a door made by human hands that could keep me out any longer. But Jimmy hissed his disapproval and pulled a pair of lock picks from his pocket. Part demon, part Boy Scout. What a combo.

He motioned for us to head around back. Wouldn't do for anyone to come along walking a dog and find us messing with the front door of Max Murphy's house. Local police trolled this street more often than any other. Cops took care of their own, especially when one of their own went down in the line of duty.

Jimmy fiddled with the locks on the back door— no alarm. Too expensive. No dog. No time. But at least Megan had invested in a dead bolt, and that would take a little concentration to bypass—I stared out at the yard.

The house was large for a city house, with a lot of shrubs and some decent-sized trees, the grass littered with toys. The Murphy kids were five, six and eight, and they owned a lot of crap. Since I wasn't all that familiar with kids, I wasn't sure if they had more than the usual number or less.

In the far corner, a garden lay fallow. Megan always made big plans to grow vegetables, maybe even a flower or two, but since she had a hard enough time getting in a shower each day, gardening wasn't really on the menu.

Something long and sleek and dark curved around the outer edge of the weedy plot. I moved closer, frowning at the statue of a panther. Megan didn't seem the type.

In the dark, the thing was hard to see. Which might have been why it appeared slightly off—the shoulders and arms more like a man's than a beast's. The entire piece was ink black, except for the spooky sheen of its jeweled chartreuse eyes. Whoever had sculpted that had been either downright strange or just plain bad at it.

A muttered curse was followed by the clink of one of Jimmy's lock picks against the porch. I spun around— I'd given him enough time; now I was just gonna break the door—and the wind picked up.

I paused, my head tilting as I listened. Not the sway of the leaves. Not the swish of the grass. What was that?

I faced the yard. The damned statue was missing.

"Shit," I murmured.

As if my whisper had brought it to life, a large, lean black panther slunk along the edge of the garden, yellow-green eyes fixed on me. He no longer appeared half human but all beast.

The smooth slice of Jimmy's switchblade announced his presence at my side. The cat shrieked, a wild, furious, primeval call that did not belong in a backyard in Milwaukee.

The animal's tail switched back and forth. His paws were huge, his claws even huger. The thing snarled and bared teeth that seemed sharper than average, though my experience with panthers was very limited.

Jimmy flipped his knife around, something he did when he was nervous, then stepped forward. I pulled my own knife and joined him.

I was so glad we'd come to Milwaukee. The thought of that thing crashing into Megan's house, hunting Megan and the kids . . .

The panther charged. I was so preoccupied with the image of finding the Murphys the same way I'd found Xander that I was too slow, and the beast slashed my arm. I dropped the knife.

Jimmy sliced the panther across the back. The animal roared, but he didn't burst into ashes.

"Fuck," Jimmy muttered.

Not a shifter. Which meant we could poke the panther with silver until we were old and gray, but he wasn't going to die. Now what?

In the past, Ruthie would have told me ahead of time what we were facing. We would have found out how to kill him through research—books, Internet, phone calls to other DKs. But now we were floundering around a bit blind, and I hated it.

The panther crouched, belly to the ground, tail twitching, rear end shifting. Jimmy shouted, "Lizzy!" and threw himself in front of me just as the cat launched himself into the air.

As the paws left the earth, the animal became a man; inch by inch the beast arched, going up a panther, coming back down a person. He crashed into Jimmy, who smashed into me, and we all fell in a tangle of legs and arms onto the dry grass.

Jimmy grabbed for the guy, but he slipped away—it's hard to get a grip on the naked. Instead of running or kicking, biting, scratching and punching, he went to his knees.

"Mistress," he said, and kissed my foot.

"Oh, brother," Jimmy muttered.

"I swear my allegiance."

"Swell," I said. "You can—uh—get up now."

He got up; then I wished I'd let him stay down. Standing, naked in the moonlight, he was disturbing. Tall and sleek, he resembled the panther he'd so recently been. His hair shiny and dark, his eyes were an eerie yellow-green.

I glanced at the garden. "You were the statue."

The man lowered his chin in agreement.

"He was a statue?" Jimmy asked. "And you didn't think this was something I should know before I stuck him with silver?"

"I didn't connect it right away."

"You see a statue of a panther, then a panther shows up, but you don't connect it."

"Yeah, weird, hey? How bizarre that I didn't realize the statue had come to life."

Jimmy lifted his eyebrows at my sarcasm but didn't comment; instead he turned to the panther man. "Gargoyle?" he asked.

The man spread graceful hands, the muscles rippling beneath his moon-pale skin. "I am."

Gargoyles had once been animals. They'd aided the fairies left on the earth after the doors of heaven slammed closed.

The fairies had been lost. They had no idea how to survive. They were suddenly human, and they had no idea how to be.

Certain beasts of the earth helped them, and as a reward they were given the gifts of flight and shapeshifting. Gargoyles can sprout wings; they can turn to stone.

Once the fairies could manage on their own, the gargoyles were charged with protecting the weak and unwary from demon attacks. The more humans the gargoyles saved, the more human they became.

"Summer sent you," I said.

The man nodded, his gaze on Megan's second-floor window. "No one will hurt her while I am here."

There was a slight cant of the Irish in his voice, but not much. I'd been told that many of the fairies had gravitated to Ireland after the fall because the rolling green hills reminded them of heaven. I'd bet money that a lot of the gargoyles had gone along.

Jimmy put away his switchblade. "What's your name?" he asked.

"Quinn Fitzpatrick."

"And you just hang out in Megan's yard all night?" I asked.

"Shouldn't I?"

"What about during the day?"

He grinned, his teeth no longer sharp and large but normal, if extremely white. "I'm the new bartender."

My eyebrows lifted. "The one who's so lame Megan doesn't believe you can walk and chew gum at the same time?"

Quinn's grin faded. "She said that?"

"Not in so many words."

"Well, I didn't want her to know, you see, that I was sent. So I had to pretend to be more human than I am."

"By dropping things?"

"How else?"

I had no idea. How did one seem more human? If I knew, I'd have tried it long ago. I'd always been considered odd, even before Ruthie had touched me and made me even more so.

"Megan doesn't know?"

"That I'm her bodyguard? No."

"Keep it that way."

Megan had told me in no uncertain terms that she didn't need any help. She was wrong, so I'd ignored her. But I wouldn't put it past her to make life hell for Quinn if she discovered he was the babysitter.

"Have there been any Nephilim sniffing around?" I asked.

"Legion."

Man, I hated that word.

"When you say 'legion,'" I continued, "I don't get a clear picture."

"Dozens, mistress." He straightened, puffing out his extremely nice chest. "They're all dust."

"Uh—nice job."

I thanked God again that I'd sent someone to watch over Megan. Thanked Him three times that Summer had actually listened, and that she'd sent someone who knew what he was doing.

"The more Nephilim I kill, the more hours each day I can remain in this form," he said. "Soon I will be completely a man." He glanced up at the window again. "Although I do not protect her for my benefit. I would protect her even if I lost my humanity instead of gaining it."

Hmm. Interesting.

"Any clues as to why they're after her?" I asked.

"They aren't after her, but you." Quinn's gaze met mine. "They think you'll come back to see your friend. Visit your home." He spread his huge paws—I mean hands. "The grave of your foster mother." He peered around nervously. "You should go."

"You'll watch over Megan and the kids."

He put his hand over his heart. "With my life, mistress."

"Call me Liz."

"Liz. I've ended more Nephilim here than I ever managed when my seer was alive."

"Your seer died?"

"In the recent purge."

Jimmy turned away, but not before I saw the pain flash across his face. He still thought it was his fault.

Technically it was. Jimmy could dream walk—stroll through a person's mind while they were sleeping and pluck secrets from the mist. That he'd been compelled to steal the names and locations of the federation's members from Ruthie's head by his vampire father did not make what Jimmy had done hurt him any less. That so many had died because of it—that Ruthie had—was something he might never get over.

"You need a new seer?" I asked.

"I work here now." Quinn shrugged. "I've no need of anything else."

Good. One less thing. If I ever got my own power back, became the seer I was supposed to be before everything went to hell—or before hell came to me— I'd take him on. I'd lost a few DKs in the purge too. I had openings.

The dead bolt on the back door clicked. All three of us froze, glancing first at one another and then at the door as it began to open.

The next instant, we were behind the thick shrubs that separated Megan's yard from the yard to the north. I hoped the neighbor didn't have a yippy dog that would announce our presence.

Megan stepped onto her porch, her gaze searching the shadows. She wore a pair of Max's old department sweatpants, cut off above the knee, and a shamrock green tank top that read: *Murphy's.*

She looked exactly the same—short and cute, with curling red hair and dark blue eyes, a few freckles on her darling pert nose. Her arms were round but toned—from lugging around three kids, their stuff, trays of food and drinks—her legs solid and sleek. Twelve hours a day on your feet will do that.

"Liz?" she murmured.

I bit my lip, forced myself to remain silent. If she knew I was here, she'd want to spend time with me, talk awhile. I wanted that too. I missed her so damn much. But I couldn't hang around, couldn't risk any Nephilim seeing me with her, knowing how much I cared. So far I'd been lucky. But luck never went my way for very long.

Megan sighed. Her shoulders sagged. I felt like a shit. I promised myself I'd call as soon as I could and do my best to reassure her that everything was fine.

Jimmy tapped my shoulder. I turned my head, and he jerked his at Quinn. The gargoyle stared at Megan with an expression I recognized—complete fascination and utter devotion.

"He loves her," Jimmy whispered. "Nothing will *ever* hurt her while he's here."

For an instant I closed my eyes and remembered what it was like to know that Jimmy loved me that way and what it had been like to destroy that love for the sake of the world.

Sucked, but I'd do it again.

I wasn't sure how I felt about a gargoyle being in love with my best friend and my partner's widow, but Jimmy was right.

That devotion would keep Megan alive.

Eventually she went back inside. I hurried along the side of the neighbor's house and onto the street a block away. Jimmy and I would only have to cut around one more corner and we'd be back at Murphy's, where we'd left the car.

Quinn emerged from the shadows with his pants

on. At least he was human enough to know that walking down the street naked would get him noticed.

"Thank you." I held out my hand, and Quinn took it. I had a flash of fire on the ocean, ice bobbing in a sea of flames.

I tilted my head, and he smiled. "If I hurt her, feel free."

I realized he'd just shown me the way to kill him, although I wasn't sure how flames could dance on water and ice survived fire, but if he hurt her, I'd figure it out. That he'd shown me such a secret made me trust him even more.

I handed Quinn my cell phone number. "If you need help—"

He pocketed it and nodded.

"We should go," I said.

Though we were alone on the street, we couldn't hang around. Someone might glance out the window. A cop could come by. We might not resemble gang members, but we had no business loitering on a street corner in the middle of the night. Who did?

Max had always told me "nothing good happens after midnight," and he'd been right. If I was still a cop and I saw us, I'd pull over and run every one of us through the system. We'd all be detained. Jimmy's record was . . . colorful, mine newly blackened and Quinn's . . . Lord only knew what would turn up.

With a nod to the gargoyle, I turned toward the car, and Jimmy followed. "We need to get to New Mexico."

"Summer's not dumb enough to go there," he said.

"I don't need her. Sawyer's been around long enough to know what a dagda is and where to find one."

"Dagda?" Quinn echoed, and I froze, even as Jimmy cursed.

"Do you know where to find one?" I asked.

"One?" His face creased in confusion. "There is only one."

"Explain."

"*The* Dagda. The good God."

I stilled as icy dread skated up my back. "The Dagda is a god."

"No. There is only one of those. Although many aspire."

Whew.

"So the Dagda is on our side?"

"Not necessarily."

"But he's good."

"Not good as in morally, but good as in all-powerful. Good at everything."

Well, I had been searching for an über-fairy.

"Do you know where he is?"

"He isn't anywhere."

"Everyone's somewhere, Quinn. Spill it."

"The Dagda has immense power. He can kill many with a single blow of his club and resurrect them simply by tapping the lifeless bodies with the handle. His caldron contains magic beyond compare."

"Just the guy I need to see." I narrowed my eyes. "Now."

"Those who approach the Dagda do not return the same."

I glanced at Jimmy, who appeared fascinated by the descending moon. "That's exactly what I had in mind."

"What do you want of him?"

I didn't care to explain the particulars of Summer's sex spell—even if I'd known them—that kept Jimmy's vampire nature dormant, unless there was a full moon, so I stuck to the facts.

"I need a spell reversed. He can do that, right?"

Quinn nodded, but still he hesitated. "The Dagda is both good and evil. He hasn't yet chosen a side."

"All the more reason to have a talk." An all-powerful fairy god just might come in handy. "Point me in the right direction, Quinn, and I'll do the rest."

"There is no direction, mistress." He cleared his throat when I gave him a narrow glare. "Liz," he corrected. "The Dagda lives in the Otherworld, a land that exists parallel to this one."

"Parallel," I repeated.

He spread his hands. "Another realm that is beneath."

"Beneath what?"

"The earth."

"How far beneath? Tartarus level?"

His yellow-green eyes widened. "No! He isn't a Grigori."

"But he lives beneath."

"The Dagda lives in the Otherworld because he does not care for this one."

"Why not?"

"Do you?"

Actually, I did care for it, very much. Otherwise I wouldn't be risking my life, love and the pursuit of all my happiness to save it. But explain that to a gargoyle.

"How do we get there?"

"I know the way."

I shot a glance at Jimmy. He still stared at the sky. "Summer didn't."

"She wouldn't. Until we chose a side—good or evil—we resided in the Otherworld. Summer chose right away."

"Wow, she's a saint," I muttered.

"She may become one if the forces of light triumph. If the forces of darkness rule"—he shook his head—"I wouldn't want to be her."

If the forces of darkness ruled, I wasn't going to want to be me. Hell, no one on our side was going to want to be us anymore if the demons ruled the world.

Which meant we had to move forward. Jimmy had to become again a darkness that was equal to my own. Ruthie had said that was the only way we could fight the Grigori that had been released and were even now repopulating the earth with a legion—that cursed word again—of Nephilim. We had to be as badass as they were.

"How do we get to the Otherworld?" I asked.

"I can open the door anywhere. All I need is a hill."

He turned and slipped into a nearby yard. I reached for Jimmy's hand, figuring I'd have to drag him, but he lifted both arms, as if in surrender. "I'll come."

I motioned for him to go ahead of me. I wasn't stupid. I turned my back, and Jimmy went poof. He'd done it before.

But he followed Quinn without complaint. Jimmy's hangdog behavior was bugging me more than his usual bravado. I almost wanted him to slug me, if only so I could slug him back.

In the yard a slight mound of grass made a pathetic hill, but Milwaukee wasn't exactly rolling in them. I think the closest knoll was a good twenty-minute drive.

"Lie down," Quinn ordered, and we did. From his pocket he drew a cloth bag.

"Dirt from the Otherworld," he explained, then dipped his fingers within. "Only those who have been there possess it."

He sprinkled the dirt over us. The falling specks felt like cool sand against my face. The scent of moist earth surrounded us. The sky appeared to be receding.

"Crap," I said. But it was too late; we sank, the dirt streaming in on us from above, the ground sinking away below.

I reached for Jimmy's hand again, managing to link our fingers together right before we were buried alive.

CHAPTER 8

I never thought it would end like this—suffocating as earth filled my mouth, my nose, blocked the starlight from my eyes. No, I figured I'd go down in a blaze of glory—sword slashing, blood everywhere—perhaps during the final battle called Armageddon.

Jimmy's fingers tightened on mine, and the panic that had threatened receded. At least we were together. At least he hadn't pulled away again.

Then we landed with a thud in a cool, gray, misty world, and Jimmy did pull away. I blinked and dirt cascaded off my lashes. I scrubbed it from my face, my eyes, my hair, then glanced up. The sky was brown; the earth beneath our feet swirled like a cloud.

"Upside down," Jimmy murmured.

We stood. The mist was so thick we couldn't see anything but each other.

"Now what, Sherlock?" Jimmy asked.

"We find the Dagda."

"By wandering around blindly, dropping off the edge of time and into a hell dimension?"

Music flowed on the mist; it sounded like a—

"Harp." I smiled. "They don't play harps in hell."

"How do you know? If I were a demon—"

"You are."

"Do you really want to throw that stone?"

Good point.

"If I were a demon," he continued, "I'd use harps to lure the unwary right into the pit."

"I'll remember that." And I would, because he was probably right.

The harp music drifted closer, became louder. Jimmy and I pulled out our silver knives. I always felt better with something sharp and shiny in my hand.

From the fog stepped a tall, broad man with a huge club slung about his waist. In one arm he held a harp made of glistening, polished, intricately carved wood, with strings of gold that he plucked with large yet nimble fingers.

His hair was the sun and his eyes the sky. His teeth when he smiled were as white as winter ice and his lips the shade of a sunset in the west.

He was huge—everywhere. About eight feet tall, several feet wide, probably three hundred pounds. How could he walk on the clouds? Big feet, big hands and a codpiece—who wore those anymore?—the size of a dinner plate, which appeared to barely contain his impressive package.

At the sight of us he paused. The harp disappeared, as did his smile. The silence that descended when the music died seemed to pulse in my ears like thunder.

He reached for his club; the thing detached from his belt and flew through the air into his hand. "How did you get in?"

"Quinn."

He relaxed somewhat, though he didn't put the club back.

"Are you the Dagda?"

He stared me up and down, the perusal as blatant

as any I'd received while tending bar at Murphy's. "Who wants to know?"

"Elizabeth Phoenix."

His smile returned. "The leader of the light."

"Word travels," Jimmy said.

"I am not completely cut off from your world. My people come here for rest, for protection, for . . ." He grinned again. "Vacation."

"Seems like a real rockin' place," I said.

"It is peaceful. No one can enter the Otherworld who has not been here before. Or who is not given entry by one of us. This is not bestowed lightly." He swung his club, one slash right and then left, and the displaced air nearly blew us off our feet. "If I am displeased by those granted entry, they die. Badly."

"People always say that," Jimmy murmured. "But really, what is 'dying goodly'?"

The Dagda scowled, seemingly annoyed by the mere sound of Sanducci's voice. "Silence your pet, light's leader, or I will silence him for you."

"You can try." Jimmy stepped forward.

I elbowed him back. "This is not a pissing contest, Sanducci."

"Could have fooled me."

"Behave," I muttered. "We need him."

"You come to convince me to join your fight," the Dagda continued.

"Eventually," I agreed. "But first things first. I'd like you to remove a spell."

"From your collar?"

I reached up and fingered the jewels. "No. From him."

The Dagda's gaze turned toward Jimmy, and he took in a deep breath, tilted his head and frowned.

"Plenus luna malum," he said, reciting the name of the spell. "His vampire is beneath the moon."

"Yes. I was told that you could release it."

"It will not be easy for me. Or comfortable for him."

"But you *can* do it."

"I can do anything."

Jimmy snorted, and I sent him a glare before returning my attention to the Dagda.

"Will you?" I asked.

The Dagda's gaze slid over me. "For a price."

"No," Jimmy said. "She's mine."

The words "since when" were on the tip of my tongue, but Jimmy narrowed his eyes, and I kept them to myself.

"Sacrifices must be made," the Dagda murmured. "You know that. Nothing is for free."

"What, exactly, are we talking about?" I asked.

"A boon. A favor."

"Could you be more specific?" I didn't like promising what I didn't understand.

"I don't know now what I might need later."

"No," Jimmy repeated. "It's too dangerous."

"You wish the spell reversed; I am the only one powerful enough to do so." The Dagda shrugged. "I wish for a boon from the leader of the light. It's simple. Say yes and get what you came for, or say no and go back where you came from. And good luck winning your battle without the proper—"he lifted a brow—"equipment."

Ruthie had said we needed to be as evil as they were to win, and I'd seen the truth of this myself when I'd fought the Naye'i. She'd had no humanity, no compassion, no restraint. She'd killed horribly and often and without remorse. I would never have been able to best her without the physical strength and the inner fury of my demon. With the Grigori loose, creating Nephilim by the minute, we needed more power than mine. We needed Jimmy's.

Since the Dagda appeared to be the only one who could remove the spell and release Jimmy's demon, the choice was even simpler than the fairy god had made out. Because I didn't have one.

"Just to be clear . . . You'll release Jimmy's demon *and* you'll join our side," I stated. "In return, I'll do something unknown for you at a future date."

"Both the spell and the choosing of sides," the Dagda mused. "This will have to be a very great favor."

"I figured that."

He smiled. "So did I."

"Don't I have anything to say about this?" Jimmy asked.

"No," the Dagda and I answered at the same time.

"How long will it take?" I asked.

"*Plenus luna malum* is not easily cast. I will do my best to be quick, but removing it is not simple either. You must leave him with me."

"But—"

"You have work to do, light's leader. You cannot tarry here."

"You'll let me know when he's—" I stopped, uncertain what to say. Not *better.* Not *cured* or *healed.* More like *worse.* Cursed and possessed and insane with a lust for blood and death, destruction and chaos.

"Yes," the Dagda agreed. "When we are finished, I will contact you." I opened my mouth to ask how—he was underground—and the Dagda held up a hand. "I have ways. Do not worry about that."

"You'll have to bespell . . . something." I traced the collar around my neck. "Or he'll be—"

"I know what he'll be, and I will take every precaution. I prefer my own blood right where it is and not soaking into the ground of the Otherworld."

I took a deep breath, glanced at Jimmy, whose face was tense and pale, but I nodded, and Jimmy closed his eyes so he wouldn't have to look at me anymore.

"The deal is made," the Dagda said. "Now it must be sealed."

"With blood, I suppose."

"A kiss is so much more binding."

"You want me to kiss you."

He tilted his head. "Is that a problem?"

"I can just imagine what the 'favor's' gonna be if you're sealing the deal with a kiss," Jimmy muttered. "But then that's right up your alley."

He was angry, hurt, betrayed. I couldn't blame him for lashing out. So why did I?

"I could use more power." I lifted one shoulder, then lowered it. "Why not his?"

Jimmy stared at me as if he'd just realized something and he didn't much like it. "You've changed."

I laughed. "You think?"

"No more talk." The Dagda reached for me. Jimmy made a move, as if he'd put himself between us, and the fairy god sent him to the ground with one sharp glare from his ice-blue eyes.

"Stay," the Dagda murmured, and then he kissed me.

As kisses went, it wasn't so bad. A mere brush of his lips, soft and almost sweet—not even a hint of tongue. Unfortunately, at the first touch I saw the truth of what he'd do to Jimmy.

It *was* going to hurt.

I jerked back, my lips forming "no" but my voice too bound by horror to set the word free.

The Dagda's intent gaze bored into mine. "Do you choose to spare him even if it means the end of the world?"

And that "no" I'd been choking on flew free.

CHAPTER 9

The next instant I was on top of the hill instead of below it. I laid my hand against the cool green grass and murmured, "Sorry."

Then I got to my feet and I left Jimmy behind.

Quinn had disappeared. I assumed he was making like a statue in Megan's garden again, which was where he should be. I should be—

Anywhere but here.

I got in the Navigator and headed for the airport. The only place I could think to go was New Mexico.

Eight hours later, I stepped off the plane in Albuquerque—flights from Milwaukee to the Southwest were few and far between—then rented a car and drove north.

Sawyer lived at the very edge of the Navajo reservation near Mount Taylor, one of the four sacred mountains that marked the boundaries of Navajo land, known as the Dinetah, or the Glittering World. In that world, strange things happened. Especially around Sawyer.

I drove through flat, arid plains that would eventually give way to mountain foothills dotted with towering ponderosa pines. Canyons surrounded by high, spiked, sandy shaded rock shared space with the red mesas immortalized forever in the westerns of John Ford.

I was still a few miles from Sawyer's place when a lone black wolf appeared next to my car. Most wolves wouldn't have been able to keep pace at 60 miles per hour, but this wasn't most wolves.

I pulled to the side of the road and stepped out. The beast paused in the mesquite scrub and stared at me, tongue lolling, spooky gray eyes fixed on my face.

"How did you know I was coming?" I asked.

He tilted his head, didn't answer. Couldn't. Sawyer might be more than a wolf, but he still couldn't talk.

"I'll meet you at the house."

I made a move to get back into the car, and he let out a low *woof*, then pawed at the dirt and shook his whole body as if he'd just climbed out of an icy cold bath.

"Why don't you shift back so we can talk?"

He lifted his upper lip and showed me his teeth.

"Oookay." I stared at him for several seconds. "You didn't get yourself cursed again, did you?"

Sawyer had been cursed by his mother, the Naye'i, or woman of smoke. For years, centuries, millennia— who knew?—he'd been unable to leave the Dinetah as a man. But since I'd torn her to shreds, the curse was broken.

I contemplated Saywer's fuzzy ears and bushy tail. Unless it wasn't.

I sighed. Sawyer obviously had no desire to return to his human form at the moment, and since making a wolf do anything, especially this wolf, was damn near impossible, I'd have to compromise.

"If you can't beat 'em." I opened the trunk of the rental, then pulled a silk robe from my duffel. "Join 'em."

A gift from Sawyer, the robe had been fashioned in every shade of midnight—blue, purple, black with sparkles of silver—the image of a wolf flickered in the folds. Skinwalkers can shape-shift, but they need a little help. Sawyer, in human form, had tattoos everywhere. They depicted mammals and birds and insects—every single one a creature of prey. To shift, he touched a tattoo and became whatever lay beneath the stroke of his fingers. I could do the same. Touch him and become them.

However, sometimes, like now, touching Sawyer's tattoos wasn't an option, so I used the robe.

Quickly I lost my clothes. The jeweled collar around my neck had been bespelled, which allowed it to shift shape along with me. A good thing, since a vampire werewolf was something I really didn't want to be.

I swirled the garment around my shoulders and embraced the familiar bright flash of light that heralded the change. A blast of cold, followed by heat, then the fall from two feet to four, the shift from human to wolf. It didn't hurt, not really, but it freaked me out every single time.

Phoenix.

Sawyer's deep, melodious voice echoed in my head—the telepathy that existed between shifters in their bestial forms.

What's going on? I asked. *The curse should be broken.*

It is.

He circled closer, slid along my body, rubbed his face against mine, and I let him. While human, I didn't trust him. He kept too many secrets, told too many lies. But in this form we were pack, joined in a way no one else could ever understand. Animals don't lie. I'm not sure they're capable of it.

If you can leave the Dinetah as a man, then why are you furry?

He whirled and took off across the deserted terrain. I hesitated, but only for an instant. In this form certain things called to me, and running was one of them.

True wolves can cover 125 miles in a day and run 40 miles per hour. Shifters are much faster, and skinwalkers can move so quickly they seem to disappear in one place, then appear in another. Part of the reason we excel in this area is that we love it. Running frees us.

I chased Sawyer until I caught him; then I jumped onto his back and we rolled onto the ground, tussling and snapping, nuzzling and nipping. But all too soon, he sidestepped and ran away again. Sawyer wasn't much for play, unless it was sex play. The man was a sexual god.

Maybe that was hyperbole. But not by much. He'd had centuries to hone his skills. He could seduce anyone, was comfortable doing anything. Unfortunately, sex meant nothing to Sawyer but a means to whatever end he was after at the time. That didn't make the sex any less spectacular. But the aftermath was a bitch.

I understood why he was the way he was. His mother had screwed him up. Didn't they always? However, Sawyer's mother had screwed him up by actually screwing him. The federation had helped to make Sawyer a head case to rival all head cases by using his talent as a catalyst telepath—he could free blocked supernatural abilities through sex. He'd certainly unblocked me.

That he'd drugged me and slept with me to do so was still a matter of contention between us, but since I'd discovered the truth about his mother, I was a little less likely to plunge a knife into his back when he wasn't looking. I still hadn't forgiven him, but I kind of understood why he'd thought it was okay. His boundaries were as fucked up as he was.

We ran for miles. It felt so good just to be out in the fresh air, with the wind in my fur and nothing else to do but be.

Night hovered at the edge of the horizon. Mount Taylor loomed ahead, towering and beautiful. Full of mystery and magic. It was on that mountain that I'd become who I was right now. I still wasn't sure how I felt about that.

There was destiny and this was mine. I hadn't wanted it. Still didn't. But we very rarely get what we want. We move on and we live or we die, but we deal.

Sawyer headed away from the mountain, across the scrabbly land. Just when I was about to ask where we were going and why, he paused, crouched and seemed to disappear from the earth.

I let out a surprised *woof* and his head popped up as if he'd been buried in the dirt. *Come*, his voice commanded me.

I followed more slowly and saw that the dry ground had crumbled away into a fairly deep hollow, one side open to the steadily descending night and the other trailing back into a twisting cave beneath a rock out-cropping the shade of sand. Sawyer stood with his head inside the cave and his tail dappled by the shadows of the setting sun.

What do you smell? he asked as I joined him.

I took a whiff. Something wild and gamey, not human but not completely inhuman, something that did not belong, yet something I recognized but could not quite put a name to.

I don't know.

Not coyote, not wolf, he mused.

No. Those I'd smelled before.

He crawled in.

Hey! Not a good idea.

What if the animal that had been living in this place came back and found us there?

Sawyer didn't respond, and he didn't reappear. I stood outside for a few more seconds; then after a quick glance behind me, I went in too.

The place was a burrow, tight and warm and dry. It smelled of whatever had found it, a lot of them.

Maddening. His thought came to me loud and clear along with the flavor of his emotions. In this form feelings were like auras, scents perhaps. Laughter smelled like syrup. Fury like fire. And right now, overlaying the smell of unknown beast, I caught a whiff like sweet-and-sour sauce. Confusion. Sawyer wasn't sure what to make of this place and this intruder any more than I was.

Why don't we go outside? Wait and watch for them to return and then we'll know.

He lowered his head in agreement. I tried to turn and trot back toward the gray oval of the entrance and so did he. His chest bumped my rear end. My tail slid across his nose. We froze, tangled together, pressed close and unable to move without pressing even closer. Then his breath brushed over me, and I understood the meaning of "being in heat."

Sawyer had lived as a wolf. He'd mated as one. He wanted to do so again, and he wanted to do so with me. I'd resisted. The idea made me squirrelly. Or at least it had until today. Today my beast was howling for release, my skin twitching beneath the fur, the scent of Sawyer, of me, of this place, making me consider lowering my shoulders, lifting my rump, then allowing him to mount me from behind and—

He moved, and I bolted from the burrow, slamming into him so hard he in turn slammed into the wall and caused dirt to sift over us like rain.

Panicked, I reached for and became myself, the air going from hot to cold as the bright flash of magic that surrounded the shift faded. I stood in the moonlight naked and panting, my body still aroused, my mind churning like a storm-shrouded sea.

Another flash of light warred against the stars in the navy blue sky, and then Sawyer stood next to me. At least he had tattoos between him and the night.

In human form, he wasn't handsome. His face was too finely angled for that, but he was striking, with silky black hair trailing past his shoulders, his bronze skin a sharp contrast to his strangely light eyes.

I'd never known a Navajo to have gray eyes, especially a full-blood like Sawyer, which led me to believe those eyes had marked him as a skinwalker, a sorcerer, a witch from birth. Since the Navajo fear the supernatural and hate witches above all else, this probably explained a lot about Sawyer.

"When we're wolves, Phoenix, we're wolves," he began.

"We're not."

I pulled my gaze away from the sleek, glistening expanse of his skin. No matter how much he infuriated me, scared me, confused me, if Sawyer took off his clothes—and he did that a lot—my mouth went dry and my mind went south. No one on earth, in any century, had a better body than Sawyer.

"Wolves can't think," I continued, "can't reason, can't talk to one another with their minds."

"Are you sure?"

I drew back my arm to slug him; I don't know why. I couldn't hurt him. I didn't know if anyone or anything could. He grabbed my wrist, quicker than the snake tattooed on his penis. I'd never been sure if that was Sawyer's idea of a joke or not.

My other hand came up, also clenched into a fist, and headed right for his blade of a nose. He snatched that wrist too. Our bodies smacked together—breast to chest, hip to hip.

His snake was awake.

I had an instant to think, *What the hell?* and then we were kissing. If you could call it that. More of a battle—with teeth clashing, tongues plunging, tiny nips at the lips and the chin. We might be human—or then again we might not be—but we were behaving more like animals than we had only moments before.

I'm not exactly certain what got into me, besides him. Sure, I was still aroused from the encounter in the burrow, and being naked in the pine-scented shadow of Mount Taylor with the breeze stirring my hair and the light of the stars dancing across my skin would make anyone moon mad.

Perhaps I needed to have sex with someone for no other reason than that. No exchange of power—I already had Sawyer's and I didn't get double no matter how many times I tried—no favors to be granted, no boons to be asked, no forgiveness to be begged. Just sex with a man who knew better than any how to have it.

I tugged on my wrists, and he let them go so I could run my open palms over his incredible body. As I touched each tattoo the essence of the beast flickered— wolf, hawk, crocodile, tarantula, snaaaaake.

The hiss of a rattler slid through my mind even as the sleek, hard skin of Sawyer slid through my hand.

He cursed, then nipped my collarbone. He was as on edge as I was.

A growl purred through the air—him or me? Hard to say. His hands at my hips, he twirled me around, my back to his front. We were nearly the same height, Sawyer maybe an inch taller, which allowed his erection to rest in the cleft of my buttocks. The sensation was exquisite. I rubbed against him like a cat.

He cupped my breasts, lifting them like an offering to the goddess of the moon, her silvery breath a hint of frost across our skin.

His lips at the curve of my neck caressed; his teeth worried a fold, a siren call to what lay captured inside of me. His tongue trailed along the collar that bound me, tickled beneath it, and the demon within me roared.

I bent at the waist, took him in from behind. As always, he knew what I wanted, what I needed, better than I did. Fast, hard, no words, only actions. Make me forget, make me feel but not think, make me come.

He held me to him with one arm around my waist, palm warm at my belly as his long, supple fingers stroked me higher and higher even as his other hand teased my nipples until they peaked and ached and burned. His body slammed into me so violently the slap of skin on skin echoed in the still and silent night, the sound as enticing as the actions.

I wanted more and he gave me more, he gave me all that he had, all that he could, until together we convulsed, our bodies shuddering against each other, within, around, as one.

When the glow faded—it always did—I straightened. He stepped back. I cast him a glance, but he was staring at the moon and not at me.

He looked exactly the same as he had the first time

I'd seen him, and he always would. Sawyer was age-
less, virtually indestructible and, for those reasons and
several others, damned dangerous. Lucky for us he was
on our side.

I think. With Sawyer, one could never quite tell.

I opened my mouth, but before I could speak, howls
erupted from the darkness all around us. Weird howls.
Howls that did not belong in the New Mexico desert.
More like calls, maybe cackles.

"Foxes?" I asked.

"No." Sawyer tensed, muscles gliding beneath
marked skin. The tattoos seemed to live, to breathe,
even dance. Since they were magic tattoos, fashioned
by a sorcerer wielding lightning rather than a biker
guy with a needle and ink, dancing wasn't completely
out of the question.

Shadows flickered, meeting, melding, then separat-
ing into strangely hunched figures that moved with a
rolling yet oddly jerky gait.

"What are they?" I whispered.

"Hyenas," Sawyer said, even as their hair-raising
laughter rose again toward the moon.

"In New Mexico," I clarified.

Sawyer cast me a quick, unreadable glance. "They
aren't real hyenas."

"Duh," I muttered, my gaze returning to the steadily
multiplying shades.

Sawyer and I had no weapons but ourselves. Good
thing we were pretty amazing.

I reached for his biceps where the image of a black
wolf howled. But Sawyer stopped me with a quick
shake of his head as he circled my wrist and drew my
hand much, much lower.

For an instant I resisted. This was no time to play

with the snake; then Sawyer spoke. "The only animals the hyenas fear are the big cats."

My gaze lit on his thigh, where the image of a tiger roamed. I laid my palm on Sawyer's leg, high up where his pulse beat thick and heavy.

"I hope you're right," I said.

CHAPTER 10

The flash came again—bright light and icy heat, the whoosh of the breeze as I fell. I'd never changed into a tiger, wasn't sure what to expect.

I'd discovered over time that shape-shifting—at least for skinwalkers—had nothing to do with our human shape. When I was a wolf, I was a wolf. Less than a hundred pounds despite being quite a bit over a hundred pounds as a human. As a snake, I was a regular-sized snake. As a tiger, I appeared to be one big mother—maybe three hundred pounds if the size of my paws and the drag of flesh on my bones was any indication.

A second flash drew my attention to Sawyer. Damn, he was gorgeous. Orange coat, brown stripes, sleek, muscular and even bigger than me.

The hyenas were toast.

Unfortunately, they didn't appear to see it that way. Instead of running for their lives as a good hyena should when confronted with a tiger, they surged forward.

Sure, there were a bazillion of them. But tigers were *mean* if the roiling, burning fury that pulsed in my blood was any indication. Seeing the hyenas here, on my land, my place, my *territory*, made me want to crunch their bones like uncooked spaghetti.

The pack came at us like a wave. I went with my

instincts; they were all I had. One swipe from my mammoth paw and the first hyena's neck broke. I sank my teeth into the throat of another and twisted, then just kept smacking and tearing, snatching and yanking, mowing through the throng on the left as Sawyer did the same from the right. With any luck, we'd meet in the middle unscathed.

If I'd been nothing more than human I would have died. I had no idea what killed a hyena shifter—silver, gold, bullets, knives, strangulation with the cursed entrails of a billy goat. However, a fight to the death *between* shifters works nearly every time, and the telltale burst of ash from each hyena proved it was working just fine right now.

That was the good news. The bad news? There were too many of them. They were legion—again.

They tag-teamed us. I began to bleed. Would a skinwalker die if bled to death by the wounds of another shifter? I didn't know.

What I did know was that to kill me, they had to kill not only my skinwalker nature but my dhampir and vampire natures as well. Not that it couldn't be done. It would just take time. But from the number of hyenas tumbling over the dunes, time was on their side.

What should we do? I thought.

Sawyer replied, *Keep fighting. Help will arrive.*

Help? From where? What? Who? How? And most important—when?

Two hyenas engaged me from the front, and as I smacked them around, a third snagged my leg and clamped down. Hyenas have the most powerful jaws in the animal kingdom. I roared as bones snapped.

The thunder of my call made the shifter flinch, and I pulled away. But I was hurt, couldn't move as fast, wouldn't heal completely until I shifted back into my human form, which I couldn't do with an army of hyenas all around.

Sawyer jabbed and parried, tossing animals willy-nilly. He was bleeding too; one particularly nasty wound flapped open on his shoulder, making him gimp as badly as I did. I began to get a little scared. We weren't going to last forever.

Help! I thought. A plea. A prayer. Right now, not much more than a platitude.

Then a roar split the heavens. Everyone froze, glanced upward. I almost expected to see fire raining down. Perhaps a huge celestial hand sweeping from the sky and scooping Sawyer and me to safety.

Hey, I *had* lost a lot of blood.

Instead, a lion stood on a nearby rise, the desert breeze ruffling his mane, the rising moon throwing silver sparkles across the golden expanse of his fur.

He loped down the hill, came at the army of hyenas with wild and savage abandon. Waded into them with claws and teeth and snarls. They scattered like pigeons. Unfortunately, they regrouped like pigeons too.

I braced myself for the onslaught, then sent out a thought to the lion: *Run, Luther!*

Luther was a street kid we'd picked up last month south of Indianapolis. He was a Marbas, the offspring of a lion shifter and a conjurer. His parents had been killed by other lions—a cadre of shifters descended from the demon Barbas—and we still weren't sure why.

Luther had become the latest addition to the federation. He was an accomplished channeler and a damn good fighter—living on the streets tends to make that happen. I should know.

For an instant I thought he hadn't heard me. Lions

and tigers are similar, can even interbreed. Ligers, anyone? Or tigons? However, we aren't the same species, and our telepathy might be funky.

But Luther cast me a scornful glance—the type every teenager gives his idiot parents—then went right back to fighting the hyenas. He seemed to be enjoying himself, crunching and munching his way through half a dozen.

My leg was healing—slowly, but I could put weight on it. With the addition of Luther, we held off the tide. However, at this rate, we weren't going to win. It was only a matter of time until they did.

Luther roared, both pain and fury, and I drove forward, finishing off every hyena in my path until I reached him. Ever since I'd met the kid, I'd felt a bizarre affinity for him, a near maternal devotion I didn't understand but couldn't shake. When I saw one of the speckled beasts with his teeth sunk into Luther's neck, I grabbed the freaky humpback by his hump and tore him free.

Luther bled from several nasty gashes, but they didn't slow him down in the least. He turned to face another wave, and I snarled. He ignored me some more.

I couldn't force him to leave; I had my paws full. But if we lived through this, we were going to have words. Despite Summer's dig that I was no longer in charge, I was. Especially of Luther.

I don't know how long we fought the hyenas, how many we killed or how many more poured into the fight. But there came a time when it was just Sawyer and I in the middle of the fray, and my chest seized up, thinking that some of the ash floating through the air was Luther.

Then I saw a flash of leonine tail at the outskirts of the melee. Luther trailed a circle of bloody footprints around the hyenas. And as he did so, they stopped fighting, milling within the confines of the paw prints, bumping against one another and snarling but never breaking the plane.

Now what? I thought. Should we slaughter them while they were confined? Or perhaps leave them within the charmed ring forever?

Get out, Sawyer ordered. *Quickly, before the spell is complete.*

Neither one of us had any problem stepping past the bloody circle. As soon as my pads touched the pristine dirt on the other side, a faint chanting arose. Foreign and rhythmic, yet still I recognized Luther's voice in my head.

Blood, the moon, a chant—magic was definitely afoot. I stood back, so did Sawyer, and we watched and listened as the kid weaved an unknown spell.

The night stilled. Silence pressed on us as heavy as a rain-drenched quilt. Then the hyenas began to glow as if the sun poured down on them alone. A tiny flame blazed on each and every one—like E.T.'s heart light—then with a final yipping laugh-howl they burst into ashes. Bizarrely, not a single fleck landed outside that charmed space.

What in hell did you teach him? I murmured as Luther turned and loped toward Mount Taylor.

Not that, Sawyer answered, then followed the lion back home.

Me, I had a car to retrieve, clothes to put on. I might not care if Sawyer saw me in only my skin, but the kid was another story. I wasn't *that* comfortable with shape-shifting. I doubted I ever would be.

Sawyer and I had run a long way as wolves, but I was able to retrace the miles just as easily as a tiger. Sure, a tiger was probably more conspicuous than a naked woman, but weird stuff happened around Sawyer's place all the time.

The locals avoided the area, especially at night. The Navajo are very superstitious. They believe that all sorts of evil spirits walk in the darkness, and they're right.

Sawyer had been outcast by his people. He lived at the edge of the Dinetah. No one talked to him, visited or even, I'd been told, said his name out loud, so I didn't have to worry about running into any of the Navajo at this time of night. And if a white person happened by and saw me, well, they'd be much more likely to write off seeing a tiger than a naked woman to their imagination.

My car was right where I'd left it, my clothes too. I slipped into both and moments later the steady hum of the tires on the pavement lulled my still-racing heart back to a more normal beat.

The hyenas had scared me.

Not just that there were hyenas where they did not belong. That happened in my world. But that there were so damned many of them. Would Sawyer and I have been able to handle the swarm without Luther and his spell? How long until something I couldn't handle came along?

Tiny sparks appeared to my right—the lights of Sawyer's place. I wheeled off the main road and headed down the dirt drive. The night was too dark to see everything, but I knew what lay at the end of the lane as well as I knew the tattoos that graced Sawyer's skin.

The house—a small ranch with two bedrooms, a kitchen, bath and living area—sat at the foot of the mountain, along with a hogan, a traditional Navajo dwelling made of logs and dirt.

Behind it, dug into a hill, was a sweat lodge, and

between the two ran an open porch that could be used for both eating and sleeping when the temperature climbed too high.

Sawyer lived in the hogan most of the time, and though he used the coffeemaker in the kitchen, he often cooked his meals over an open flame. Right now that flame leaped toward the sky, sending flickers of shadow and light across the two figures in the yard.

Since Sawyer often wore the traditional breech-clout of the Navajo several centuries in the past, I was surprised to see him in a pair of jeans. He'd tied his long hair back with a strip of rawhide, throwing the planes of his face into sharp relief.

Luther was dressed nearly the same as he'd been the first time I'd seen him. The clothes were just newer and a whole lot cleaner. Sneakers, jeans several sizes too large and a T-shirt. Plain. Olive green. Something an army recruit might wear in basic training, which is kind of what this was.

He appeared to have put on some weight. A good thing; the kid had been far too skinny. He was tall—probably six-two—and his feet and hands revealed the promise of more growth to come.

His skin was darker than mine, lighter than Sawyer's, his hair kinky and a gorgeous combination of gold and sun-streaked brown. His eyes were light—hazel right now, turning amber when his beast began to purr.

I climbed out of the rental and confronted the boy. "I told you to run."

He rolled his eyes. "Why would I run away when I came there to save you?"

"To save us." I glanced at Sawyer, who shrugged. "Did you know he could do . . . whatever that was?"

Sawyer shook his head.

"Who taught you?" I demanded. "Summer?"

The fairy had struck up a friendship with Luther, or perhaps it was vice versa. The kid had issues with strange men. I didn't blame him. I'd seen what lay in his past, and it was much the same as what lay in Jimmy's and my own—people we should have been able to trust proving untrustworthy.

"The fairy has been obsessed with Sanducci, as usual." Sawyer took a drag on a cigarette he hadn't had an instant before, then blew out a stream of smoke on a sigh. "She's been no help training the boy at all."

"So you've been training him?"

"Some."

My gaze sought Luther's. "That's okay?"

Luther nodded. Where, at first, he'd been unable to stand near Sawyer without twitching, would sidle closer to me whenever possible, now he seemed more confident, less uncertain and no longer frightened at all. Might have been teen bravado and very good acting, but I didn't think so.

"You're sure," I pressed.

"I'm as powerful as he is." The kid lifted his chin. "He tries anything, I'll tear him up."

Behind the boy's back Sawyer's smirk was illuminated by the red-orange glow of his cigarette. We both knew better, but there was no point in telling Luther. If he felt safer believing he could take Sawyer, then let him. Sawyer would never touch Luther inappropriately. Sawyer had been touched that way enough himself.

"Why'd you fight at all if you knew a spell to get rid of them?"

"Because I could," the boy said with all the arrogance of his youth and the pride of his lion.

"Just because we *can* fight doesn't mean we should.

Especially if there's a way to end the Nephilim without bloodshed."

Luther's gaze flicked to mine. "I needed blood."

"Theirs?" He shrugged, which I took as a "yes." "You aren't ready to fight yet."

The boy's shoulders straightened. "Am too. I been fightin' all my life."

"Not things like this."

"I did fine." He spread his big hands wide. "Not a mark on me."

"Anymore."

"I heal just like you and him."

"We aren't indestructible, Luther. We can die."

"Speak for yourself," Sawyer murmured, and I shot him a glare. He wasn't helping.

"You brought me here to become one of you," Luther insisted. "I can't if you don't let me."

"But—"

"He's right, Phoenix," Sawyer interrupted, flicking the remnants of his cigarette away. "He's more prepared than you were."

Luther had known there were demons out there, had sensed them and fought, if not actual Nephilim, then humans who were close enough. When I'd discovered the whole demon deal, I was more shocked than I should have been.

I was a cop once. I'd seen things that still made me start up in the night, sweaty and shaking. I should have figured out the score long before Ruthie's death opened my eyes.

I contemplated Luther. "You need to be more careful."

He snorted. "They're all toast. I think they need to be more careful."

Which reminded me.

"If Sawyer didn't teach you the spell and Summer didn't, then—"

The air stilled, yet my hair stirred in an impossible breeze. Luther's carriage changed; his head tilted in a way that was more feminine than masculine; his shoulders rounded so that he seemed ancient and tired with it; even his eyes grew darker, appearing brown instead of hazel.

He opened his mouth, and Ruthie's voice came out. "I taught him, child. Who do you think?"

CHAPTER 11

"That still freaks me out," I muttered.

Since I'd released the vampire side of my dhampir nature, Ruthie no longer spoke in my head or my dreams but through Luther's mouth.

"Don't matter how I talk to you, Lizbeth, just that I do continue to talk. We do what we gotta do to win this war."

"You should know."

Ruthie had taken me in when no one else would. She'd loved me more than anyone else in my life ever had, and because of that I'd adored her. I'd have done anything for Ruthie Kane. When she'd died in my arms, I'd been devastated.

Or at least I would have been devastated if the transfer of power hadn't knocked me into a three-day coma. Then, when I'd woken up, I'd had my hands a little full with the end of the world raining down and monsters I hadn't known existed all trying to kill me.

"You wanna explain that comment, Lizbeth?"

I really didn't but probably should.

"Jimmy said—" Sawyer made a derisive sound, which I ignored. The two of them had been at each other's throats—sometimes literally—forever, it seemed. "He said that you only took in kids with special talents. Ones you could send off to fight this war."

"Not all of my kids are fighters."

My heart lightened. Maybe what I'd always believed about Ruthie was partially true, that her devotion to those who needed someone to love them so badly was real.

"Some of them didn't have the talent," she continued. "It was nearly impossible to gauge power until I got them under my roof."

My hope sputtered and went out. "So you took us in to use us. To sacrifice us on the altar of Armageddon."

Ruthie-Luther tilted her-his head, studying me with eyes that were so much like Ruthie's, set in a face that wasn't, I got chills. "I believe I was the one sacrificed, Lizbeth."

"Just because I'm still alive doesn't mean I haven't lost things." I rubbed my hand over my face. "Some of them were more important to me *than* my life."

Ruthie, for instance. And then there was Jimmy.

Those eyes continued to stare at me, and they knew so much. "You ain't gonna forgive me for that, are you?"

"I'm not sure I can."

I'd discovered only recently that Ruthie's betrayal hadn't just been in her deluding me into believing I'd been chosen by her for my charming personality and not my psychic abilities. Ruthie had also ordered Jimmy to break my heart by sleeping with Summer. She'd wanted me to "see," to hate him so much that when he left me to become a demon killer, I wouldn't search for him.

"I knew what I was doing," Ruthie said.

"So did Jimmy."

"You gonna punish him for that forever?"

"Forever isn't as long as it used to be."

Ruthie-Luther's mouth curved, but the expression was more than a little sad. "You'd have done exactly what I did if you'd been me."

"I am you now."

"And are you any different? You made him change you into a monster, though he begged you not to. You left him with the Dagda, and you saw what he'd do."

I flinched, then fell back on the same pathetic excuse used by every goose-stepping moron from the beginning of time. "You ordered me to."

"We all have our orders," Ruthie-Luther whispered, and in her-his voice lay all the sorrows of the ages.

"I don't like it," I muttered.

"You and everyone else who's ever had to take orders."

She had a point, but then Ruthie usually did.

"If there's a spell to end Nephilim without battling them by hand, why don't we just cast it over the earth and watch them burn?"

"Nothing's ever that simple, child. The spell I taught Luther was for Boudas."

"Witches that can shift into hyenas." I'd seen one before.

"Since a big cat is the hyenas' only predator, the spell required someone of African descent, with the blood of an African big cat. Spells are very specific."

"How is it that you knew this one?"

Luther's lips curved. "I've been 'round a long time, Lizbeth. You'd be surprised at what I know."

"Probably not," I muttered. What I wished was that along with Ruthie's power, she'd also passed on all she'd learned. It would have saved everyone a lot of hassle.

"Boudas are from Africa," I pointed out. "What are they doing here?"

"There are things all over the place that don't belong. When the Grigori first arrived, Africans lived in Africa, but they don't anymore. Or at least that's no longer the only place to find someone with the DNA of a matriarchal witch from the ancient country of Bouda."

I rubbed my forehead. "So there's no telling what kinds of beasties are going to crop up now that the Grigori are back."

"No. The Grigori might not even know what they're creating."

"They won't care as long as it's bad."

"Everything they bring forth is gonna be bad," Ruthie-Luther said. "The Grigori are pure evil. They're injecting a strain of wickedness into the population that hasn't been seen since the fall. I have no doubt that there'll be Nephilim created now that haven't ever walked the earth before."

"And we'll have no clue how to end them." Not that I had much of a clue as it was.

"We need to come up with a new plan," Ruthie said.

"What's wrong with the old one? Kill them all, ruin Doomsday."

"That's been workin' real well so far."

Sarcasm. Goody.

"Doomsday was set in motion when the leader of the darkness killed the leader of the light," Ruthie continued. "Me."

"Doomsday being a period of chaos that leads up to the final battle between good and evil."

"Armageddon," Ruthie agreed.

"But in the interim, the Grigori are released from the pit of hell and repopulate the world with Nephilim."

"Creating the army to fight that great battle."

"What do the Grigori even look like?" I asked.

As far as I knew no one had seen any yet, which was just plain weird.

Sawyer had been silent, but now he chimed in. "The Grigori are chaos spirits. They look like whomever they've possessed."

"Across the globe," Ruthie said, "there's been a significant increase in possession and insanity, a rash of rapes, suicides, murders and unexplained deaths."

I'd heard this already—on the television, the radio, the streets. Chaos spirits were spreading chaos. It was what they did.

I imagined all the innocent people who didn't understand what was happening. Hearing voices that told them to do horrible things, having dreams of murder and mayhem, of violent sex with a stranger, or even someone they knew, then waking up covered in blood the next day or pregnant the next month, and the only clue was the memory of that horrible dream.

What if someone you trusted, loved, suddenly became violent, abusive, evil? What if they hurt you or your children? What if you began to see someone else behind eyes that should have been familiar? Would you think you were crazy or that they were?

I shivered. Doomsday, chaos, Apocalypse—they were all the same thing. A time when the surreal became real. Horror became commonplace. The beginning of the end.

They were now.

"I haven't seen anything strange, felt anyone"—I moved my hands helplessly—"weird."

"You've been a little busy with eclipse demons," Ruthie said. "Among other things."

"Wouldn't the Grigori attack us?"

Luther's head shook. "They leave that to the Nephilim. Right now, all the Grigori are concerned with is making more supernatural half demons. They don't want to bring themselves to the attention of the DKs or the seers and have their fun interrupted."

"How is it that we've got a shitload of Nephililm running around," I asked, "and the Grigori have only been free a few weeks?"

Ruthie frowned. "I don't follow."

"Nephilim are *born* of demon and human. Being born takes a while. Usually nine months."

"Only breeds and . . ."—she paused and jerked her chin in Sawyer's direction, which I took to include those who were "other" as well, "other" being offspring of two Nephilim—"are literally *born* of a woman as children who grow and become something different. Nephilim are created; they spring forth fully grown."

"Spring forth how?" I asked, imagining all sorts of bad things.

"Many ways." When Ruthie didn't elaborate, I knew that most of the bad things in my head were true. They usually were.

"How do we kill the Grigori?" I blurted.

"We can't kill them," Sawyer said. "They're demons."

"So are the Nephilim. We've been killing them since they were invented."

"Nephilim are half demons. It's their humanity that allows them to die."

"You're saying we're screwed?" What else was new? "That we just keep killing the demon seed but we can never end the demons themselves?"

"No," Sawyer murmured. "That's not what I'm saying."

He went silent, and I wanted to shriek in frustration.

He was always so calm. I guess living forever, or close enough, could do that. But if there was ever a time to get excited, now was that time.

"What do we *do*?" I managed to keep from shouting, but barely.

"We find the *Key of Solomon*," he continued in the same calm voice. "Read the instructions for dealing with the Grigori; then we deal with them. Preferably before they repopulate the world with that army and deal with us first."

"Works for me," I said. "But how are we going to search for the key *and* keep the steadily multiplying demon horde from overrunning the earth."

I remembered the varcolacs—how they'd kept coming and coming, how much harder they'd seemed to kill than the average Nephilim and how I'd had to release my beast to do it. The Boudas hadn't been any easier. Without Luther, Sawyer and I might not be having this conversation.

"The Nephilim I've faced lately seem more confident," I said slowly, "if possible, even more vicious."

"Imminent victory will give anyone confidence," Sawyer said.

"They aren't going to win."

He lifted a brow and then a bare, laconic shoulder. "If you say so."

"I do. And so does the Bible."

His lips curved. "But there's the *Book of Samyaza*, which tells another story."

"I choose not to believe in fairy tales."

"Why not? You believe in fairies."

Why did I even try to reason with the man? There was no reason in him.

"Children, children," Ruthie-Luther admonished; the words when formed by that childish mouth almost made me laugh. "Eventually we'll need to find the *Book of Samyaza* and destroy it. Without the thing, they have no instructions for winning and no talisman that guarantees invincibility."

"Just because the book guarantees invincibility doesn't make it true."

"What is there about 'guarantee' that you don't understand?" Ruthie asked.

"So it is true?" I asked. "Possess the *Book of Samyaza* and win?"

"We won't know until—"

"They win," Sawyer finished.

"If the book is so damn important, then why are they after the *Key of Solomon*?"

"Could be they don't want us to have it, just like we don't want them to have the book."

I remembered what the varcolac had said. "Or one of the little people wants to command the demons."

Ruthie-Luther's dark gaze sharpened. "Whoever commands them becomes the Prince."

"Of Darkness?" I asked.

"Pretty much."

"I'm confused. When the Grigori flew free, whoever released them should have been possessed by Satan."

"Theoretically," Sawyer murmured.

"Explain."

"My . . ." He paused, unable to utter the word "mother." "The woman of smoke, if she actually released the Grigori, is dead. So—" He spread his nimble hands.

I blinked, trying to connect the dots. "So he's floating around looking for a host?"

Sawyer shrugged. Ruthie did too.

"Fan-damn-tastic," I muttered.

We remained silent for a moment.

"I thought if I killed the leader of the darkness, we'd get a replay." Or at least that had been the rumor.

"Even if that was true," Ruthie said, "and we don't know for sure, the Grigori were released before you killed her."

"Great. I became a vampire for no reason at all."

"If you hadn't killed the woman of smoke when you did, they'd be one step closer to victory. The Naye'i would be the Prince, and I think we'd all be dead."

Ruthie was right. At least I'd managed to end that bitch before she became the most powerful evil on earth. Point for me.

"How did she release the Grigori?" I asked.

"No idea," Ruthie said. "Though there might be a clue in the key."

"If she'd had the *Key of Solomon*, the Nephilim wouldn't be searching for it now."

"Regardless of how she released them," Ruthie said, "she released them. We need to—"

"Find the key, find the book," I interrupted. "Unfortunately, the guy I put on that task wound up a little dead."

Ruthie-Luther frowned. "Xander Whitelaw is dead?"

"How can you not know this?" I asked. "I thought you had a hotline to heaven." On the heels of those thoughts came another, better one. "He's on the other side. You can ask him what he found out."

My heart rate sped up. Maybe we weren't doomed after all. Maybe we could find the key tonight, perform the spell and rid the earth of demons by morning.

"He's not in heaven," Ruthie murmured.

My heart stuttered. "He went to hell?" Hadn't seen

that coming. Not that Xander had been a goody-goody. I hadn't known him well enough to know what he'd been. But he hadn't felt evil.

"No," Ruthie-Luther said slowly. "Not hell."

"You aren't making any sense. There's heaven and hell and here."

"And then there's where I am."

"You said you were in heaven."

"Not quite."

"What do you mean, 'not quite'?"

"I have a place for little ones to get used to the idea. Not heaven yet. More like the waiting room."

Ruthie's version of heaven was a house with a white picket fence and kids who'd died too soon. Even in the afterlife, Ruthie was still the mother to every lost soul.

The thought gave me pause. Obviously mothering was in her DNA, and that it was made me think that she *had* loved me for more than my talents.

But thinking and believing, then accepting and forgiving can be pretty far apart, and they can take a lot of time to draw together. Time was one thing I didn't have much of right now.

"Is there another waiting room for adults?" I asked.

"No. Adults understand death a little better than children."

"Then what are you saying?" I asked. "Xander's dead. He has to be somewhere, and it isn't where the living walk."

"You're certain of that?"

There hadn't been enough left of him to be anything but dead, even before we'd burned the place down.

"Yes."

Ruthie-Luther lowered her-his chin toward the thin, olive drab–shrouded chest. "If he isn't in heaven or hell, then his spirit's still on earth."

Sawyer drew in a sharp breath, but when I glanced at him, his face remained stoic, and I returned my attention to the woman speaking from the boy's mouth, resolving to get to the bottom of that later.

"Xander's a ghost," I clarified.

"Yes."

"Why?"

"Spirits remain on earth for a lot of reasons. Unfinished business, a violent death."

"Two for two," I murmured. "We need to ask him what he wanted to tell me, that'll finish up his business, and he can . . ."—I made a fluttering, *move along* gesture with both hands—"go into the light. Win-win."

"Not that simple," Ruthie said.

"Why not? Just ask him."

"I can't ask him, Lizbeth. I'm dead."

"So's he."

"Not in the same way."

"There are degrees of deadness?"

"No. Dead is dead. But for some, not really."

I smacked myself in the forehead. "Fine. You can't ask him. The world's gonna end; we're all gonna be Satan's bitch because the guy with the info can't get his deadness to fit just right."

"Watch that mouth!"

"Yes, ma'am," I said automatically. I couldn't help myself. Years of respecting Ruthie, loving her, practically worshiping the ground she walked on, died hard, perhaps never. But anger, hurt and fear died hard too, and I'd always been a sarcastic, snotty pain in the ass when any of those emotions were involved. Sometimes even when they weren't.

"I didn't say we couldn't find out the information," Ruthie soothed, "just that *I* couldn't talk to the man."

"Who can?"

Ruthie-Luther turned her-his head toward Sawyer. "Him."

CHAPTER 12

Him.

I should have known.

"You can talk to ghosts?" I asked.

"It's one of the gifts of a skinwalker."

"Then I can do it too."

"No. It's a talent tied to my magic."

A skinwalker is both witch and shifter. The shifting comes at birth; the magic comes later.

I could be as gifted as Sawyer. I could toss people across the room with a flick of my hand; I could talk to ghosts; I could heal wounds at the speed of sound. All I'd have to do was kill someone I loved.

I'd decided to pass.

Most days I had a hard time believing Sawyer was capable of loving anyone. Killing yes, loving no. However, I'd seen into his head, into his past. I knew he'd lived as a wolf; he'd had a mate, but he didn't have her now. Maybe he'd killed her.

Or maybe he'd killed someone else. When I'd touched him and seen the frighteningly long and lonely aeons of his existence, he'd hidden things from me, blocked me in a way that no one else ever had.

"Why are we standing here chatting?" I asked. "Open up the phone lines. Talk to Xander and find out what he knows." I frowned. "Knew. Whatever. Just do it."

"Just?" Sawyer repeated. "It's not that easy."

"Do whatever voodoo you do."

"I'm not a bokur."

"A what?"

"Voodoo dark priest," Ruthie-Luther said. "Very dangerous."

"And he isn't?"

Sawyer's lips curved. He loved it when someone called him dangerous. Sometimes I thought he purposely cultivated the fear that surrounded him, fed the legends by doing just enough creepy stuff to keep them circulating. I had a feeling that people being scared of him had kept Sawyer alive on more than one occasion.

"I can't just talk to Whitelaw," Sawyer said. "I've got to bring him forth."

"From where?"

"The realm where he walks."

"You're talking about raising the dead. That doesn't sound like a good idea." I glanced at Ruthie-Luther. "Does it?"

"He won't actually be raising him to life," Ruthie said, "just raising his ghost."

"So that's okay?"

"What else we gonna do?" Ruthie asked. "We need the key, the book, somethin'."

"All right," I said, glancing at Sawyer. "What do you have to do?"

His lips quirked, and suddenly I remembered what Xander Whitelaw had told me about Navajo skin-walkers.

They have sex with the dead.

I made a face. "Uck."

"I didn't say anything," Sawyer pointed out.

"I've never been clear on all the powers of a skin-walker."

"And you never will be," he returned.

I narrowed my eyes. I wished I could make him tell me, but Sawyer still trumped me in power. Which might be why he refused to let me in on all his secrets. He wanted to keep it that way. He was so damn annoying.

"Whitelaw had a lot of theories," I began.

Sawyer's smile died. "So he did."

"How many of them were true?"

"Hard to say."

I started ticking off all that I knew. "Shape-shifting. Check. Witchcraft. Bingo. Cannibalism?"

Sawyer didn't answer.

"Killing from afar by use of ritual?"

The smile returned, but he still didn't speak.

"Travel on storms?"

That legend probably came about because skin-walkers could move faster than the wind. So, technically true.

"Power from lightning?"

I'd seen his mother throw lightning like Zeus. Never had seen Sawyer do it, but that didn't meant he couldn't.

"Associated with death and the dead."

Obviously, since he planned on raising Xander's ghost and asking him some questions.

"Incest."

Sawyer's face went as still as the dark mountain behind him.

I guess I wouldn't call the last a power but rather

the source of any weakness. Another curse. The first but not the last Sawyer had received from his mother.

"Sorry," I murmured.

What had happened to him at the hands of that psychotic evil spirit bitch wasn't his fault, and I shouldn't be reminding him of it now. Or ever again.

Sawyer continued to make like a mountain. I glanced at Ruthie-Luther and spread my hands—code for *Do something*.

She sighed. "Sawyer."

Her voice was gentle, the one that had soothed me when I was sick, strengthened me when I was weak, taught me what I needed to know and told me what I needed to hear. No matter what she'd done for the sake of the world, the fact remained that she'd done a lot for me as well. Regardless of her motives, Ruthie Kane had saved me from the streets and myself. She'd saved a lot of people. I was going to have to cut her some slack.

Eventually.

Sawyer's dark gaze moved to Luther's face and softened. I wasn't sure what lay between Ruthie and Sawyer. She'd sent me to him when I was fifteen to learn how to control what I was. Hadn't worked completely; I'd had to come back recently and learn some more.

Sure, it had been beyond strange to send a fifteen-year-old girl to spend the summer alone with a grown man in the New Mexico desert. But I wasn't an ordinary fifteen-year-old girl and Sawyer wasn't really a man.

If Social Services had found out, they would have yanked me from Ruthie's care quicker than a starving cat snatched a baby mouse from its nest, but they hadn't found out. I now knew that Ruthie had controlled more than just the federation—or rather, the federation had members just about everywhere in very high places, and if things were discovered that weren't supposed to be, it was an easy task to wipe memories from human minds. Or, in some cases, wipe those human minds from the face of the earth and move on.

Besides, Sawyer had never touched me inappropriately. The first time. Not because he had any morals to speak of but because he was scared of Ruthie. Considering Sawyer, I had to wonder what lay in their past and just how much power Ruthie had that I didn't know about.

Ruthie reached out for Sawyer with Luther's hand, and Sawyer took it. Seeing the two of them connected like that was kind of weird. But right now Luther was Ruthie and the touch seemed to help. Sawyer straightened, removing his hand from Luther's as he got down to business.

"I'll need something from him."

"From him," I repeated, confused.

"A part of the person who is now a ghost. Hair, nails, skin."

"He's dead."

"Oh, well," Sawyer said, and headed for his hogan.

" 'Oh, well'?" I glanced at Ruthie-Luther. "That's it? 'Oh, well. Have a happy end of the world.' "

"What do you want me to do?" Sawyer stopped, turned. "Conjure something from nothing?"

"Uh . . . yeah," I said in my best "duh" voice, which Sawyer ignored.

"There has to be a connection. Something to tell the . . ."—he waved his hands vaguely—"powers that be who we want to bring forth."

"This is such BS," I muttered.

"Lizbeth," Ruthie murmured. "Think. Where can we find a part of Xander?"

"Got me. We burned him," I said. "Had to. He was a mess."

Ruthie winced. "Nevertheless, humans leave little pieces of themselves all over the place."

"We burned his office too."

"Didn't realize Sanducci was a pyro as well as an asshole," Sawyer murmured.

Sawyer might be as old as dirt, but he could also be quite childish. Especially about Jimmy.

"His apartment," Ruthie said. "Hairbrush, toothbrush, nail clippers, hat."

"Hat!" All eyes turned to me as my shout echoed back from the mountains. "I took his hat."

"You didn't think to mention this?" Ruthie asked.

"What for? It's a cool hat. I didn't want it to—" I broke off. I hadn't wanted it to burn. I'd liked Xander. I wished I'd had time to get to know him better.

I went to the rental car, leaned in and came back out with the felt hat. Sure enough, several blond hairs were stuck in a ribbon that went around the inside of the crown. I handed the whole thing to Sawyer.

"Bury hair beneath a lightning-struck tree," Ruthie murmured.

"That's to kill a person," Sawyer said. "Not raise their ghost."

I cast Ruthie-Luther a quick glance. "Where'd you learn that?"

She lifted a bushy light-brown brow.

"Oh," I said, and turned my attention to Sawyer. "I guess you really can kill from afar by the use of ritual."

"I guess I can."

"We could end a lot of demons that way."

"Doesn't work on demons," he said absently.

"Of course it doesn't," I muttered. "That would be too damn easy."

"What do you have to do?" The voice was Luther's. On closer examination, the eyes and the body were now his too.

"Where's Ruthie?" I asked.

The kid shrugged. Obviously gone. Her work here—for now—was done.

"We must wait for the lightning." Sawyer contemplated the perfectly clear sky. "The fire of its strike is needed to raise a ghost."

"We have to wait for a storm?" Even though storms were common around here in the summer, we might be waiting for weeks. "And the lightning has to strike . . . what? Where?"

Sawyer didn't answer. This time when he headed for his hogan, he disappeared inside, and he didn't come back out.

I took a step in that direction, and Luther put a hand on my arm. "He doesn't like it when you go in there."

"I don't care what he likes." And I knew better. The last time I'd gone in there, he'd liked it a lot.

But I paused and contemplated the boy. "How have things been here? With him?"

"All right. He knows stuff."

"Living forever will do that," I said dryly. "You aren't uncomfortable with him? He doesn't scare you?"

Luther had been beating on his chest—as wild animals and young males can't help but do—when he'd said he would kick Sawyer's ass, but I wanted to know the real truth. So, with Luther's hand still on my arm, I opened my mind and saw into his.

Luther and Sawyer beneath the noonday sun. Stripped to the waist, sweating, laughing. Sawyer seemed almost . . . human. I got distracted.

Luther moved away, breaking our connection. My eyes met his.

"You don't have to do that," he said.

I tilted my head. I'd never told him what I could do.

He looked away. "Ruthie speaks through me, but she also speaks to me. She tells me things I need to know."

"Okay."

"Sawyer wouldn't hurt me," Luther said. "Well, he would. He has. If I let my guard down, and he knocks me ten feet into a wall or some rocks, it hurts, and I heal. But he wouldn't . . . you know."

"I know. Otherwise I wouldn't have left you here."

"No?" he asked. "Not even if my being here would make me into the type of killing machine you need?"

"What's that supposed to mean?"

"I know what's at stake. I know that some of us will die, maybe all of us. We don't have any choice. You didn't have any choice. I am what I am. I'm this way for a reason. I need to learn how to control my lion, how to kill Nephilim, and Sawyer's the best one to teach me. If there's a price to be paid for the knowledge, I'll pay it."

"*I'll* pay it," I corrected. "Not you."

Luther's gaze went to the hogan. "I think that's been his plan all along."

CHAPTER 13

Luther went into the house, and a silence as cool and navy blue as the sky settled over the land.

"How do you plan to pay me, Phoenix?"

I turned, half-expecting Sawyer to be right behind me, so close my breasts would brush his chest. I'd gasp, stumble back, nearly fall, and he'd catch me.

But Sawyer wasn't there, and he wasn't standing in front of the hogan or in the doorway of the house or anywhere that I could see.

"How were you paid in the past?" I asked.

"The usual way."

His voice seemed to come out of the darkness, seemed to *be* the darkness, and I shivered. His mother had been the darkness. Sawyer had warned me often enough that she was a part of him. I should probably kill him, but I didn't know how.

I moved toward the hogan. "When you say 'usual,' where are you headed with that?"

"Blood, guts, the souls of children."

"You aren't funny," I said.

"I didn't mean to be."

"You aren't ready to turn over a new leaf?" I asked. "Start helping us out of the goodness of your heart rather than . . ." I paused.

Jimmy had said Sawyer trained federation members for money, but Sawyer didn't seem the type, and I knew now that Jimmy lied.

I reached the arched dwelling, pulled back the woven mat that served as a door and peeked inside. The place was empty.

Sawyer hadn't disappeared into thin air, as much as it might seem so. I'd been distracted. So had Luther. Our gazes had not been on the hogan the entire time, and Sawyer only needed an instant to turn into whichever one of his beasts he desired; then in a blink he'd be gone.

"Can't do that."

His voice came from farther away. He still sounded as if he were all around me, but fainter. More the wind than the night. Could he turn into the wind? I had no idea.

"Can't do what?" I backed out of the hogan.

"Help you out of the goodness of my heart."

"Why not?"

"I don't have one."

"Goodness or a heart?"

"Exactly."

I rubbed my forehead. Whether I was woman or wolf, talking to Sawyer always gave me a headache.

"What are you going to charge for training Luther?" I demanded.

I had a pretty good idea. With Sawyer it was always about sex. His powers were based in sex. His body was built for sex. His mind was filled with sex.

Or perhaps that's just what he wanted everyone to think. If he were dismissed as a supernatural nymphomaniac, he didn't have to connect with anyone. He didn't have to put himself out there. He didn't have to risk rejection or heartache. If Sawyer was all about sex, then no one ever expected love. I certainly didn't.

Besides, according to legend, loving Sawyer, or having him love you, was a one-way ticket to Deadsville.

"I'll put it on your account," Sawyer answered.

I didn't like the sound of that. I already owed the Dagda a favor.

"Can't I just . . ." I paused. What? I had very little money. My power was minuscule compared to his. The only thing I had that he wanted was me, and he'd already had that. Many times.

"I think you already did," he said, seeming to echo my thoughts.

"Then we should be even."

"Not yet," he whispered.

"Great. Put it on my account," I snapped. "At this rate, I'll be doing you until the end of the world."

"That should work."

My only consolation was that the end of the world appeared to be right around the corner.

As we'd been talking, I'd been strolling around the yard, behind the hogan, the house; I'd peeked into the sweat lodge and the ramada. No Sawyer. I gave up.

"Where are you?" Supernatural hide-and-seek just wasn't my thing.

"Remember the lake? On the mountain?"

I turned, staring up at the shadowy expanse of Mount Taylor, and as I did so, thunder rumbled in the west. "Yes."

"We need to do something about that lightning."

"What kind of something?"

"Bring it forth."

"You said we had to wait for it."

"I say a lot of things."

Not really. Sawyer was the least likely sayer of a lot in this world.

He took a breath, let it out long and slow. "I don't want the boy to know, to follow. He should stay here."

I glanced uneasily at the house where Luther had disappeared. "But—"

"He's safe. He's a lion when he wants to be."

"There are so many of them now."

"And so few of us," he agreed. "He's going to have to go out on his own soon. I've nearly taught him all that I know. All he lacks is practice."

The thought of ordering Luther—who insisted he was eighteen, but I had my doubts—to kill demons made me slightly ill. I'd sworn I wouldn't send teenagers out to die. But once again, I didn't have much choice.

"He'll be fine, Phoenix." Sawyer's voice was soft, low, and he sounded so certain. "I need you here. We have to bring the lightning."

"How is it that I can hear you?" I asked.

Not telepathy. I wasn't a beast, and I was hearing him on the wind, or the air or the stars—who knew?—but not in my head.

"Magic," Sawyer said. "I can do all sorts of great things."

"If you're so damn special, why do you need me to bring the lightning?"

"You'll see."

The last time I'd gone up the mountain to the lake I'd been on two feet. The trip had taken a good portion of a day.

This time I didn't have a day. The storm was rumbling. I didn't need Sawyer to tell me I had to move my ass. I didn't need him to tell me to make my ass furry and run like the wind. I just did.

As a wolf, I loped up the overgrown path. Bushes

and branches pulled at my mahogany coat, brambles stuck here and there. Tiny, wild things skittered out of my way. Because I was both wolf *and* woman, I could ignore them.

However, the spill of the moon dazzled. I found my gaze pulled to it, and my throat ached as I stifled the call. I wanted so badly to sing to that nearly full moon and to hear others like me answer.

I caught the scent of smoke and water long before I would have if I'd been wearing shoes. My paws dislodged rocks on the path that tumbled downward, spilling me out of the overgrown fir and pine boughs and into the small clearing that fronted the clear mountain lake.

The moon flared off the water like a spotlight, the glow illuminating the hogan at the base of a mound of rock. A fire blazed higher than Sawyer's head, turning every color seen upon the earth.

He was naked. What else was new? He kept extra clothes in the hogan, but Sawyer preferred to walk around with only his tattoos for adornment. He always had.

I reached for myself, and in a blast of light and ice I became a woman. I headed for the hogan and Sawyer lifted a hand.

"No," he murmured.

"No what?"

"No time," he said, then lifted his arms to the starry sky.

I expected the fire to leap higher, to swirl, perhaps to speak. He'd done funky things with fire before. Tossed in strange Navajo herbs that had made me do . . . him. Conjured a woman from the smoke who had turned out to be the mommy dearest of all time.

But the fire remained the same—too high for

safety, too colorful to be only fire—and when his fingers pointed heavenward, the sky split wide open.

I tensed, expecting lightning to spark. Instead rain tumbled down, drenching us in seconds as the fire continued to dance on unharmed.

"Come closer," Sawyer whispered, and I did, drawn by his deep, commanding voice as well as the warmth of the flames against the sudden chill of the night.

Xander's hat sat on the ground near his feet, a circle drawn in the dirt around it.

"What . . . ?" I began.

"Touch me."

"Huh?"

Sawyer's dark gaze swept to mine. "Touch me."

"I don't—"

"Now. I need help."

"You've never needed anything or anyone. Ever."

In his eyes, something flared. Fire? Fury? I couldn't tell. "You're wrong."

The earth trembled. Sawyer's mouth thinned, and he seemed to tremble too.

I glanced up, but the sky was as clear as a sterling winter night. The moon and the stars continued to shine through the falling rain. However, the wind began to swirl and the rain began to sting. Strangely enough, Xander's hat stayed right where it was.

"Phoenix," Sawyer said between gritted teeth. "I can only do so much on my own. I'm bringing the storm when there is no storm. The lightning is going to require more power than I have."

"Nothing requires more power than you have."

"Touch me," he ordered, and his eyes blazed silver.

I slapped my hand to his waist. The sharp smack of flesh on flesh was followed by a sharp hiss, and steam rose from his skin as thunder rumbled ever closer.

As always, when I touched him the essence of his beasts called to me. They wanted out—every last one of them. Sawyer's tattoos were predators; hell, so was he.

Sometimes when we came together, those animals seemed to swirl in the shadows, waiting to be called at his command. I looked for them now where the light met the darkness and saw nothing. They didn't dance in the flames or float through the smoke, yet still I sensed them hovering.

The wind stirred my hair; the rain pattered against my cheeks and I lifted my face.

"Ah," I murmured. There they were. Appearing and disappearing in the shapes of the clouds that now gathered. Behind them sparks flared, and the air sizzled.

"Almost," Sawyer whispered. "Just need a little more . . ."

He shifted and his slick naked body slid against mine. He lowered his gaze from the sky to my face. That sizzle in the air seemed to scoot along every nerve ending I had.

"A little more what?" I managed.

"Power," he said, and kissed me.

Static flared, a sharp spark between my lips and his. His tongue soothed the burn. I thought: *Moisture and electricity. That can't be good.* Then all my thoughts disappeared as it became very good indeed.

The storm erupted. Wind whipped our hair; rain pelted our bodies; thunder shook the mountain. I held on to him more tightly, kissed him more deeply. He was the only warmth, the only reality, that I had.

His arms were still raised—calling down the lightning, controlling the wind, bringing the chaos. My lips opened, I welcomed him in. The man could do more with his mouth than most could do with their entire body.

I traced his tattoos. Whenever my fingertips skated over one, the image of the animal flared behind my closed eyelids, yet I felt no difference in the texture of his flesh. These tattoos had not been carved into his skin with a needle but emblazoned by magic and—

"Lightning," I whispered into his mouth.

"Soon," he returned. "Very, very soon."

"You did them," I murmured, catching for just an instant a flicker of the past. Sawyer on this mountain, the wind swirling, the rain falling, the storm raging.

"Mmm." His voice was absent, his attention on my breasts, my neck, the curve where my waist became my hip, where my thigh became my ass.

I tried to focus, managed but barely. "You did those tattoos. You said they were made by a sorcerer wielding the lightning. It was you."

He shrugged. The movement shifting his bones in ways bones should not shift.

"You're a sorcerer," I clarified.

"Medicine man, skinwalker. I'm many things, Phoenix."

"Your powers . . ." I paused, uncertain what I meant to say, what I wanted to ask.

"Did you think murder would give me nothing?"

I jerked, the movement knocking me against him hard, though our wet bodies glided together so soft.

"What did it give you?" I asked.

His gaze met mine, and the centuries swirled. "Everything," he whispered, "and nothing at all."

Then he kissed me again, making me dizzy with his past, with his power. I was lost, couldn't fight it or him any longer. Maybe later.

More kissing, more touching. The slide of my hands

across his skin, my breasts skidded over his chest, my nipples pearling from the friction and the chill. His penis pressed against my belly. I couldn't help it; I rubbed against the hard length.

His tongue mimicked the act I was considering committing on the wet ground. In and out of my mouth, in and out. I sucked on it, played tag too. He bit me, just a nip, so I bit him back. The sharp pain, the tang of blood, seemed to increase the wind; the rain became a torrent.

Everywhere we touched flared both hot and cold, sizzling and slick; the air buzzed. Something was coming.

I held on to Sawyer. I wouldn't, couldn't, let him go, so I kissed him harder, deeper, and suddenly everything stilled.

The ground jerked, as if the very dirt were a carpet about to be pulled from beneath our feet. My body and Sawyer's too convulsed, shuddering and shaking as ozone, acrid and dark, burned all around us. The whole world seemed to go bright with silver light. I was afraid to open my eyes for fear my corneas would be fried to a crisp.

But the earth didn't open and swallow us. The lightning didn't strike us. The rain no longer rained down on us. Even the breeze had died.

As I came back to myself, I realized three things. Sawyer and I were still pressed together, the remnants of what felt very much like an orgasm tingling along my skin.

The air still smelled like something sizzled; I could almost hear it crackling.

And we were no longer alone; I sensed something, someone, very near.

Cautiously, I opened my eyes. The lake remained

smooth as glass. The nearly full moon shone serenely on its surface. Mount Taylor loomed. Sawyer's hogan remained exactly where it had always been.

However, the hat in the charmed circle was gone, and Xander Whitelaw now stood in its place.

CHAPTER 14

He looked exactly the same as the last time I'd seen him.

No, not the *last* time. I wanted to forget the last time.

Xander Whitelaw looked the same as the last time I'd seen him alive.

Khaki trousers, blue button-down complete with a tie, loafers and rimless glasses. Total geekazoid, but handsome if you liked blond-haired, dark-eyed long-distance runners with a brain. I was sure someone did. Or had. Hell.

"Miss Phoenix?" he asked in his soft, slightly southern voice.

I nodded, unwrapping myself from Sawyer. Our skin peeled apart with an audible *fwonk*. Sweat and rain, as well as a little mud, covered us; we were a mess. I badly wanted to jump in the lake, but first things first.

"Clothes," I muttered, and ran for the hogan.

"It doesn't matter," Sawyer called after me. "He won't care. He's beyond that."

"I'm not." I ducked inside the structure.

There wasn't much there. Sawyer didn't care who saw him in the altogether, and this was his place, even more so than the one down the mountain. Sawyer came to the lake when he wanted to perform rituals no one else should see. Or perhaps he came to perform rituals that could only be performed here.

The Navajo refer to Mount Taylor as their *sacred mountain of the south* or *the turquoise mountain*. Once, long ago, it had been an active volcano. Maybe that was why Sawyer lived at its base, why magic happened at its peak. Volcanoes never really went away; they only fell asleep. I wouldn't put it past Sawyer to wake this one up. Considering the way the ground had rumbled, maybe he had.

Inside the hogan all I could find was winter clothes—a plaid hunting shirt and heavy denim jeans. I'd swelter in them unless—

I yanked off the arms of the shirt—with my superstrength, I didn't even need scissors—then I tore off the bottom half; I did the same to the jeans above the knees, leaving just enough material to cover the important parts. After the adjustments for the temperature, the items fit fairly well. Sawyer's aura, his strength and power and wisdom, made him seem larger than he was. If not for the muscles on him and the hips and chest on me, we'd be the same size. I didn't even have to loop twine through the belt loops before I rejoined the men outside.

Sawyer lifted his brows but didn't comment on the destruction of his clothes. I was sure he had more somewhere and equally sure he rarely wore these. It would have to be a cold day in . . . the mountains before he deigned to put on a stitch.

Xander still stood within the circle. I joined Sawyer and murmured, "Can he move?"

"Move, yes," Sawyer answered low enough so Xander couldn't hear. "Leave, no."

"Why?"

"We don't know where he's been, who he's seen, what he's been offered."

"Offered?"

"There is a hell, Phoenix, and some of us will go there."

I cast him a quick glance. He was working for the good guys—as far as I knew. Why was he worried about hell?

I opened my mouth to ask, but Sawyer kept talking. "You'll agree to anything to avoid that."

"Me personally, or the general 'you'?"

Sawyer lifted a brow and didn't bother.

"What's the last thing you remember?" Sawyer took a step closer; Xander took a step back. His heel brushed the circle, and he drew in a sharp breath as he jerked it away. I scowled at Sawyer. The guy had been through enough.

Xander's brow creased, which only served to remind me how uncreased his brow had been. Whitelaw was undoubtedly one of the youngest Ph.D.s in history, and I'd gotten him killed long before his time. Guilt flickered, but I was getting used to it.

"I called Miss Phoenix." Xander's dark, confused gaze met mine. I wanted to take his hand, say I was sorry, but as Sawyer had said, I didn't know where Xander had been, what he'd agreed to, who he'd become.

Instead, I nodded encouragingly. "That's right."

"You were coming to see me." He glanced around, and despite the press of darkness it was easy to tell that we weren't in Indiana anymore. "Or did you say you were going to bring me to see you?"

I opened my mouth, then shut it again. Was I supposed to tell him what had happened? I didn't want to.

"We brought you," Sawyer said, which was technically true. We'd just left out the part where I'd gone to him first and he'd been dead.

"Fascinating," Xander murmured.

"You said you had information for me," I reminded him.

"I do. Yes." The professor lifted his hand, rubbing his forehead as if he could make the information within tumble free. "The *Book of Samyaza*."

Sawyer and I exchanged a glance. Double damn. I was really hoping that was a myth.

"You found it?"

"No. There are so many rumors, but not a single solid clue as to its whereabouts or even what it looks like."

"Swell."

"Relax, Phoenix," Sawyer murmured. "That means they don't know anything about it either."

"Or they're better at keeping secrets than we are."

"If they knew what it looked like or where it was, they'd have it and we'd all be—" Sawyer flipped his dark, supple hands over so that the palms faced the starry night sky.

"Cannon fodder," I muttered.

"Would you like to know what I learned about the *Key of Solomon*?" Xander smiled.

I straightened. "Where is it?"

"The key is with the Phoenix."

I'd heard that before. It didn't make me any happier this time.

"I don't have it," I said.

"Not you. An actual phoenix."

"Say what?"

"A legendary ancient Egyptian bird."

"I know what it is," I muttered. "A myth."

Xander's gaze went to Sawyer. "Myths aren't so mythical anymore."

Everything I'd ever considered legendary—werewolves, vampires, ghosts, you name it—was a helluva lot more real than I was comfortable with.

"We have to go to Egypt?" I asked. "That's gonna take a while."

Xander, who'd seemed so with it, suddenly didn't. His face crumpled; he began to blink as if trying to recall something that was long gone.

"Xander?" I said, alarmed. "You okay?"

"Give him time," Sawyer murmured. "It isn't easy to walk between worlds."

Xander stopped blinking. "I was at my office," he said. "And I heard footsteps. I thought it was you—"

"But it wasn't. Did you see who—?"

Xander shook his head. I wasn't surprised. Ghosts don't know who killed them, which is often what makes them ghosts.

Whitelaw's gaze fell to his feet. He kicked a bit of dirt at the circle, and when it fell back on his shoe as if it had hit an invisible wall, he lifted his gaze to mine. "I'm dead."

Then poof—he disappeared.

"Hey!" I ran to the circle, but the only thing there now was the hat. "Bring him back!"

"Can't." Sawyer leaned over and scooped the hat off the ground, then handed it to me.

"Bullshit," I muttered. "You can do anything."

"No," he said softly. "I can't."

"Where did he go?"

Sawyer twirled his hand toward the sky, then let it fall and pointed to the ground as he shrugged.

"I wasn't finished asking him questions."

"Once ghosts realize they're dead, or once they've completed their unfinished business, they're no longer ghosts."

From nowhere, Sawyer produced a cigarette; he snapped his fingers and produced a match the same way. After lighting the end, drawing smoke deeply into his lungs, then letting it trickle out through his nose, he contemplated the fire.

"Have you ever encountered an actual phoenix?" I asked.

"I've seen so many things." Sawyer took another drag, then blew the smoke upward in a steady, gray stream.

It didn't pay to point out that smoking was unhealthy. Breathing had become unhealthy for members of the federation, and since killing Sawyer was damn near impossible, I didn't think mouth, throat or lung cancer was much of an issue.

If I were the Pollyanna type—and I wasn't—I'd think that facing constant death and eternal destruction did have an upside. We could practice every vice we'd once given up without a care. Smoking, drinking, drugs, STDs—go nuts—they were no longer going to kill us any time soon.

Of course other cares had taken their place. We might not have to worry about cancer or AIDS, but there were always demons, fiery hell pits and the end of the world.

Sawyer tossed his cigarette onto the fire, then stared into the distance with a thoughtful expression. I moved closer, figuring he was going to impart all the wisdom he'd compiled on the Phoenix. Or at least tell me where I could go to get it.

Instead, he slapped his palm to his biceps. The resulting flash of light made me shield my eyes, and when I opened them again, he was gone.

"What about me!" I shouted to the night.

I waited until dawn streaked the sky before I headed down the mountain. When I'd come up the hill, I'd done so as a wolf—better eyes, better nose, better traction. Since I'd left my robe behind and Sawyer was gone, I'd be returning as a human. Yes, I was nimble and quick; I was strong. But the mountain was stronger. If I left in the dark, I might end up sliding into a culvert and breaking my neck.

Not that I couldn't heal a broken neck, but I really didn't want to. Just because my body could mend when broken didn't mean it didn't hurt like hell when the break occurred.

What was the rush anyway? Sure, Sawyer had been in a helluva hurry, but I had no idea why. If he'd needed me along, he wouldn't have left me behind.

By the time I reached the foot of the mountain, I was hot, tired and thirsty. If Sawyer were lounging around drinking lemonade, I just might try to kill him again.

But he wasn't. No one was. Which made me nervous. Where was the kid?

I checked the house, the hogan, the sweat lodge and the ramada. Not a sign of him. Maybe Sawyer *had* come back here; then they'd left together.

I began to touch things—Luther's huge Nikes, Sawyer's pillow—maybe I'd get a hint of where they'd gone. But Sawyer had always been good at blocking me, and it appeared that ability extended to his inanimate belongings as well, since I saw nothing. As for Luther, he'd worn those shoes to town, where he'd bought . . . comic books. Which wasn't really very helpful at all.

My car sat in the yard. I retrieved my duffel and my cell phone, although getting a signal in the shadow of the mountain was iffy at best.

I'd get cleaned up, changed, eat a bit and then head to the nearest burg where I could boot up my laptop and research the Phoenix. Sometimes I missed Ruthie's whisper more than I missed . . .

I tried to think of something I missed more than that and couldn't.

"Okay," I muttered. "I miss Ruthie's whisper more than I miss anything." But missing the voice wasn't going to bring that voice back. I wasn't sure what would.

I fingered the dog collar still latched around my neck. Perhaps if I got rid of this demon, but I didn't know if that was possible.

I turned on the water and, as I waited for it to warm, lost Sawyer's tattered, sweat-encrusted clothing. Exhaustion weighed on me. Fighting evil wasn't easy. Fighting the evil inside of you . . . Well, that was downright excruciating sometimes.

I stood under the stream, letting the heated mist curl around me, breathing in the steam like a balm, allowing the familiar pulse of the water to soothe the prickling unease that had followed me down the mountain. By the time I finished, I almost felt human. Quite a feat, considering I wasn't.

The door opened and then closed. Beyond the filmy white shower curtain, the shadow of a man loomed. Though I assumed it was Sawyer, I leaned down and palmed my knife, which I'd laid on the lip of the tub.

"We need to talk," I said.

The only answer was a long, rolling growl. Not a wolf. More like a big cat. Again.

My head tilted. "Luther?"

This time my answer was a roar that shook the mirror over the sink. Not Luther. A bigger, badder lion.

I glanced at the blade in my slick hand, wishing I hadn't left the gun loaded with silver bullets in the duffel bag. The knife was going to be tricky in such close quarters.

Suddenly the shower curtain was yanked violently from the rod and I stood face to chest with a man I'd never seen before: tall and broad, his skin as dark as the continent his ancestors had roamed and his eyes as golden as his shaggy hair. Even without the rumble that continued to roll from his throat, I'd have pegged him for a lion shifter.

"Where is de boy?" he asked.

"What boy?" I stalled.

The man let out another roar, snatched the knife from my own hand with speed that blurred even for me and planted it in my chest.

Why did every evil thing want to stab me in the chest? I have to admit it was a pretty big target, but come on. Be original. Try a kidney, the jugular, something, anything, else. None of those shots would truly kill me anyway.

However, the pain made me drop my guard, and the still-roaring lion man knocked my head against the ceramic tile. I heard the thunk and watched as the world fell away. My temple conked the lip of the tub as I went down, and I slid along the smooth side, coming to rest with my neck at an odd angle.

The water that swirled past me ran a rainbow of reds—maroon to fuchsia, fuchsia to petal pink. My heart thudded, stuttered, almost failed, and the rainbow began all over again—maroon, fuchsia, pink.

I needed to remove the knife. I wasn't going to be able to heal with that stuck inside of me. But I couldn't seem to lift my hand.

I watched the water's rainbow swirl and wondered absently what would happen next. I couldn't die, but I couldn't heal.

And by the way . . . where was that lion man?

Right before I lost the last thread of consciousness, I heard a distant roar, followed almost instantly by a sound that made me fight against the dark spots overtaking my vision.

A second roar, a familiar one.

Luther.

"No," I whispered. But, as usual, no one was listening.

The kid wasn't ready for this. Someone had to help him, and the only someone available right now was me.

I managed to grip the side of the tub, even pulled myself half over the edge before the dark spots dancing in front of my eyes collided, and then the whole world went black. But it didn't stay black for long.

During most of the occasions when I'd almost died—yes, I did this a lot—I awoke in the dreams of others. The ability was known as dream walking, and I'd caught it from Jimmy.

In the land between life and death, the place where dreams live, I would be drawn to the unconscious meanderings of the one with the answer to my most desperate question.

Opening my eyes, I expected the darkness to end, but the world was black. The air was hot, yet I was so cold, and something smelled really, really bad.

I tried to sit up and rapped my head against a very low ceiling. Lying back, I felt along my prison, the sides, above, behind. Surrounded by solid walls covered with satin, and when I stretched my feet, my toes—oddly bare—brushed satin too.

"Hello?" I shouted, startled to discover I had an accent—melodic, deep and dark and foreign. How strange.

Usually when I dream walked, I found myself in a person's head. I could talk with them. I could stroll through the corridors of their mind and peek at things they didn't want anyone to know. This was the first time I'd actually *been* the person whose dream I'd invaded. I couldn't say that I cared for it.

I was trapped. Closed in. Buried.

My mind spun; a chittering insanity threatened. I slammed my hands against the roof, and a loud *crack* split the silence. Dirt sifted across my face.

Arise. The word drifted through my head, a faraway, maddening whisper. *The time is here.*

A compulsion, sudden and impossible to ignore, filled me. Before, I'd desperately wanted to get out; now I just had to.

I clawed upward, a nearly impossible task, through six feet of hard-packed earth. My nails broke; my fingers ached, as did my legs, which I kept pushing against whatever lay beneath. My heart beat a rapid and painful cadence. My ears and nose, my mouth and eyes, were stifled by dirt.

This journey brought back memories of my descent into the Otherworld, confusing me a little, because that memory was mine and this was . . . not. I'd never been two people before. If the body I inhabited now actually *was* people, and I didn't think so.

People don't rise from the dead.

The whisper returned. *The promise is fulfilled. Your fate awaits. Arise!*

I couldn't resist that voice. It lured me onward, and soon my hand burst free.

Heated, humid air caressed my cool, cool skin, so heavenly I surged ever higher. First my shoulder, then my neck, then my face emerged into the approaching dawn. On the eastern horizon, the sun would soon rise and with it a brand-new me.

In the half-light I caught a glimpse of my arms. The shade of the skin was dark, the texture supple and young. As I watched, the scratches I'd sustained from my battle with the earth faded first to thin white lines and then away completely. My lips curved. What had been promised was now delivered.

I was *free*.

Morning kissed the horizon. As the flames spread across the sky, strength spread through my body, blazing away every ache, every doubt and every last remnant of exhaustion.

The sun—ahh, the sun. It had been so long.

Is it all that you remember? asked the voice—louder now, no longer muffled by earth, but still far away and maddeningly familiar.

"More."

It will be yours if you do what you promised.

"I will."

I patted a rough-hewn sack that hung from a strap looped across my chest. My clothing—some kind of sarong-type dress—was in tatters, but that sack, though dirty, had remained in one piece, and inside rested something hard and rather large for a necklace.

There is a place prepared for you. Come.

I had no choice but to obey. In truth I wanted nothing *but* to obey. I ran past crumbling headstones. The spindly limbs of ancient trees reached toward an increasingly colorful sky as beneath my bare feet the earth rumbled and shook. The dirt spilled out its dead and they began to walk.

I lifted my arms to the dawn. As the warmth radiated over my skin, power returned and with it all of the magic.

CHAPTER 15

"Son of a—"

Pain yanked me out of the dream, but a final image flashed inside my head.

The sun rising, red lava against a gray sky and a woman flying straight into that fire, arms becoming wings, hair and skin turning into feathers brighter than the colors surrounding them, as she headed slowly toward a familiar, seductive whisper.

The sight of Luther with my own blood-covered knife in his hand made me bite off the end of the curse. Not that Luther hadn't heard it all before, and he'd probably hear worse before this was over; I just didn't like him to hear it from me.

"You okay?" he asked.

I sat up, my hand instinctively reaching for the wound, even though, now that the knife was out, it had nearly healed. My chest slick with blood, I was also naked.

Everything came rushing back. The shower. The shifter. The knife.

"Turn around!" I ordered. After tossing me a towel, he did.

The floor was slippery, the water pink. I'd bled a lot and the shower had continued to run even after the lion man had killed me.

"Where is he?" I asked.

"Hell, I hope." Luther took a cautious peek, turning when he saw I was decent. Or as decent as I got sitting naked beneath a tiny towel.

His head tilted, and his curling, tangled golden-brown hair shifted over one hazel eye. "Do the demons go to hell when we kill them?"

"Not a clue, kid."

"If they do, then they would just fly right out again now that hell is an open doorway."

I lifted my hand to rub my forehead, saw the blood and let it drop back to my side. "I guess."

"Which would defeat the purpose of killing them."

"Since they turn to dust, I think they're just . . . gone."

Luther considered that awhile and then nodded. "I think so too."

We might be deluding ourselves, but right now I needed a better delusion than the one I'd just had, which I didn't think was any delusion at all. But I couldn't figure out just *what* it was.

I managed to get to my feet without falling on my ass. The slightly slimy sensation of bloody water squishing beneath toes would have turned anyone's stomach, but not mine. As long as I—or someone I cared about—wasn't dead in that bloody water, I'd grit my teeth and move on.

Another mantra—I had a hundred of them.

I quickly washed off my hands, my feet, then shooed Luther ahead of me and into the hallway. "Wait here," I ordered, and ducked into the bedroom where I'd left my duffel.

Quickly I donned my usual costume of jeans and a tank top, good socks and tennis shoes. Once, I'd been partial to sandals, but that was before I had to fight for my life all the damn time. Flip-flops just aren't any good on a battlefield.

My fingers brushed against a plastic sandwich bag that held two items of jewelry I'd once never left home without looping around my neck. Now, one could give me quite a burn and the other . . .

I sighed and pulled the bag free of the rest. Through the sheer container, Ruthie's silver crucifix gleamed. I missed wearing that almost as much as I missed her.

The remaining item was a chunk of turquoise culled from Mount Taylor. Sawyer had drilled a hole, strung the stone on a chain and given it to me when I was fifteen. I hadn't known it then, but the turquoise not only protected me from his mother but also was a type of homing device. When I wore it, Sawyer knew where I was.

Why I'd continued to wear the stone right up until the jeweled collar had made a second necklace overkill—not to mention that the chain had caught on the stones and I'd feared one day it would break and disappear forever—I wasn't sure. Sawyer had scared the pants off me back then. He'd also fascinated me, and that he'd given me a gift had charmed me. Back when I hadn't known what true charm was.

Before Jimmy.

I winced. I'd been trying not to think of Sanducci. About where I'd left him, and what was being done to him.

My fingers convulsed around the turquoise, and thunder rumbled from the mountain. Did the mountain call to the tiny part of it that had been taken away? Did it mourn this bit of stone like a little child lost?

I snorted and dropped the plastic bag back into my

duffel. The mountain *was* magic, but that was going too far.

I zipped the duffel and took it with me when I left the room. I wasn't staying, though I wasn't sure yet where I needed to go.

Luther wasn't in the hallway, and for an instant I panicked until I heard someone moving around in the kitchen. I went to the doorway and watched the kid pilfer through the cabinets for food.

"I told you to stay."

He turned with a bag of chips clutched between long, dark fingers. "I'm not a dog."

No, he was a teenage boy with more power than was good for him. I'd left him with Sawyer and Summer because they were the best choice at the time, but now—

"You're going to have to come with me."

"Not."

I blinked. "I can't leave you here alone."

"I've been alone most of my life. Believe me, this"— he spread his arms wide, the bag of Ruffles swinging merrily—"is easy street. Ain't nothin' round here that can do me any harm."

"Listen—"

"No," he snapped. "I'm waiting for Summer. She'll come looking for me here when she—"

My eyes narrowed. "When she what? Do you know where she is?"

Luther shook his head, and his kinky golden-brown locks jiggled. Funny, but suddenly I didn't trust the kid at all.

So I reached out and touched him, but I didn't see what I thought I would. With my gift, that happened a lot.

I couldn't read minds; more's the pity. Sure, when I

touched people, and un-people too, I saw things—where they'd been, what they'd done—but I couldn't see everything.

Situations that packed strong emotions—love, hate, joy, terror—came through the quickest and the strongest. Often, if I asked a question, then followed up with a brush of my hand, I could "hear" the answer.

But not today.

With the kid I didn't see Summer. Instead I got slammed with his memory of the fight with the lion man.

Luther training in the desert, running, rolling, kicking, jumping. Suddenly he pauses as the wind rustles his hair and Ruthie's voice whispers, *Barbas*.

I'd believed the man who'd invaded my shower had been a lion shifter, but there was more than one kind. That he'd been the same kind that had killed Luther's parents, the same kind as Luther's mother, was not a coincidence. Not in my world.

The memory continued to play out, and as long as Luther let me I continued to watch.

The roar of the barbas splits the suddenly still air. Luther's eyes flare from hazel to gold. His head turns toward Sawyer's house as the man emerges, already shedding his clothes and shifting to his true form.

I expect Luther to grab a knife, a spear, preferably a gun, and take out this guy. Instead, Luther strips too, and then he shifts.

They come at each other just like the lions on *Wild Kingdom*. Fast and furious, all snarls and claws and teeth. Blood and spittle fly. Horrible gashes open in their sides; chunks of fur and flesh thunk against the ground.

I yanked my hand from Luther's arm and lifted my gaze to his.

Luther's eyes, ancient despite the youth of his face, stared into mine. For an instant they flared gold, and the lion inside peered out. "Seen enough?"

His voice was a rumble—part beast and part man. I blinked, and he was just a kid again. Tall, gangly, he gave the appearance of being too awkward to do much but trip over his own massive feet. But I'd seen him fight in human form, and that appearance was deceiving.

"You could have shot him," I murmured. "Silver plus shifter equals ashes."

"Not with a barbas. I'm surprised you don't know this."

"I've been a little busy," I muttered, but he was right. It was my job to know. The instant I'd heard the word "barbas" the first time, I should have found out how to kill one. "Clue me in."

For an instant I thought he might refuse. Since I'd returned from LA, he was behaving as if he could barely stand the sight of me, as if he trusted me even less than a stranger. I couldn't blame him. He'd been there before Sawyer and Jimmy had managed to cage the new and not-so-improved me behind my fancy jeweled collar. It hadn't been pretty.

The kid reached into his pocket and pulled out a white flower with a few crumpled green leaves attached. "Hellebore." At my frown he continued. "A plant used in witchcraft to invoke demons. Specifically demons of Barbas."

"You brought that thing here on purpose?" My voice rose, cracking on the last word.

"You think I was out there?" He flung his long arm and nearly clipped me in the nose with one huge hand. "All alone? Just for fun?"

I didn't know what to think. "Why would you—?"

"It's better to face them on my terms. Right here. When I'm ready for them, one at a time, rather than have them sneak up on me in a group."

The words *like they snuck up on my parents* were left unsaid.

I digested that for a second. I liked this scenario a whole lot better than the one where the barbas had somehow found Luther at Sawyer's compound. This place was supposed to be shielded from prying eyes by Sawyer's magic.

I let out the breath I hadn't known I'd been holding on a long, relieved sigh.

"They've been searching for me all along."

My breath stuck in my chest again. "Excuse me?"

"I've always known it." He shoved the hellebore back into his pocket. "I always felt stalked. When the feeling got to be too much, I'd run. Thought I was paranoid, but like they say, you aren't paranoid if they're really after you."

"Why are *they* after you?"

"I didn't ask. Don't care. They killed my family. They die. End of story."

He sounded so much like Jimmy my mouth fell open. If the kid continued to lure in demons and dust them with ease, he'd *be* another Jimmy—the best demon killer in the federation. Which wasn't such a bad thing considering how short my list of available demon killers had become.

"Now that I know what they are," Luther continued, "that I'm not crazy when I feel evil, when I see things, hear things, now that I know how to kill them . . ." His eyes flared golden fury once more. "I plan to."

He lifted his chin as if he expected me to argue. I didn't. The idea of sending him out alone was hard to swallow, but I'd swallow it. I had to.

Besides, the kid had Ruthie now. Theoretically, I was in more danger than he was.

"So you lured him in with hellebore?" Luther nodded. "But how'd you kill him?"

Luther grinned. He was going to be so handsome—if he lived long enough. "Not only does hellebore bring them forth, but if you use it right, damn stuff kills them."

"How do we"—I made quotation marks in the air with my fingers—" 'use it right'?"

"Boil the plant in oil, then dip the tip of a weapon into the juice. Pow!" He slammed a massive fist into an equally large palm, then flipped his hands outward. "Whoosh."

"Where'd you discover this info?"

There was a brand-new federation database where DKs and seers could enter what they'd learned about the Nephilim from their personal encounters. But I couldn't recall giving Luther the code.

"Sawyer," he said shortly.

"Hmm," I murmured. I wasn't surprised. "You know where he is?"

The kid frowned. "I thought he was with you."

"There's a lot of that going around."

"Huh?"

"Never mind. So, to be clear, you dipped a weapon in boiled hellebore oil. What weapon?"

Luther's smile was thin and just a little scary. "Me."

CHAPTER 16

I'd been looking toward the mountain, wondering if, perhaps, Sawyer was still up there, but at the kid's words I looked right back. "Say what?"

"The spell required a weapon of fury coated in hellebore."

"A weapon of fury could be anything."

"In this case, that weapon was me. I rubbed hellebore all over my body."

"Dammit, Luther!" I clenched my hands to keep from throttling the kid. "You could have been killed."

"I wasn't."

"Don't do that again."

His expression became mulish—a quick switch from strong, able man to sulky little boy. "I'll do whatever I have to. Seems to me it's a lot safer to take a bath in hellebore than to coat some weapon and hope like hell you've got that weapon at hand *if* a barbas shows up. This way, I'm always ready."

The kid thought like me, which made it hard to argue with him. Knowing that he was protected the next time a barbas tried to kill him took a small portion of the load off my heavily overloaded mind.

"It would be good to know why they keep coming after you," I murmured.

"Does it matter?"

"Maybe. Seems their time would be better spent wreaking havoc wherever they can like the rest of the Nephilim. That they're obsessed with you is . . . disturbing." To say the least.

"They killed my parents"—Luther shrugged—"but they never found me. Maybe they just can't let it go."

"So they keep searching for the next fifteen years? Awful long attention span for a kitty cat." I thought back to my short encounter with the lion man, and I tilted my head as I heard again his heavily accented voice. "He was African."

Luther snorted. "Why? Because he was black?"

"He had an accent. He said, 'Where is de boy?' "

The sudden shift in expression on Luther's face made me pause and ask, "What?"

"Just like that?" he asked. "He sounded *just* like that?"

"Yeah," I said slowly. "Why?"

"My mother had an accent. She was from Kenya." His lips curved into a small sad smile as his eyes gazed toward the mountain. "She would walk in the house, and she would call, 'Where is de boy?' and I would come running."

My eyes got a little misty at that picture. I'd never had a mother—at least one I remembered. By the time Ruthie had taken me in, I'd been far too old to come running and she'd had far too many children in her care to call.

You'd think I'd have flashes of someone—a hazy, ghostly face in the night, a cool hand on my brow, the echo of a voice, a scent that brought back . . . anything— but I didn't. Before the first foster home there was only a great black void, one I often wished had reached forward to encompass several of the places I'd lived thereafter.

"You're saying the man who came searching had the same accent as your mother?" I clarified.

"Since I didn't hear him say anything but—" He opened his mouth and roared so loudly if I were a cartoon I'd have been blown back three feet by the current, then shrugged. "Got me."

As I'd thought before, it was too damn coincidental that a cadre of barbases had killed Luther's parents and one had shown up here. Even if Luther had called the thing in, from its question to me in the shower, the barbas had been looking for the kid, and as the boy had pointed out, you aren't paranoid if they're really after you.

"Relatives?" I mused.

"Of my mother?" At first Luther appeared intrigued, until he realized that though he might have gained family, that family wanted him dead.

I remembered when I first realized that people— things, demons, whatever—I'd never met and hadn't personally hurt wanted to kill me. It took a little getting used to. Luther got over it a lot quicker than I had.

His face hardened; he lifted his chin and murmured, "Gonna dust every last one of the bastards."

"That's my boy."

"I'm not your boy."

The kid still didn't trust me, and I couldn't blame him. Without this collar, I'd want to kill him too. Without this collar, I'd probably do worse than kill him for a long, long time.

And wouldn't that be funnnnn? the demon whispered.

I shivered. I hated this thing inside of me. That I'd

sent Jimmy to have his released only made me hate myself nearly as much.

I ignored Luther's jab. What choice did I have? Pointing out that he *was* my boy, as in under my command in Armageddon's Army, would only force another confrontation about having lost my connection to the army's true general. Since I needed that connection now, pissing off the conduit wasn't advisable.

Hey, I *could* be taught!

"Can you bring Ruthie?" I asked.

Luther frowned. "Now?"

"No, I thought maybe next Friday. After we're all dead."

"You don't have to be bitchy about it," he murmured.

"Obviously you don't know me very well at all."

His lips curved just a little. "I've never tried to *bring* her. She's always just—"

"There," I finished.

"Yeah."

Boy, I wished she were just "there" for me right now.

"Close your eyes and—"

"Open," Luther interrupted. "I know."

Considering he'd been working with Sawyer for several weeks, I was certain he did. Sawyer was big on being open. Which was downright hysterical considering how "closed" the man was.

Luther shut his eyes, took a deep breath, let it out and waited. I stood helpless, able only to watch, to hope and pray that he'd succeed, but also kind of hoping he didn't. I'd been able to reach Ruthie solely in my dreams. I couldn't call her up on a whim no matter how much I might have wanted to.

Time passed. I sighed, shuffled, opened my mouth

to tell the kid to forget it, he'd tried, but then his eyelids fluttered, opened, and the eyes that stared back at me were no longer hazel but a deep woodsy brown.

My lips tightened; I glanced away. "Overachiever," I muttered.

"Lizbeth," Ruthie's voice came out of Luther's mouth, sweet and gentle as a spring rain at dawn. "Jealousy don't help anyone."

I shrugged. "I'm supposed to be the most powerful seer in centuries, but I can't *see* anymore, and I could never bring you like he can."

"We all have our talents, child. Right now yours are in a different area."

"Will I ever be a seer again?" I asked, my voice so wistful it surprised me.

In the past, all I'd wanted was to be normal, for God to take away the psychometric gift I'd been born with. Then Ruthie had given me *her* gift, and I'd wished that away too. Now that gift was gone, and I ached to have it back again.

"Time will tell," Ruthie murmured.

If I closed my eyes I could delude myself; I could forget—momentarily—about the boy channeling the woman and once again see Ruthie Kane.

Nearly everything about her was sharp—her mind, her elbows, not to mention her spiky hips and knobby knees. I never could figure out how a woman who resembled a bag of bones could give the softest, sweetest hugs on the planet. The kind of hugs people lived—and died—for.

She'd fold me into her arms, and the fluff of her steadily graying Afro would brush my face as I listened to the sturdy thud of her great big heart. I missed those hugs so damn much.

I opened my eyes. The kid looked nothing like her,

and if I tried to hug him, I'd probably wind up with a black eye. Not that I needed a hug or anything.

Yeah, I didn't believe it either.

"What's that mean?" I asked. "Time will tell?"

"The future is . . . murky."

My eyebrows lifted. "I thought the future was written."

"It is. Unfortunately, the way it's written . . ." Luther's huge hands spread wide. "Could mean anything."

I rubbed my forehead. Why did I even *try* to make sense of my life?

"Listen." I dropped my hand. "I had a . . ." I paused, frowned. "Well, I thought I was dream walking, but—" Quickly I explained what I'd seen and how I'd seen it.

Luther's mouth turned down, just the way Ruthie's always had whenever life threw her an unpleasant curve. "Not dream walking," she muttered.

"You're sure?"

Those familiar eyes in that unfamiliar face met mine. "Coffin, dirt, graveyard. The dead don't dream, Lizbeth."

"If you say so."

"I do. This was a message."

"From whom?"

"The usual messenger," Ruthie said, obviously still thinking. "This woman was dead, and then she wasn't."

"And how does that happen exactly?"

"Someone, or something, raised her."

"Zombie?" I'd never met one, but that didn't mean they weren't around.

Luther's curls flew as his head moved left, right and left again. "Zombies don't run; they shuffle. They aren't very pretty either. The decay don't go away just 'cause they're above ground instead of below. But what zombies really don't do is turn into birds and fly."

"What does?"

Ruthie held up one long, brown finger. "First, tell me about the bag she carried. Size. Shape. Weight."

I placed my hands four inches apart. "About like this." Then I did the same lengthwise and added a few inches to the space. "And this. Weighed a pound or so."

Ruthie's gaze remained on mine. "If you had to guess, what would you say was inside?"

I closed my eyes, imagined again what it felt like to be the woman in the grave. I shivered at the memory—the dirt in my nose and mouth, the darkness all around me, the press of the earth, the smell and the madness that hovered very close to the surface.

"Focus, Lizbeth. What was in the bag?"

I stood in the exquisite rays of the rising sun, felt the cool, damp morning dew on my feet and my face; then I lifted my hand—scratched and bleeding, but already healing—to the satchel looped around my neck.

As soon as I touched it, I got a flash so strong it made me stagger and open my eyes. "Whoa, what the hell?"

I'd never been able to touch something in my memory and see it. Of course I'd never been able to enter anyone's mind without first physically touching them; I'd never "become" someone the way that I'd become the woman in the grave.

"What did you see?" Ruthie's gaze was intense; Luther held his breath.

"A book. Very old. Had a crest on the front." I scowled, staring into the distance, thinking so hard I risked a brain embolism. "A star."

"Five points or six?"

I closed my eyes and laboriously counted as I held on to the image in my head with all the power that I had. A bead of sweat slid from my brow, tickling first my cheek and then my neck. "Six."

"Hexagram." Relief colored Ruthie's voice.

I opened one eye. "That's good?"

"Yes and no. Pentagram—five points—can be white or black magic. Just depends."

"But a hexagram?"

"Jewish magical symbol. Legends state it came into use after being discovered on a signet ring transcribed with the secret four-letter name of God."

"Which is?"

Luther's eyes rolled. "A *secret*, Lizbeth."

I lifted my hands, surprised to discover they were shaking. I put them behind my back, clasping my fingers together in an attempt to still the trembling. "Forget I asked."

"What else?" Ruthie pressed.

I reached again into the dark recesses of another mind. "Lions?"

Luther's head bobbed. "The seal was used to mark magical icons of legend and the sacred name was replaced with lions, which were a symbol of Solomon."

I started, but Ruthie continued to speak. "The hexagram with the lion accents is known as the Seal of Solomon."

Solomon. Swell.

"The key is with the Phoenix," I murmured.

Which explained how the dead woman had come back to life, then turned into a brightly colored bird and flown into the sun. I don't know why I hadn't caught on before. My only excuse, one I'd used many times before, was that I'd been a little busy to connect the dots since I'd been dealing, again, with half demons that were trying to kill me.

"Now what?" I asked.

"You'll have to infiltrate the Nephilim."

"Excuse me?" My voice was so loud I startled a bird from a nearby bush.

"How you think you're gonna get the key back?"

"Kill them all and take it?"

"Could." Luther's bony shoulders lifted, then lowered. "But there's a lot more of them than there were, and they're gettin' stronger every day. Infiltrating is a better bet."

"They know me. I'm not going to be able to sneak up and pretend to be one of them."

"Don't sneak, child; walk right in the front door and volunteer."

"And they'll believe my sudden change of heart because they've all had recent lobotomies?"

"No, Lizbeth." Luther took a deep breath, then let it out slowly, looked toward the mountain, up at the sky, back to the house, the hogan and finally me. "They'll believe it because the Phoenix is your mother."

CHAPTER 17

I was speechless. Might be a first. But seriously, what could I say to a revelation like that?

"I—uh—" I blinked several times and finished with, "What?"

"Did you think your name was plucked out of a hat?"

"Sure."

"It wasn't."

I wrestled with the word "duh." If I let that comment past my lips, I'd only get smacked. I swallowed hard; it felt as if the comment were literally a rock in my throat, but I forced it down.

"Isn't this something I should have been told before she rose from the dead and flew off with the key to ruling the world?" Or at least all the demons in it.

"What good would it have done?"

"What good?" My voice rose; hysteria bubbled just beneath the surface. "What *good*? Isn't knowledge power?"

"She was *dead*, Lizbeth. I had no idea she would crawl out of her grave and fly away."

"Isn't that what a phoenix does?"

"Not exactly." Luther's full, youthful mouth puckered in a very Ruthie-like way. "A phoenix dances upon the flames of its funeral pyre, then rises from its own ashes to live another thousand years."

"Fan-fucking-tastic," I muttered. "My mother was—*is*—a Nephilim."

It was a revelation on par with discovering that the Uncle Charlie everyone was always referring to had the last name of Manson.

"Not exactly," Ruthie repeated.

"*What* exactly?"

"She's other."

"Like Sawyer?"

"No one's like Sawyer."

Another comment that deserved a "duh" but wouldn't be getting one.

I thought back to what I'd been told about those who were "other." Grigori plus human equals Nephilim. Nephilim plus human births a breed. But a Nephilim breeding with a Nephilim gave rise to something apart from both humans and monsters. A being that could never truly be either one. By combining two forces of evil, those that were other could become stronger than either of the parents who created them.

"My mother is other," I murmured. "The product of two Nephilim."

Somewhere in the back of my mind, the demon began to laugh. I ignored it. I was getting better at that by the minute.

"What kind of Nephilim?" I asked.

Luther shrugged. "Seers see the Nephilim at hand, not their entire family tree."

"Someone should know."

Luther glanced toward the mountain again, then quickly back. "Perhaps. But not me."

"What about my father?"

"What about him?"

"Who is he? Where is he? Should I expect him to try and kill me any time soon?"

"I've never heard a word about your father."

"I'm supposed to believe that?"

"I've never lied to you, child."

I laughed. "You told me I was an orphan."

"You were as far as I knew. Your mother *was* dead, your father a mystery."

I stared into the familiar dark eyes set in a face that was far too young for them and wondered. Had Ruthie ever lied to me? She'd omitted a helluva lot, but an out-and-out lie? I wasn't sure. I did know that if she'd lied, she'd had a good reason. I also knew that if she'd lied for that good reason, she certainly wasn't going to admit the truth to me now just because I'd asked.

"You'll meet her soon," Ruthie said, "and then your questions will be answered."

All my life I'd craved a mother. Even after I'd found Ruthie, or she'd found me, and the constant ache had faded, I'd still wondered; sometimes I'd dreamed. Now I had a mother, and she was a double-damned half demon. Or maybe a quarter demon. So what did that make me?

Same thing I'd always been.

A freak, but a very, very powerful one.

"Okay," I managed. "Where do I go from here?"

"Infiltrate the Nephilim, take the book, do whatever's necessary to send the Grigori back to Tartarus."

"I don't believe the Nephilim are going to buy my defection."

"There'll be tests." Ruthie sighed, and glanced away again. "There always are."

"What kind of tests?"

A long, dark finger tapped against the glittering

stones of my dog collar. "There's a reason for this. A reason for everything."

"The only way to fight them is with a darkness as complete as they are," I murmured.

"Exactly."

"Jimmy——" I began.

The boy's huge palm cupped my cheek, but Ruthie stared out of his eyes. "I'd never send you there alone, child."

Then the kid blinked, and she was gone.

"Wait——" I began. But it was too late. "Shit."

Luther dropped his hand from my face and backed up. I tried not to be offended when he rubbed his palm on his pants.

"Sounds like you need to go," he said.

"Wish I knew where. I doubt the forces of evil are all gathering for a convention in a town called Hell."

"You never know."

My gaze sharpened. "Do *you* know?"

He shook his head and silence settled between us. I wasn't sure what else to say. *Take care. Watch your back. Trust no one. Kill first; ask questions later.* He knew all that, had probably known it before he'd met me.

"Well"—I cleared my throat—"no sense hanging around."

"You gotta fly to Milwaukee? Have the gargoyle let you back into . . . ?" He pointed to the ground.

"No." I reached into my pocket and pulled out a plastic bag containing a spoonful of dirt. "I have a key."

"Stole earth from the Otherworld." Luther's mouth curved. "Nice."

In truth, I hadn't stolen it, though I should have. I hate to admit it, but possessing the key to the lock on the Otherworld was nothing short of an accident.

If I'd been thinking clearly, if I'd still been the me I once was, I never would have left Jimmy behind with no way of getting him back. That I had only showed how far away from the old me I'd come.

When I'd returned from the Otherworld, I'd found grit in my hair, underwear and socks, so I'd gathered it into my palm; then I'd put it into this bag.

"If Sawyer shows up . . ." I paused and Luther tilted his head, waiting. I sighed. "Never mind."

"He could help," Luther said. "Just let me know where—"

"No," I said. All I needed was for all three of us— or four, or even five if Luther told Sawyer and Summer where we'd be—to go charging into Nephilim land. That would *really* look suspicious. I still wasn't sure how I was going to manage it.

I headed for the nearest hill, which in New Mexico was more of a mountain. I wouldn't need to go all the way up. Considering how I'd gotten in the last time, I figured a foothill would do.

On the way, I glanced back at Sawyer's place. I thought Luther would be watching, maybe he'd even wave, but he was gone.

The wind swept across the desert, dry and hot, ruffling the short, shaggy length of my hair. I found myself straining to hear Ruthie's whisper on that wind, missing it and her all over again. Sometimes I was so damn lonely.

I'm here, the demon whispered.

"Not for long."

The only response was more laughter.

I lay on the crackling dry scrub, ignoring the rocks that cut into my shoulders. Quickly I took a pinch of earth, held it up to the clouds, thought better of the angle considering the wind and lowered my arm before releasing it.

The remnants of the Otherworld cast across my cheeks and chin like silt, and like before, the ground beneath me churned as the sky fell away, and the earth closed in.

Darkness reigned. I didn't dare breathe. For a long, terrifying instant, I lay caught between one world and the next. My muscles tensed as I prepared to fight my way out; then the earth beneath me loosened, and I tumbled free.

At first I thought the dirt in my ears was scratching together too close to my eardrums and creating a god-awful racket. Then I shook my head; the dirt came out, and the sound became even louder.

Someone was screaming.

I jumped up; earth fell like hail all around me, disappearing through the clouds billowing at my feet. The sky remained the shade of tree bark, and mist shrouded everything.

"Hello?" I called.

The screaming grew louder.

"Shit." I pulled my silver knife—since Jimmy had given it to me several months ago the thing rarely left my possession—and moved toward the sound. Whoever, whatever, that was, I had to make the shrieking stop.

Then it did. Abruptly. Completely. The resulting silence seemingly louder than the screaming had been.

The mist thickened, brushing against my face like cobwebs of ice, curving around my neck, sliding down my back, so slick it almost seemed to whisper.

Lizzy.

I paused, straining my eyes, my ears. Was that the mist? Or was it Sanducci?

I was glad the shrieking had ended, and then again I wasn't. The sound was crazy-making, sure, but without it I was lost in a world I didn't know.

What had been screaming? More important, why?

"Hello?" I called again, and something in the swirl of white shifted.

My fingers tightened on the knife. Who knew what lurked here? Who knew if silver would do anything but piss it off? Nevertheless, silver was better than nothing.

I waited, trying to slow my breathing, to blend into the mist. But I was too big. I glanced down at my hot pink tank top and winced. Too bright. And my heart was beating too hard and fast.

I was a target, plain and simple. Luckily I was a target that was very hard to kill.

CHAPTER 18

I narrowed my eyes, squinting at the place where I'd seen the shifting sliver of darkness, but it was gone. My imagination, perhaps?

A scuffle behind me. I turned.

Nothing.

Something there? Or perhaps there?

Only the mist swirled.

I had to stay where I was. In this place, I could be lost forever. I could walk into a black hole. I could fall and never again get back up.

So I continued to wait and watch. I don't know how long I stood there, knife clasped in my sweaty hand. Eyes and ears straining. Heart thundering despite my best efforts to make it slow.

I drew in a long, deep breath and caught a whiff of cinnamon and soap. Familiar hands slid around my waist; then familiar lips nuzzled my neck.

"You came back," Jimmy murmured. "You didn't leave me here to—"

I frowned. I *had* left him here to—

So why wasn't he?

"Where's—?"

"Shh." He spun me around. I caught the sparkle of dew like diamonds in his dark hair; then he kissed me before I could stop him. Not that I wanted to.

The kiss was pure Jimmy—all I'd once loved, all that I still did. I should push him away, but I couldn't. He hadn't kissed me like this since—

My eyes burned. I couldn't remember. There'd been so much between us—hatred and sadness and pain. Sure, we had our memories. First kiss. First love. First time. How did you ever get past that?

Making each other into vampires was a pretty good start.

So why was he kissing me now as if he meant it?

I didn't ask. I was afraid if I did, I'd break whatever spell we were under. And it had to be a spell, because this certainly felt like magic.

The mist swirled faster, cooler and thicker. The only warmth in this place was him. I stepped closer, pressing my body the length of his, and realized something.

He wasn't wearing any clothes.

Mist clung to my eyelashes, making them so heavy to lift. That was all right. I didn't want to see any more than I wanted to speak.

He smelled like Jimmy, and he tasted like Jimmy too. For just a little while, I wanted to remember what it had been like to be loved like this. Back when forever wasn't a curse but a promise. Back when everything was fresh and new and full of hope. Even me.

His palms traced my waist, my rib cage, skated over my breasts to smooth my shoulders, then skimmed down my arms. One hand cupped my wrist, squeezed just a little, then his fingers spread over mine, and I was shocked to realize I still held the knife. Shocked further when I let him take it.

I tensed, but the soft thud as he dropped it to the ground was reassuring. Not that a knife could hurt me.

No. That wasn't true. It would hurt, but it wouldn't kill. A major distinction these days.

His tongue moistened my lips, tickled my teeth. My hands no longer clenched; I was free to run them over him. Jimmy's face might be just short of pretty, but his body wasn't short of anything. That olive skin was slick and smooth, rippling over sleek muscles. His body lithe and long, I'd once spent hours learning every dip and curve until they were as familiar to me as my own.

I knew how best to touch him, where to stroke, how hard and for how long. I knew his moans, the way his breath would catch if I traced his nipple with a fingernail. How his belly would clench, the muscles rolling against my hands, or my lips, like the lap of a river against the shore.

I buried my face in his neck, drew in the scent of him, one that always caused competing waves of peace and lust. Jimmy was safety—or at least he *had* been. He'd protected me; he'd killed for me.

But he was also sex and danger—a lethal, irresistible combination. As teens, we'd had to hide what we felt, definitely what we did. Ruthie would have killed us. So we'd had sex in closets, on countertops, against the wall in the upstairs hall while Ruthie and the little children had put away groceries downstairs.

Hey, I never said we were smart. We were hormone-driven kids.

I suckled his neck, teased a fold with my teeth. He tasted of summer and salt, the only warmth in a world that had become so damn cold.

Blood, whispered the demon. *You know that you want it.*

And I did. So badly I could almost taste the flow.

You won't hurt him. You can't kill him.

That wasn't true and I knew it. So did the demon. Sneaky, lying bastard.

I took a deep breath and lifted my mouth from Jimmy's skin. It was a lot harder than it should have been.

I imagined shoving the demon—which in my head was a misshapen, cloven-hooved monster—behind an iron door. I slammed it shut; the sound made my ears ring. The demon began to fling itself at the door, screaming and pounding, throwing a tantrum like a child. I turned my back on that door and tossed away the key.

Ah, that was better.

The mist had thickened further; I couldn't see anything but the shadow of Jimmy's head so close to mine. Mist that thick didn't exist.

On earth.

"Remember the night we snuck out?" Jimmy's voice was disembodied, though his breath brushed my cheek.

I gave a short, sharp laugh. "Which one?"

"Close your eyes," he whispered as his lips skimmed my temple, then each of my eyelids before skimming over my cheekbone. "See if this rings any bells."

His teeth grazed my chin and memory flickered. A chill in the air—October—the scent of just-fallen leaves from a pile beneath the big maple tree in the yard, the crunch of my bare feet across a few that had been torn free by the autumn wind. Me cringing at the sound, which seemed as loud as thunder in the secret navy-blue night.

"You gave me a note," I said as his fingers crept beneath my tank, his palm against my stomach large and hot. I rubbed myself against him and tried not to purr.

"Meet me at midnight." His face to my neck, he licked the throbbing vein, pressing his tongue to the pulse, scraping his teeth back and forth to the rhythm of my heart.

I wanted him to bite me; I wanted him to drink from me as I died.

"Shit," I muttered. We were both so fucked up. But then we always had been.

We might lie to ourselves that the demons within us were new, but Jimmy and I had always had demons. The only thing new was our letting them out.

"I thought Ruthie saw," I continued, voice more breathless by the minute. "I flushed the note, just in case."

He laughed, the movement brushing our chests together. I ached to feel skin on skin. Maddened, I leaned back and yanked the tank over my head. Before it even hit the ground, he'd released the catch on my bra with a deft twist, then lifted my breasts into his palms, cupping and caressing, lowering his head, letting his breath trickle over the gooseflesh raised by both the mist and our memories.

"Touching you made my hands shake." He pressed a kiss to my collarbone, skimmed his fingers there too, and I felt him tremble. "It still does."

My throat felt funny—thick and tight—and my eyes burned. There must be something in the mist besides water.

What had happened down here? The Dagda was supposed to have released Jimmy's demon. Instead he seemed to have brought back the Jimmy I'd lost. The boy who'd needed me and loved me, the almost man I'd adored.

"The moon was full," he continued, "but it was foggy. Like this."

"No," I corrected. "It was warm that night. Clear. Indian summer."

"And then a front came through."

Funny how memories can be both the same and completely different. I remembered the heat, the sky and Jimmy. But now that he mentioned the front, I could almost feel the cool, autumn wind and the fog that had padded in, twirling around our ankles like a smooth gray cat.

"You wore that skirt I liked."

"You told me to." Another reason I'd flushed the note.

"I didn't tell you not to wear underwear."

My lips curved; I leaned forward and put my mouth against his ear. "Some things I can figure out for myself."

His fingers flexed, the pressure against my breasts just short of pain; his thumbs stroked over the tips.

"I dreamed of you in that skirt. Every time you wore it to school, I'd sit in Chemistry and imagine getting you out of it."

"As I recall—" I took in a quick breath when he slid two fingers beneath the waistband of my jeans, brushing the lace at the top of my panties before flicking open the single button. "As I recall," I tried again, "you never did get me out of it."

"Didn't need to." He drew the zipper down, the sound muffled by the thick, heavy air. He yanked the jeans and the panties past my hips; I kicked them away along with my shoes. "I just lived out my dreams."

I tilted my head; my lips parted, and his mouth crushed down on mine. As his palms traced up my thighs, then cupped my ass and lifted me, everything came rushing back.

The night, the moon, the fog—the heat of the air,

the chill of that incoming front. Midnight. Everyone asleep but us. In the distance, a dog barked, too far away to matter. Not that anything would have stopped us then. Nothing was going to stop us now.

He'd taken my hand; we'd raced to the backyard where the shadows were deep and we could be all alone.

That skirt, he'd said, lifting the hem, which reached to mid-calf, floaty and flouncy, nearly black with a cast of purple that made me think of enchanted, starlit skies. I'd found it at Goodwill—we did a lot of our shopping there; just because Ruthie was the leader of the supernatural forces of light didn't mean she was rich in anything but power. The skirt had probably belonged to an old woman, a former hippie perhaps, but it had looked almost new and had fit me so well.

You'd think a teenage girl would go for a shorter hem—not that Ruthie would have ever let me wear anything higher than my knees—but not me. Not the way I'd lived—on the streets, in foster home after foster home, a pretty child who'd turned into an exotically beautiful young woman who'd developed earlier than most. I'd wanted to cover myself, to hide from everyone but him.

Every time you wear it, all I can think of is sliding my hands underneath.

I wasn't completely certain if the voice I heard was only memory or if he was speaking the same words now. He was definitely performing the same ritual. His calloused fingers scraped deliciously along the backs of my thighs as he parted my legs and setting my knees across his slim hips.

Then, he'd braced me against the back of the house. Now he was bigger and stronger—he had supernatural abilities—so he merely lifted, then entered me. I crossed my ankles at the small of his back, wrapped my arms around his neck and settled in for the ride.

With my eyes closed, the mist drifting seductively across my skin and the scent of Jimmy all around, I was transported into the past. All that had happened since—the pain, the betrayal, the infinite changes—disappeared. If I let myself believe we were in Ruthie's backyard instead of the Otherworld, that it was October and not August, that we were still kids, still human—or at least believed that we were—it was easy.

I clung to him, let him take the lead, his hips advancing and retreating, his mouth covering my face, my neck, my breasts, with reverent kisses. Back then he'd worshiped me; I'd idolized him. It hadn't lasted, but while it did the world had been such a glittering, glorious place. There'd been hope and love and chances. There'd been so many possibilities in life.

Now there were a lot more possibilities in death, or at least possibilities *of* death, which might be why I was letting reality slide. Time enough to worry about vampires and demons and the end of the world later. They'd all still be there after I came.

As good as this felt, the pressure wasn't quite right. I tightened my ankles, arched my back, which pushed my breasts right into his face. He didn't mind; he'd always liked them.

He took a nipple between his teeth, tugging, suckling, before gifting the other with the same treatment. The sensations danced across my skin, skated lower, yet still this just wasn't right.

"Let go," I murmured against his hair.

"Never." He kissed one swell, rubbing his cheek against the other.

I tangled my fingers in his damp, curling hair. "Put me down. Please? I need to feel you—"

He lifted his head, and for an instant I could have sworn I saw a telltale flash of red at the center of his dark eyes. But it couldn't be. If his demon were free, he'd never touch me so gently. When his demon was free, Jimmy was into—

I shuddered, remembering the time I'd spent in captivity in Manhattan.

"You need to feel me?" he murmured, laying his face once again against my chest. "I must be losing my"—he flexed his lower body, and I gasped as he slid ever deeper—"touch."

"I didn't mean that. I just—" I shifted, tugging on one leg.

For an instant I thought he might hold me there, and I panicked a little. The last time he'd forced me to do things I didn't want to do, I'd been his slave and he'd been the psycho master of my prison. But he let go, and my feet fell to the ground as he slid from my body.

"Don't tell me we're done," he said, voice tight.

I took his hand, planning to draw him down with me onto the soft, misty ground we couldn't see. "Not yet."

This place was so strange. We stood on something solid, yet clouds swirled all around our feet and the sky was the shade of the earth. As I lay back, the cool mist enveloped me, shutting out everything in this world. If I hadn't taken hold of Jimmy's hand, I'd never have known he was there.

One tug and he followed, covering my body with his. "This is what I needed," I whispered.

He didn't speak; I couldn't see. He could be anyone.

Except I knew his body, his scent, the sounds he made right before—

Jimmy tensed, the movement causing his body to rub against me just right. His breath caught; for a second I thought he might call me baby. I'd always hated the term, but now it had been so long since I'd heard the word, I held my breath too.

Instead he cursed the way he always did when he was trying to hold back, to wait for me to catch up so we could come apart together. But I didn't need to catch up, I was already there, so I arched, taking him deeper, running my palm over his back, pulling him closer as he pulsed within.

"Jimmy," I murmured, and in my voice I heard everything. Past happiness, present pain, future pleasures—only with this man had I ever been truly whole.

Because he knew me, body and soul, he shifted, pressing harder where I needed him to, and I came in a rush, his name again on my lips, my hips pumping. I could have sworn I felt him swell, pulse and come again. Inhuman, sure, but wasn't he?

That thought brought me out of the moment, tore away all the magic. The interlude was over. We had to go back—to both the present problem and the real world.

His head against my chest, I tangled my fingers in the unusually long hair at the nape of his neck, opened my mouth to ask what had happened down here, how he was. But before I could say anything, he jumped lithely to his feet and disappeared into the mist. In the distance, the screaming began again, trilling through the night like a long, lonely song.

I scrambled up, cast my hands around for my clothes and knife. I didn't like that screaming. Liked even less being naked while it rolled around me, bristling along my bare skin, causing sharp, painful gooseflesh to rise in its wake.

When the last zipper, catch and tie were fastened, I moved toward the shrieks, knife once again held tightly in my fist.

The sound had started up again too quickly to be Jimmy, I assured myself. But the assurances were merely that. Jimmy could move quicker than a high wind when he chose to. Although why he'd choose to rush toward something that could make him scream like that—

"He wouldn't," I murmured. "So it can't be him."

My demon started to laugh. I guess it had managed to pry open the door in my mind and slip out. Swell.

"Shut up!"

The demon laughed louder, and whoever was screaming . . . they screamed louder too.

"Jimmy!" I shouted. He didn't answer. I doubted he could hear me above the screaming.

How was I going to find him and get out of here?

The same way I'd found him and so many others in the past. My gift. The one I'd been born with.

I could touch people and know things about them, but I could also touch what they'd touched and find them. It had been a very handy talent when I'd been a cop. The power wasn't any less useful now; I just used it a lot less because I had so many others.

I let the mist settle on me like a summer rain. Closing my eyes, I breathed in, then lifted my free hand and laid the palm over my stomach, right where Jimmy had touched me. And I saw him—in what appeared to be a cave: rock walls, the trickle of water, the flicker of a fire across his face.

"Another cave," I muttered. "Figures."

The last time his vampire nature had sprung free, I'd tracked Jimmy to a cave in the Ozarks. I wondered at the attraction. Caves gave me the willies.

Nevertheless, I had to find this one. I brushed my fingertips across my skin as he had, and saw the path Jimmy had taken as if he'd trailed phosphorous footsteps through the fog.

Sometimes this worked and sometimes it didn't. I was so damn grateful my radar was functioning now my knees wobbled. I stopped that by striding forward, letting my mind be my guide instead of my eyes, which would only deceive me in this misty Otherworld.

My shoes scratched against earth that could not be seen. I caught the scent of grass, leaves, greenery, could have sworn that a bush caught at my knee, a low-hanging branch brushed my neck.

The distant ping of water on water brought me up short, and my eyes snapped open. I took a step back. I'd nearly slammed nose first into a wall of rock.

I trailed my hand along the face, first to the right, then back to the left until I found the opening. Seconds later I found Jimmy.

His back to me, he contemplated the fire. Water trickled down the stone wall, dropping bead by bead into a tiny bowl just big enough to wash your hands. Shoulders slumped, head hanging, he worried me.

"Hey." I came up behind him slowly. "You okay?"

When I got closer I saw the welts across his back, as if he'd been whipped with chains of gold. I was surprised I hadn't felt them when I'd run my fingers over his skin. Though they were fading fast, already more like red lines from a minor accident than raised welts from a serious injury.

I stepped closer still and discovered similar marks

on his wrists, around his neck and waist and ankles. I drew in a shaky breath as I reached out to run a gentle finger along his shoulder. My hand trembled.

"Ah, Jimmy," I began.

He spun around with that freaky dhampir speed, grabbing my wrist and yanking me close. His eyes flared bright red.

"Gotcha," he said, and then he bit me.

CHAPTER 19

He went for my wrist and not my neck. The dog collar was good for more than decoration and keeping my demon on a leash. It protected my jugular from out-of-control vamps. Lucky me.

Perhaps I should have Summer bespell one of those black leather collars with spikes. That would work even better, and in truth, this bejeweled poodley thing was just embarrassing.

Jimmy latched onto the vein in my wrist and without thinking I reached over with my free hand and smacked him upside the head. I didn't pull my punch—why would I?—and he flew a few feet. Unfortunately, he took some of my arm with him.

Blood arced through the air, decorating the dirt between where I stood and where he fell. I had an instant to wish I'd knocked him into next week, or at least into the wall, before he started to laugh.

The blood dripping down my hand, off the tips of my fingers and into the ground slowed from a torrent to a drip. A quick glance at the wound revealed it *had* begun to close, but not with the usual creepy speed, the skin growing back together between one blink and the next. Wounds made by a Nephilim always took longer to heal, and right now Jimmy was one of the bad guys.

I returned my gaze to Jimmy as he wiped the back

of his hand across his mouth, smearing red from his chin to his cheek. Wow. Attractive.

"The Dagda did what I asked," I said.

"Did you think he wouldn't?" Jimmy climbed to his feet, no worse for a knock in the head. If he'd been human, I'd have rattled his brains. He might not have gotten back up. Too bad he'd never been human. "You're queen of the world, Elizabeth."

My mouth tightened. He knew I hated it when he called me Elizabeth, but protesting would only encourage him to do it more. Besides, did I really want him calling me Lizzy or baby in that mocking evil voice?

Hell no.

"Not queen," I murmured, my gaze darting left, then right, hoping to catch a glimpse of a bracelet, a ring, another collar, any item the Dagda might have bespelled to control this thing. Except—

Jimmy, when he was Jimmy, would never have taken it off.

"Leader, ruler, blah, blah, blah." Jimmy lifted one hand to his chest and rubbed my blood into his skin. I looked away again. I hated him like this.

So what, exactly, did it mean that Jimmy was evil and there was no trace of a control? No trace of the Dagda either for that matter.

"Fuck."

Jimmy grinned and licked his lips. I caught a hint of fang. "I love it when you talk dirty. Do it some more."

If Jimmy had killed the fairy god before he'd created a leash we had more problems than . . . Well, just about anything.

"Where's the Dagda?" I demanded.

"You think I . . ."—he skimmed his hand over his

belly, leaving another trail of red—"have more power than a fairy god?"

"Yes."

He laughed again. I'd always despised his vampire laugh. Cold, with not an ounce of humor, mocking and—okay, I'll admit it—downright scary. That laugh made me want to put my hands over my ears and shriek until he stopped.

"You know I don't have that much juice, Elizabeth. But you might."

My eyes narrowed. "What are you talking about?"

"You want all his power on top of your own? Baby—"

"Shut up," I snapped, unable to stop myself. "Don't call me that."

"Because he does?"

I blinked. This was the first time I could remember him referring to Dhampir Jimmy as a separate entity from Vampire Jimmy. Myself, I had to agree. They were two different beings. But when Jimmy had been evil before, he'd been completely evil, with no hint of the man who was not. In fact, when I'd tried to seduce the old Jimmy free by bringing up happy memories of our pasts, the new one had hurt me until I stopped.

"Why the seduction?" I asked. *I'd* had a good reason. He didn't.

"I get bored with always taking what I want. Sometimes it's fun to make them want me."

"Them?"

"Women. Or men. Depends on my mood."

Jimmy the vampire liked sex—any way, any time, with anyone. How could I have forgotten?

Because I'd *tried* to forget—that and everything else about this version of Sanducci.

"Getting back to my plan," he continued. "You

fuck the Dagda—I'll watch." He winked. "I've always wanted to see you in action, but it's a little hard when you're on top of me. Actually"—he grabbed himself like Michael Jackson on a *Thriller* reunion tour—"it's a lot hard when you're on top of me."

Vampire humor. Gotta hate it.

"Once you absorb his power, I'll kill him"—he shrugged—"or you can. We'll toss that stupid collar of yours into the fire and then—" He flipped his hands over in a voilà gesture that would have been more nonchalant if a few drops of blood hadn't flown free. "Together we'll rule every world that there is."

"Let me ask you something." Jimmy lifted his eyebrows as I strode closer, then I knocked on his forehead with my knuckle. "Are there more voices in there than two? Is one of them named Samyaza?"

"You think I'm the Antichrist? No, baby." He rolled his eyes when I snarled. "I think that might be you."

"Me?" I squeaked.

"You didn't guess?"

"Huh?" Why was I always three steps behind? Sure, I'd been a little lax when it came to listening in church, but still—I was the leader of the light. Why didn't I *know* anything?

"The destroyer, the beast—whatever they're calling him these days—possesses the one who releases him."

"So?"

"The Grigori flew free when you killed the woman of smoke."

According to Ruthie, they'd already been freed and not by me. But I should see where he was going with this, find out what Vampire Jimmy knew.

"Again I say, so?"

"It must have been something you did."

"Which was?"

"Got me." He tilted his head, and one dark lock fell over his black and red eyes. The gesture was so Jimmy. The eyes were so not. "You been hearing any whispers in there?" He smirked as he repeated my own question back at me. "Are there more voices in there than two?"

"Enough." I turned away before he could see the truth. He'd scared me. "Where's the Dagda, Jimmy? Don't make me beat it out of you."

"You'd enjoy that."

"I would." I took a deep breath and faced him again. He was so close my breasts brushed his chest, and as usual, I'd never heard him move. I slammed the heels of my hands against him. "Back off."

He must have been prepared for that reaction, because he didn't move an inch. Instead his gaze lowered to what I first thought were my breasts, then realized was my neck. More specifically, my collar.

"I could take that off," he whispered. "You and me, together, we could do some damage."

I stepped out of his reach. "I think that's what Ruthie has in mind. You and me. Doing some damage."

His lip lifted, like a dog, except dogs didn't have such pointy fangs. "I don't take orders well. Even when I'm Stupid Jimmy."

"Stupid?" Sanducci was a lot of things, but stupid had never been one of them.

"Wimpy, whiny. Everything this one—he slammed his palms against his chest with a solid thunk—"isn't."

"Keep that up and you'll break some ribs," I said.

His snarl became a smirk. "Worried?"

"No, I'd just rather do it myself."

The screaming, which had continued in the background all this time, suddenly stopped.

"What *was* that?" I murmured.

"One of the Dagda's women."

I jolted. "What?"

"He likes it when they scream."

"And you think I'm going to do *that* guy just to get his magic?"

His eyes when they met mine were more black than red, and when he spoke I heard the old Jimmy far more than I liked. "Sooner or later you'll have to sleep with someone just for their power."

"Maybe. But I'll choose later and someone else."

The red flared brighter. "I don't think you get to choose."

"*You* certainly don't."

I thought he might attack, and I wanted him to. Right then nothing would have made me happier than beating the ever-loving crap out of Sanducci.

"He will kill you, light's leader."

I whirled at the soft-voiced comment. The Dagda had slipped into the cave and now seemed to fill every inch of spare space. No wonder his women screamed. He was huge all over.

I yanked my gaze from the Frisbee-sized metal that covered his privates. "I'm not that easy."

The Dagda's ruby lips curved. "With this around your neck . . ." He reached out, his long, long arm stretching farther than I'd have believed possible, and drew a finger along my collar. "You are yet human. He is not."

"I could beat him."

"But you wouldn't kill him, because you need him for the coming fight. And that weakness would be your undoing."

"I can't take him anywhere like this." I inched back, removing my neck from the Dagda's touch.

"No." The Dagda let his arm fall to his side. "Which

is why I made you a gift." He held up a thin, circular piece of metal.

"What's that?" I asked.

"Bespelled," the Dagda hedged. "When Sanducci wears it, he will again be . . . as human as he gets."

I held out my hand, and the Dagda dropped the circlet into my palm. It was bigger than a ring, smaller than a necklace.

Frowning, I glanced from the metal to Jimmy's biceps, then his wrist. Still not gonna fit.

"Where—?" I began, and then suddenly I knew.

The thing tumbled to the ground. Here, in the cave, the mist was absent and the earth was actually earth. The circlet hit with a tinny clank and lay still.

"That's . . . That's . . ." I couldn't finish the sentence because I wasn't certain of the term, though I knew very well what something that size would fit. I'd had my hands—among other body parts—around it often enough.

"A cock ring," Sanducci muttered.

Even though I'd known what it was, the words shocked me. I might be a sexual empath, but that didn't mean I had much sex. In truth I'd had very little. No telling what I might "catch" if I wasn't careful. Unfortunately, for me, there were things much worse than an STD.

"Was that really necessary?" I asked.

Jimmy and the Dagda glanced at me in confusion. I wasn't sure who I was addressing either. Jimmy for saying the words or the Dagda for creating the borderline-obscene control?

"What would you have me do?" the Dagda answered. "This will be hidden, not easy to remove unless removal is what is desired."

I'd certainly have preferred a less visible means of

control myself, but considering this—I frowned at the circlet, which still lay in the dirt, the reflections from the fire casting red, orange and yellow sparkles across the stone walls—I'd stick with what I had. No telling what the Dagda might come up with for me if he put his mind to it.

"I'm not wearing that," Jimmy said.

"I can bespell something else," the Dagda offered. "But it would take time. I'd have to wait for another sacrifice."

I stilled. "Sacrifice?"

"For the spell."

"Tell me you're talking goat. Pig. Chicken."

Jimmy's annoying laughter swirled around the cave once more.

The Dagda's brow creased. "What good would an animal do? For a spell of this magnitude, the blood of the innocent is needed."

"Goats are innocent."

"The blood must be freely given and not taken. A *sacrifice*," he said slowly, as if I was dim-witted, which I guess I was.

I whirled on Jimmy, who was still laughing. "Is that what Summer did? To this?" I patted my collar, my fingernails clicking against the glittering, glass jewels like rain on a tin rooftop.

"Of course." He smirked. "Though it was a little hard to find innocent blood at the time."

"What did she do?" I demanded.

I had visions of Summer and Sawyer creeping into a sleeping Navajo village and stealing away a sweet-faced cherub or a nubile virgin.

"You'll have to ask her," Jimmy said. "I was . . . indisposed."

Oh, yeah. He'd been screaming at the top of his

lungs and throwing himself against the golden door of his prison like a lunatic.

"Your women." I turned back to the fairy god. "They give themselves freely?"

His lips curved into a seductive smile. "Wouldn't you?"

"Not so much."

The smile froze. "I bring joy beyond compare. I am very good at my job."

"You're killing women with sex."

"What?" he roared. "Who says this thing?"

I glanced at Jimmy, and the Dagda took a step toward him. "Whoa!" I put up my hand. "You said it yourself. As much fun as it would be to kill him, he's needed."

The Dagda blew air out his nose like an enraged bull, causing a puff of dirt to swirl across his feet. "I kill no one. They scream with *pleasure*, not pain. They give themselves; I do not take."

"Unlike some people," I murmured, narrowing my eyes at Jimmy, who smirked and shrugged.

Asshole.

"These women," I continued. "They're human?" The Dagda nodded. "And they sacrifice themselves why?"

"For gain."

"Money? Power? Love?"

"Yes."

"How do they know about you?"

"Some still follow the ancient ways. Not many, not anymore, which is why it may take a while for me to bespell another item." He leaned down and picked up the ring, twirling it around his finger as he straightened.

I thought of the Phoenix rising toward the sun,

carrying the *Key of Solomon* Lord knew where, to do Satan knew what.

"No." I plucked the ring off the Dagda's finger. "We don't really have any time to waste."

"Fuck," Jimmy muttered as I turned. His eyes flared red and he showed me his fangs. "I'm not gonna let you put that on me."

"I'd be disappointed if you did." I glanced at the Dagda. "Wanna hold him down?"

The fairy god's gaze remained on Jimmy. "I thought you'd never ask."

CHAPTER 20

I could probably have done it myself, but it would have taken longer and, as the Dagda had pointed out, Jimmy, in this form, didn't care if he killed me, himself, everyone—if there was anyone—in a fifty-mile radius. He'd enjoy it. While I had to worry about what would happen to the world if I died, if he did, and carry the guilt if Jimmy ripped out the Dagda's throat and took a shower in his blood.

Jimmy backed up, gaze flicking from the fairy god to me several times. "He won't like this," Jimmy said, referring, I assumed, to the Jimmy who waited on the other side of "this."

"I don't care." A lie. I cared, but I had no choice.

Jimmy whirled to run; I tensed to chase. The Dagda threw up one hand like a crossing guard miming *stop*, and Jimmy crumpled to the ground.

"Hey!" I hurried to Sanducci's side. "What happened to holding him down?"

Jimmy's eyes were closed; that didn't fool me for an instant. I wouldn't put it past him to fake unconsciousness, then tear out my liver for lunch.

"I thought this was what you meant," the Dagda said. "You didn't actually expect me to use my hands when all I had to do was—" He lifted one huge shoulder. "Cuff him and be on your way."

I hesitated. The fairy god gave an impatient huff. "My magic is not so weak. He will not move until I wish him to."

I eyed the Dagda. That magic would be handy to have. However, when my gaze reached his codpiece, I changed my mind. Not happening.

My lip curled as I slid the ring over Jimmy's flaccid penis. Halfway up I checked his face. His eyes were open—just as I'd suspected, not unconscious—and red still flared at the center. White lines radiated from his tight mouth, and tiny rivulets of blood ran down his chin as his fangs pricked his lips. He was furious. I hoped the Dagda's magic held.

Springy pubic hair brushed my fingertips as the ring reached the base, and the red spark in Jimmy's eyes went out like the flame of a snuffed candle. His fangs retracted equally fast, though the tension in his face did not dissipate. I recognized sadness instead of madness; the demon had successfully been caged.

"Let him go."

"Are you certain?" the Dagda asked.

"Release him and leave us alone."

"Very well." The fairy god twirled his hand downward, as if executing a fancy upper-class bow, then ducked through the opening in the cave and disappeared.

I figured Jimmy would grab me—hit me, strangle me, or at least try—and I'd let him. Maybe it would help.

Instead, he got to his feet, then moved slowly to the shadows where he bent, picked up his clothes and started to dress.

"Don't you want to—"

He whirled. "We already *did*, Elizabeth."

"Don't call me that."

"Because he does?"

I started. They were so different, the two Jimmys, yet also very much the same.

"Yes," I whispered.

"You're the one who wanted him back."

"I didn't *want* this, and you know it."

"I know no such thing. You're the leader. You make the rules."

"I don't. You know that too."

He sighed and put on his T-shirt. A bright, tie-dyed kaleidoscope that advertised *Sesame Street*. I didn't even want to ask.

"Yeah," he said. "Sorry. It's just—" His hands fell back to his sides like the arms of a puppet whose strings had been cut. "I hate being like that. Until I am and then I love it. The pain, the blood, the fear, it's . . ." He drew a deep breath, in through his nose, then let it out through his mouth as if he was trying to calm himself, or perhaps trying to catch the scent of the blood, pain and fear. "Seductive," he finished. "But later I remember. You know?"

I nodded, though he wasn't looking at me. I knew. Boy, did I know.

"As soon as I'm me again, everything I did and said and—" His voice cracked; he swallowed, coughed, then lifted his hand and rubbed his face, freezing when he saw the streaks of dried blood.

"Shit." He strode to the tiny basin where water still trickled merrily, and plunged his hands in to the wrists. "Are you okay?"

"Of course I'm okay. I'm just like you."

"You're a whole lot worse than me."

I blinked, shocked to discover his words could still hurt. Since he faced away, scrubbing at his fingers like Lady Macbeth—I had a sudden flash of another cave, other water, but the same Jimmy, scrubbing frantically at blood that was already gone—he didn't see my pain. I waited to speak until I was certain he wouldn't hear it either.

"How you figure?"

"You're a vampire *and* a skinwalker." He paused momentarily in his scrubbing. "Anything else you've become while I was away?"

"No," I said shortly. "And being a skinwalker doesn't make me worse."

"More powerful. That's what I meant."

"Sure you did." He didn't answer, just kept scrubbing at his hands. "Jimmy, I think they're clean."

"I doubt that," he murmured, but he lifted them from the water and dried them on his pants. I didn't point out that beneath the shirt advertising happy puppets he also had blood all over his chest. If I did, we'd never get out of here.

Unable to stop myself, I moved closer, and when he saw me coming he tensed.

"What do you think I'm going to do?" I asked.

"I don't know." He rubbed his palm over his chest as if it ached. I knew the feeling. "I miss you."

"I'm right here."

He shook his head. "When I look at you I remember the other you. I can't bear to touch you or have you touch me. It used to be whenever I was tired or sad or sick I could bring out my memories of us and I'd be . . . better. But the bad ones seem to have drowned all the good ones. Now any memories of you make me—" He swallowed

I could fill in the blank. Memories of me made him sick.

"How did you get past it?" he asked. "What I did to you?"

For an instant what he'd done to me was right there—a kaleidoscope of horror. Then I gritted my teeth and I made it go away.

Lifting my chin, I met his eyes. "That wasn't you."

He snorted. "It is now."

We weren't getting anywhere. We might never get past what he'd done, what I'd done. So many people couldn't, and they had less to forgive and forget than Sanducci and me.

"We should go," I said.

"Lizzy," he began, and I couldn't help it; my heart lightened to hear him call me that again. "I'm sorry about before."

At this rate we were going to be saying, *I'm sorry*, until the day that we died.

"I'm fine." I lifted my wrist. "Healed right up."

"I meant earlier. Out there." He jerked his head at the opening of the cave, and his dark hair flew. "That thing inside me pretended to be . . . me, and I—"

"Your vamp fooled me," I interrupted, not needing or wanting a replay. "I should know better. Not your fault."

"You think that makes it easier on me? I can still see myself forcing you—"

"You didn't force me; I wanted to."

"You wanted me. *This* me." He smacked himself in the chest again. He was really going to have to stop that. "But it wasn't me." He choked and stared at the ground where my blood still darkened the dirt. "That's . . . fucked up," he finished.

"What isn't?"

His laughter was harsh, not quite vampire laughter but close. "It doesn't bother you?"

To my amazement, it didn't. I had so many other things to be bothered by.

"No," I said, and his breath rushed out in a huff.

"Then you're much more forgiving than I am."

I doubted that. I'd held a grudge against him for a long, long time. Probably would still be holding one if I hadn't been forcibly taught that there were a lot better issues to be angry about.

I crossed the short distance between us and reached for his hand. He flinched, but I took it anyway, then traced my thumb over the still-fading mark that circled his wrist.

Before I'd left, I'd seen what the Dagda would do to him, and it hadn't involved any whips or chains. There'd been fire, I thought, perhaps a knife. Pain and blood, nothing was ever easy. But I hadn't seen this.

I stroked my thumb over him again, breathed in, opened my mind . . . and I didn't see anything at all.

I lifted my gaze. "What did he do to you?"

"Does it matter?"

It would always matter. There just wasn't anything I could do about it. What had happened had happened. That I'd let it, that I'd basically ordered it, even if I hadn't been the one to hurt him, did matter. I'd had the power to stop the horror, and I wouldn't.

I understood that a lot of Jimmy's anger, his inability to touch me and let me touch him, stemmed from the knowledge that if we had to do it all over again, I'd do the same thing.

Since I could practically feel his skin crawling beneath mine, I let him go. In this form, there was only so much torture I could stomach.

I had the ability to separate Vampire Jimmy and Dhampir Jimmy; I knew that what the first one did and said had nothing to do with the other. I thought Jimmy understood the same about Vamp Liz and Lizzy. I'm sure he did—in theory.

But men are visual, which is why porn really turns them on, and for women, who are emotional, not so much. So while I could separate the two Jimmys because of the way I felt about each one, even though they looked exactly the same, Jimmy might be having a bit of difficulty getting past his conflicting feelings over what appeared to be exactly the same woman.

The problem was that the Lizzy I'd been, the one he'd fallen in love with, was gone, and I didn't think she was ever coming back. Which left a woman he didn't know and one he didn't like in the same package.

"There are things we have to do that we don't want to do," I began.

"You think I don't know that? I was eighteen, Lizzy, when Ruthie made me—" He stopped and shoved a shaking hand through his sweaty, tangled hair.

"Kill?" I prompted.

He blew air through his lips in a halfhearted Bronx cheer as he dropped his arm back to his side. "I was a killer long before that."

I hated it when he called himself a killer. I didn't think dusting Nephilim was killing. However, Jimmy had been on the streets a lot longer than I had, and he'd done things before coming to Ruthie's that even I didn't know about. Things I probably didn't want to know about.

"You remember what she made me do," he said, referring, I assumed, to his sleeping with Summer. "I knew it would hurt you," he murmured, "but I did it anyway."

"Why?"

"It had to be done."

"There you go." I threw up my hands. "So why can't you forgive me?"

"I don't know. Have you forgiven me?"

I thought of Summer's beautiful face, her tiny, adorable body, her blond hair and blue eyes and her everlasting, unbreakable devotion to Jimmy Sanducci. "No."

His lips curved just a little, and I saw again the boy who'd taken my heart and then broken it apart.

"I didn't think so," he said.

Jimmy was putting on his sinfully expensive Nikes, which he'd probably gotten for free after he took the most recent publicity photo of Venus Williams or Tiger Woods or whoever the top shoe hawker was this week, when he suddenly paused and asked, "What now?"

"We find the Dagda and get out from under."

"And then?"

Jimmy was a little behind the times. Quickly I told him everything.

"Your mother," he repeated, seemingly as stunned as I'd been. But what seemed to be true and what was true these days were often two completely different things.

"You didn't know?" I watched him closely. Jimmy was an extremely good liar. He had to be. I could probably separate truth from fiction if I touched him. However, if I touched him one more time today, one or both of us would probably wind up bloody. Again.

"I thought she was dead."

Hmm. Voice casual, gaze direct. He didn't appear to be lying, but I couldn't be sure.

"You thought she was dead, but you knew she was a phoenix? Or you just thought my mother, whoever she might be, was dead?"

"I choose door number two." He finished tying his silver-tipped laces and stood.

My eyes narrowed. "Sanducci—"

He held up a hand. "I didn't know, okay? I thought you were an orphan like me."

"You weren't an orphan."

The past flickered in his eyes, and I was sorry I'd even brought it up.

"I wasn't," he agreed. "But I am now."

"Not necessarily." His eyes widened, and I held up my hand just as he had. "I'm just saying, parents seem to be coming out of the woodwork lately. Your dad. Sawyer's mom. And now mine."

"And they're all such fantastic finds," he muttered.

"Yeah, the reunions are a hoot. Although . . ." I paused, thinking. "I haven't met my mother. Maybe—"

"Don't go there," Jimmy interrupted.

"Where?"

"Thinking that maybe she's not evil, maybe you can have a relationship, maybe things will be different. They won't be. She rose from the dead, Lizzy. That can't be good."

"It was once," I muttered.

"And once is all we get. Anyone rising from the dead these days is gonna be a problem."

He was right. Still—

"Sawyer's other, and he's not evil."

"You sure about that?"

"Yes!"

Jimmy just raised his eyebrows. My voice *had* been too loud, the word too emphatic, for him to believe me. Hell, *I* didn't believe me.

"Think about it," he said. "Guy up and disappears."

"He does that."

Sanducci stared at me until I squirmed. Everything I said was too loud or too quick and not very believable at all. Why couldn't I lie like he did?

"Don't you find it strange that Sawyer can raise the dead and suddenly the dead are being raised?" Jimmy asked.

"He can't raise the dead, only ghosts."

"So *he* says."

I opened my mouth, shut it again, then said, "What?"

"*Someone* raised the Phoenix."

"You think it was *Sawyer*?"

"Lizzy, I *always* think it's Sawyer."

CHAPTER 21

"I don't believe Sawyer would do that," I said. "Even if he could, which he can't."

"Let's go see."

"How?"

"Find her, find him."

"We won't," I insisted.

"Wanna bet?" He held out his hand, then realized what he was doing and yanked it back.

The two of them had always been like junkyard dogs, circling each other, hackles raised, teeth bared, with me right in the middle. More often than not, whenever they shared the same air they tried to kill each other. It was exhausting.

I headed for the cave entrance. One thing Sanducci was right about was that we needed to get out of here, and the only way to do that was to find the Dagda.

Outside, the mist still roamed, impossibly thick.

"Dagda!" I shouted.

"I'm here."

The voice was so close I jumped, but I couldn't see him anywhere near no matter how hard I tried. You could go blind in this place straining to see your hand in front of your face.

"Where?"

"What do you need?"

I opened my mouth to tell him I needed to see who I was speaking with, and Jimmy murmured, "Just get us out of here."

Understanding that Jimmy didn't want to see the fairy god again—I couldn't blame him—I swallowed the words I'd been about to utter. "We need to get out."

"Where you came in or somewhere else?"

I glanced at Jimmy, but I couldn't see his face. "That's possible?"

The Dagda's chuckle slithered across my skin as chill as the mist. "Here, all things are possible."

Jimmy snorted.

"Where should we go?" I asked.

"Did you see anything in your vision, or whatever it was," Jimmy said, "that might give us a hint where the Phoenix flew?"

Before, I'd been able to close my eyes and access the images. I tried, but time had faded them. I could still see the graveyard, the sky, the Phoenix, but I could no longer put myself into the scene and deepen it.

I sighed and opened my eyes. "She went into the sun."

"Rising sun, so east."

"Considering we don't know east from where, not helpful."

Jimmy let out his breath in a huff. "We'll need to find out where there are disturbed graves."

"And then visit every site?" My voice rose in exasperation.

Jimmy had told me once that no matter what we did to prevent it, the Apocalypse just kept on coming. At the time, I'd thought he was overreacting. Now, not so much.

"The Phoenix has the key," I continued. "I don't think we have that much time."

"You got a better idea?"

"Not really. If we had an Internet connection, then the Dagda could pop us out at the first tumbled graveyard. Don't suppose you're computer literate," I called out.

"You'd suppose right." The Dagda's huge form solidified from the mist. Jimmy tensed so fast I thought he might snap his spine. "However, I have something much better than a computer."

"Better?" Jimmy and I said at the same time.

"Follow me." The Dagda ducked into the cave, and after a quick exchange of shrugs we did too.

In the few seconds it took us to catch up, the Dagda had retrieved a heavy iron caldron from somewhere and hung it over the fire. The sound of something boiling, bubbling, filled the still, damp air of the cavern, and the Dagda beckoned.

I moved forward, and Jimmy caught at my shoulder. "Don't."

"I think I have to." He shook his head, frowning in the Dagda's direction. Though I wanted to stand with Jimmy's hand voluntarily on my shoulder for as long as he'd let it stay there, I inched away. "I'll be right back, and then we'll leave together, okay?"

"You don't have to talk to me like I'm a scared little kid who just woke up from a nightmare."

"How should I talk to you?"

"Like you always do."

"Rude, crude and downright mean?"

"I'd feel less like a crystal vase you're terrified you might break."

I contemplated Jimmy for several seconds. Despite

the natural olive cast to his skin, he was pale, his lips a thin, bloodless line. The circles beneath his eyes were the shade of a ripe eggplant, and no matter how hard he tried to hide it, his hands shook a bit.

He *was* fragile, and I was desperately afraid I'd already broken him. But it wouldn't do any good to tell him that.

"You stay here," I said. "I'll go there, and if I want your opinion, I'll beat it out of you."

I was halfway to the Dagda's caldron when I heard him laugh. It was almost, but not quite, the laugh I remembered. Maybe Sanducci could be fixed after all. Though probably not by me.

"Ask it what you wish to know." The Dagda pointed a finger the width of a kielbasa at the caldron.

"I—uh—" I'd never asked anything of a pot before.

Whatever was inside—obviously liquid from the way it boiled—really heated up. Snap, crackle, pop— several of the bubbles burst, spewing trickles of a tar-like substance into the air, then onto the ground.

The Dagda made an impatient noise and jabbed his hand at the caldron again. "Ask!"

"Where is the Phoenix?" I blurted.

As suddenly as it had boiled over, the liquid stilled, the surface going smooth as ice beneath a moonless sky.

"Look." The Dagda shoved me with his shoulder, and I nearly went headfirst into the pot.

Cautiously I peeked over the edge. All I saw was my own face reflected there. "Doesn't seem to be working."

The Dagda's visage appeared next to mine. "*You're* the Phoenix," he said.

"My name is Phoenix; I'm not one." At least not yet. "I meant *the* Phoenix. The one who was raised from the dead. The one who carries the *Key of Solomon*."

Before the last word had left my mouth, my reflection disappeared and another took its place. I recognized it instantly. The graveyard where I'd first seen my mother. All the graves were tumbled open, the place as still and empty as a postapocalyptic world.

"That's where she was," I said. "Where *is* she?"

"Wait," the Dagda whispered.

The image wavered but did not disappear. Instead, the focus widened, as if we were a camera and the black smooth liquid the lens. The view pulled back, revealing more and more of the area around the cemetery. To the right stood a sign.

"'Cairo,'" I read. "'Population three thousand, one hundred and fifty.' Seriously?"

I thought Cairo was huge—and in Egypt. Which made the grass and the trees in the foreground as well as the small-town streets spreading into the background a mystery.

"There's more than one Cairo," Jimmy said.

I glanced over my shoulder. He'd actually stayed where I'd put him, which I attributed to the Dagda's presence rather than Sanducci's obedience.

"How many more?"

"Not sure about other countries—"

"It's in the U.S.," I interrupted. I'd seen signs like that a thousand times.

"Well, then." Jimmy took a breath. "Cairo, Kentucky. West Virginia. Illinois. New York. Georgia."

I cursed quietly.

"Relax, light's leader. I'm not a jinn. You get more wishes than three."

"Jinn?" I cast him a narrow glare. "As in genie?"

"He's kidding," Jimmy said.

"Does he know how?"

The Dagda smiled. "I have learned much in all my years beneath the earth. Humor is only one joy of many."

"So there aren't any genies?"

"I didn't say that," Jimmy murmured. "They just don't hand out wishes."

I rubbed my forehead. I really didn't have the time for this, so I turned back to the caldron. "Which Cairo are we talking about?"

The view in the black water began to pan to the right, slowly, but still it made me dizzy. I couldn't pull my gaze away even though my stomach rolled. Right before I considered throwing up just to feel better—hey, it worked with a hangover—the picture stopped moving.

Another sign—huge, more like a billboard, with a hokey pyramid, a doofy Sphinx and a stick figure Pharaoh that seemed to be dancing the "King Tut" mambo—appeared.

" 'Come to Cairo,' " I read. " 'A beautiful city along America's Nile, right at the foot of Little Egypt.' " I scowled. "Is this a riddle?"

"It's Illinois," Jimmy answered.

I turned. He was still way over there. "You sure?"

"I *am* a globe-trotting portrait wizard," he said.

Better and better. He was starting to throw my sarcastic digs back at me.

"You've been to Cairo?"

He shook his head. "Cairo, Illinois, with a whopping three thousand souls is not exactly a hotbed of high-profile faces with pockets deep enough to pay my exorbitant, though well-deserved, fee."

"So, basically, you don't know dink. You're guessing."

"I was in Carbondale—also located in Little Egypt.

The top pick in the NBA draft last year came from Southern Illinois University. Macon Talmudge."

Sounded vaguely familiar, but I wasn't much of a basketball fan.

"And I suppose the NBA sent you."

"Of course. But I only took the job because I had to check out a few rumors."

"Werewolf? Vampire?"

"Egyptian snake demon."

"Tell me it wasn't Talmudge."

Jimmy and I had already been involved with the death of one NBA star—we hadn't killed him; he'd been one of us—but if we started leaving trails of dead basketball players, we'd wind up locked in a cage without a key. Not that a cage would hold us, but the less hassle the better, and I really didn't need my picture plastered in every post office from Corpus Christi to Anchorage.

"It wasn't Talmudge," Jimmy obliged.

"But the snake demon, you got it?"

Jimmy looked down his nose at me. Of course he'd gotten it.

"I'm sensing a theme here," I mused. "Egyptian snake demon. Ancient Egyptian shape-shifting firebird. Both found in a place called Little Egypt. Why?"

The Dagda shrugged and spread his massive hands, but I hadn't been asking him. I lifted a brow in Jimmy's direction.

"I did some research on the area," Jimmy said. "The origins of the name are unclear. Some say it started around the Civil War. Illinois was a free state; however, the section that became Little Egypt was given a pass so the saltworks in the region could be mined. People up north began to refer to that part as Egypt."

"Because they kept slaves."

"Yeah. Another theory is that the conflux of the Mississippi River—America's Nile—and the Ohio River creates a basin similar to the Nile Basin. Which is why they named the town on the peninsula where the rivers meet Cairo."

"That would explain why Egyptian creepy things are drawn there," I mused. "It feels like home."

"The Nephilim are descended from the fallen angels. They don't really have a home."

"No, but when they settled all over the world and gave rise to the legends that named them, they adopted one."

"True," he agreed.

"If Egyptian supernatural creatures traveled to America for whatever reason, I can understand why they'd gravitate to an area that was similar to where they'd spent centuries—if not in climate, at least in terrain and name. Shall we head for Cairo?"

"May as well," Jimmy agreed.

I glanced at the Dagda. "You'll be coming with us?"

"I will remain."

"But"—I clenched my hands into fists—"you agreed to fight on my side."

"And fight I will, once you grant my boon."

"Which is?"

"I haven't decided."

Jimmy made an impatient sound. "And he never will. He's as sneaky as a leprechaun."

"I am nothing like a leprechaun." The Dagda appeared insulted.

"They're cunning and slick." Jimmy narrowed his eyes. "They twist words to suit their purpose. They deceive every chance that they get."

The fairy god tilted his head. "Perhaps I *am* like a leprechaun."

"If he never requests a boon," Jimmy said, "then he never owes you his allegiance, which is how he'll remain down here and out of the fight."

"Are you afraid?" I asked the Dagda.

I expected him to reach for his huge club, and then use it on my head. Instead, he laughed. "I fear nothing, light's leader. However, I'd prefer to choose a side when the winner is more certain."

"We'll win," I said.

"When you believe that with both your heart *and* your head, let me know."

I turned back to the caldron. "What does the Phoenix look like?"

The water had gone black again, but as soon as I spoke the murk cleared.

"Not me," I muttered impatiently, lifting my hand to rub away the dirt across my cheek. *"The . . ."*

I paused, cursing when I realized why the reflection had not lifted her hand and rubbed at her face too.

The Phoenix looked a helluva lot like me.

CHAPTER 22

"What is it?" Jimmy started forward, but I held him back with a lift of one finger. I wanted to study the face of the Phoenix, to catalog the differences, and I needed a little quiet time to do it.

Hair curlier than mine, maybe because it was longer, darker too, more the cast of Jimmy's blue-black tresses than the auburn I called my own, eyes also dark. Guess Daddy was the source of my blue eyes, or perhaps one of his relatives. Her skin reflected a lifetime beneath a hundred thousand suns. I'd always known I wasn't white, that I was at least part something else. But I'd figured African-American, Native American, even Italian-American, never Egyptian.

If you saw her in the shadows, if you saw me in the dark, we could easily be mistaken for the other. Which might work out to my advantage, or it might yet get me killed.

"We need to go." I glanced at the Dagda. "To Cairo, Illinois."

"Follow me." He ducked through the opening of the cave.

I motioned for Jimmy to proceed, but he was already moving. I suppose getting out of the Otherworld was worth anything. Even getting out of here with me.

"You will hold hands," the Dagda ordered.

I could barely see Jimmy. The damn mist was thicker and colder than ever. I inched closer, but he inched back. I reached for him, and he lifted his lip like a cornered dog.

"Knock that off before I smack you with a rolled newspaper," I muttered. "I won't bite."

"Yes," he said simply, "you will."

I grabbed his hand anyway, holding on tightly in case he took it into his head to pull away. I was treating him like a little kid again, but if the behavior fit . . .

As soon as I touched him a warm, dry wind stirred my hair. We were no longer in the cool, misty Otherworld but standing on a decent-sized hill above a tired small town bordered by a lot of muddy water. I'd seen the Mississippi River often enough to recognize it.

"Welcome to Cairo," I murmured.

Jimmy was looking around, blinking as if he couldn't believe his eyes. "Freak-y," he said. "I didn't even see him . . . anything."

"Guess it pays to be a fairy god."

"Probably not well."

Jimmy was joking again. That was good. It just had to be, so I smiled, even though he chose that moment to yank his hand out of mine as if I'd recently been infected with leprosy.

I tried to make conversation, so I wouldn't have to deal with the fact that the only time he could bear to touch me was when he was evil.

"Nice hill." I kicked the grass, which was more like hay, and a puff of dirt rose around my foot. "Back where I come from, we call those from the Land of Lincoln *flatlanders*, with good reason."

"Back where I come from too." Jimmy headed for Cairo, his pace speeding up more than it should have despite the downward dip, probably because he didn't try to slow his pace.

The better to get away from you, my dear.

"This part of Illinois has more hills than the rest." He gestured toward the water. "The rivers."

I nodded. The area around the Mississippi in Wisconsin was downright craggy.

Since we'd popped out of the Otherworld without benefit of a car, we had little choice but to hoof it in the direction of Cairo. I could see houses in the distance and beyond them another body of water, the Ohio River, I assumed.

"Who thought it would be a good idea to build a town between two major rivers?" I asked.

"Probably the same guy who thought New Orleans was a fabulous concept."

"New Orleans *is* a fabulous concept," I argued. I'd been there once, for a bartenders seminar—code for tax-deductible drunk fest—and I'd been charmed.

"Except when it's getting hit by a category five and caskets start floating down the street." I cast him a quick glance, and he shrugged. "When you bury people above ground, which is actually below sea level, shit happens."

"And Cairo?"

"Gets flooded a lot. The highest ground around here is the levees." He pointed to a bridge with the word "CAIRO" painted across the front. "There's a gate they shut when it gets really bad. Cuts the town off and sends the floodwaters into the fields."

"Why settle here?"

"In the eighteen hundreds, this place was hopping. Major port on both rivers."

"And now?"

"The ships don't need a port between Minneapolis

and New Orleans. No passengers, no need to fuel up."
He shrugged. "I hear the place is pretty ghostly."

The sun had nearly set, casting everything in sepia.
Shadows loomed. I hated shadows.

"What did you see when you stared into the pot?"
Jimmy asked. "At the end, I mean."

"My mother looks oddly like me."

"How oddly?"

I slid my gaze in his direction, then back to the
road. "Just don't kill me by accident."

"I'll try," he said dryly. "I don't suppose you know
how to kill a phoenix."

"I was hoping you did."

"Never met one. Considering the legend, there
might be a reason for that." At my curious glance, he
continued. "A phoenix lives for a thousand years and
is reborn for another thousand from the ashes of its
funeral pyre."

"Still not catching a clue."

"Maybe there's only one."

"Seems like a waste of a good legend," I said.
"There could be a thousand of them. None of which
ever truly die, but are instead reborn again and again."

"An army of virtually indestructible birds," Jimmy
mused. "I hate it when that happens."

"Ha-ha," I said, but I didn't feel like laughing. "You
think that's why she's been raised? To lead the army
of indestructible birds?"

"Why stop there? Why not lead the whole damn
indestructible army of the Apocalypse?"

I'd been thinking the same thing; I just hadn't
wanted to say it.

"Nice to meet you," I muttered. "They call me the
daughter of the Antichrist."

"She hasn't taken over yet."

"She has the key; it's only a matter of time."

"I think if the Antichrist had taken form—whatever form—we'd know, don't you?"

"Why? Is there a sign? Big red letters in the sky? A rain of fire? Perhaps a mass e-mail?"

Jimmy stared at me for several seconds before answering my original question. "The end of the world is predated by wars and rumors of wars, famine, disease, lawlessness, earthquakes."

"Check and mate." I frowned. "Except that's been going on since forever."

"Because there's been the possibility of the end over and over and over again, but we've always stopped it."

"We'll stop it this time too."

"It's never gotten this far before. We're one step away from Armageddon."

"The final battle is now," I whispered, paraphrasing the last words a living Ruthie had ever spoken to me.

"Ruthie!" Jimmy exclaimed. "She'd tell us if we were fighting a losing battle."

"Would she?" I asked. "What good would that do?"

At his confused expression I continued. "If she told us the Antichrist had taken form, that all of our efforts weren't enough to stem the demon tide, people would give up, crawl in a hole or surrender. Hell, maybe they'd even join the other side."

"Would you?"

I gave him an evil glare. As if.

"The end is just the beginning," I said. "Ruthie knows that. We've got prophecy coming out of our ears and none of it is exactly crystal. There's always a way out if you just keep searching."

"It ain't over until . . ." Jimmy stopped, tilted his head and glanced back at me. "When's it over?"

"When I say it's over."

His grin made me catch my breath. Sure, he still appeared as if he'd just spent several days worshiping the porcelain god, then another two or three unconscious in a garbage dump. Regardless, his physical beauty shone through. It would take more than a torture session with a fairy god to erase that. Thank goodness.

Because his smile, and that face, made me think of things I shouldn't, I kept walking.

"There's another problem," I said as Jimmy hustled to catch up. "Even if Ruthie *would* tell us that the end of the world is nigh, she can't." I tapped myself on the temple. "Cable's on the fritz."

The reminder that I no longer had a direct line to Ruthie because of what he'd done—and how I'd made him—caused Jimmy's smile to disappear like the last ray of sun before the storm of the century. His gaze returned to the horizon where bits of pink and orange had faded to a thin, purple line.

"Maybe this isn't such a good idea," he murmured.

"It's *the* idea. Ruthie's idea. Only by becoming the darkness can we overcome it."

"I've never been real clear on how we do that."

I wasn't either, but I wasn't going to tell him that.

"Ruthie said to infiltrate the Nephilim."

"Because walking straight into the lion's den is *always* a good idea."

"Worked for Daniel."

Jimmy rubbed his eyes and didn't answer.

"Relax," I said, then remembered something Sawyer had told me once. "To win, we have to believe that we will."

Dropping his hand, Jimmy began to laugh. "You think they don't believe *they* will?"

"You have to have faith, Sanducci."

He sobered as quickly as he'd lost it. "Do *not* quote George Michael to me, Lizzy."

And then I was laughing. It felt good.

We reached the outskirts of Cairo. The place had a haunted air that I didn't think had anything to do with the Phoenix. My laughter died. I wished like crazy we'd popped out of the Otherworld when the sun was still shining.

"It does feel like a ghost town," I murmured. "You don't think—"

"I don't know," Jimmy interrupted. "Maybe."

I didn't point out that I hadn't finished my sentence. Jimmy wasn't psychic, but he wasn't human either. However, his ability to know what I was thinking, to finish my sentences, stemmed from something that wasn't, for a change, supernatural. It stemmed from being raised together, loving each other, sharing everything, at least until we'd stopped. That he was acting like he used to, before the world fell apart, was too precious to question and risk driving away.

"Where do you think she is?" I murmured.

"That would be your department, not mine."

My gaze wandered over the street, the buildings. We'd passed by beautiful stately homes—some restored, others broken. In front of us lay the main street, which appeared to be more of the same—storefronts that had been renovated to resemble small-town America and others that had been left boarded and empty.

The quiet was so loud it seemed to hum, or maybe that was just the power lines overhead. I stepped forward and felt a jolt, as if I'd licked my finger and pressed it to a light socket.

Jimmy, who'd been right on my heels, started, cursed and froze. "Did you feel that?"

"Yeah," I said. The roots of my hair still prickled. "What do you think it was?"

"Magic," he muttered, dark eyes flicking from one side of the street to the other. "You okay? Any weird urges?"

"No urges," I said. "I'm fine." Or as fine as I would ever be with a dog collar around my neck and a demon murmuring in my head. "You?"

"Just dandy. Come on."

As we walked past the hardware store, the outside light snapped on, the door opened and a tall, thin man stepped out.

His hair was so blond it was nearly white and his bugged eyes and buckteeth only contributed to the image of an overly excited palomino.

"Hey there," he said, staring straight at me. "What's your name?"

Jimmy stepped in front of me. "Why do you want to know?"

The man's face creased in confusion. "Just bein' friendly."

"Then why don't you want to know *my* name?"

"Jimmy." I tugged on his arm. "It's a small town and we're strangers. Relax."

He didn't. Not completely, but he at least let me move out from behind him so I could converse with the man.

"You must be here to see the new gal," he said.

"How'd you guess?" Jimmy asked.

"Well." The guy hitched up his pants, which were in great danger of drooping past parts I did not want to see. He hadn't taken his gaze off of me once. "One glance at your face, and I figured you for a relative or somethin'."

My smile was tight, but he accepted the expression for the "yes" that it was.

"You look just like your . . ." He waited for me to supply my relationship.

I tried; I really did. But I just couldn't get "mother" past my lips.

"Mother," Jimmy murmured, and shrugged when I cast him a glare.

The man slapped a huge hand across a bony knee. "I knew it. Sure enough. Though your ma, if you don't mind my sayin', appears nearly the same age as you."

I bet she does, I thought sourly.

"Good genes," Jimmy said.

"Or no genes," I muttered.

Jimmy elbowed me in the ribs, but the man didn't seem to notice. "Don't have many newcomers to Cairo. Not much goin' on here these days for em-*ploy*-ment but the one factory. Biggest thing to happen in a coon's age was your ma showin' up."

He had no idea how big. Or how lucky he was that we'd arrived before she'd started stringing the street-lights with dried intestines and using severed heads to decorate the fence posts or doing whatever else she might have to do to become queen of the end of the world.

I shivered.

"Cold, miss? Chilly when the sun goes down on the river. But don't worry; it'll heat up tomorrow."

"I'm sure it will," I said.

"So"—he rocked back on his heels—"just you two come to town?"

"You see anyone else?" Jimmy asked.

"What is *with* you?" I muttered, but he ignored me.

The man didn't take offense; I wasn't sure why. "Just wondered if you'd need a place to stay is all."

"Uh-huh." Jimmy's voice was as skeptical as his expression. "So, where'd you say she lives?" Jimmy asked.

The man pointed to the far end of town. "She's in the biggest old house left standin'. Probably a half mile out. Just follow this street. Red brick. Pert' near big as a hotel. Can't miss it."

"We won't," Jimmy said.

I caught a strange sound, one I recognized but couldn't place right away because it didn't fit. Not until the talkative, friendly townsman turned to dust right before my eyes. One minute he was solid; the next tiny particles sluiced into a pile at my feet, then drifted away on the wind.

Jimmy flipped his wrist, causing his silver switchblade—the source of the odd yet familiar noise—to fold back in two before he slipped it into his pocket.

The guy hadn't burst into ashes, as if he'd been incinerated with a flame hotter than any known to man, as he would have if he'd been a Nephilim. No. He'd turned to dust like a—

I hadn't a clue.

"What in hell was that?" I demanded.

"Could you be a little louder? I don't think they heard you in Panama."

"There's no one here."

"You're wrong," Jimmy said quietly, his gaze intent on something farther up the street.

The chill I'd felt earlier came back and gave me gooseflesh on my gooseflesh. When Sanducci moved into the road, I followed.

The sun was completely gone, the sky an icy gray. The streetlights hadn't yet kicked in, so the figures at the outskirts of Cairo seemed to loom up from the ground, materializing out of nowhere. Hell, maybe they had.

"There are a few other signs of the Apocalypse I left out," Jimmy said.

"I take it those are one of them?"

"Revenants."

"And you left them out why?"

"There are thousands of signs, which come from just as many interpretations of prophecy. I can't remember every one. And until they actually happen"—he spread his hands—"they're just a theory."

The crowd of shadows began to move forward. "These look a little more solid than a theory. What are revenants?"

" 'When hell is full,' " Jimmy quoted, " 'the dead will walk the earth.' "

"Revelation?"

"George Romero. *Dawn of the Dead*."

"They're zombies?" I thought of the graves spilling upward as the Phoenix sprinted over them.

"Kind of." At my evil glare he continued. "They're a special type. Not your garden-variety zombie or they'd be decaying all over the place."

"But they're not Nephilim."

"Nephilim turn to ashes, and zombies—"

"Turn to dust," I finished.

"Uh-huh. They're dead, not demonic."

"How'd you know what he was?"

"Wasn't sure. Had to stick him and see."

"What if he'd been a person?" I snapped.

"He definitely wasn't a person. I knew that much."

"How?"

"Can't you feel them?"

He jerked his chin toward the advancing shades,

which appeared to have increased greatly in number in the few seconds we'd been chatting.

That buzzing I'd sensed earlier, which I'd thought was too much silence or cancer vibes spreading from the power lines, I now recognized as the hum of supernatural entities—a lot of them.

A scuffle behind us and I spun, only to discover that there were even more revenants closing in from the rear. My knife was in my hand, and I didn't remember how it had gotten there; I was just glad that it had.

I pressed my back to Jimmy's. "How'd you kill the first one?"

I knew there'd been a silver knife, pointy end into the revenant, but when killing supernatural boogies, where the knife went was sometimes as important as there being a knife at all.

"Silver straight through the heart."

"Heart only?"

"Yes."

"Shit," I muttered. Hitting the heart dead on isn't as easy as it sounds, especially when you're outnumbered a helluva lot to two.

"Do you want to surrender first?" Jimmy asked. "Or should I?"

"Huh?"

"Don't you remember?" Jimmy turned his head, met my eyes. "Getting into that house is what we came here for."

We had monsters to the north, monsters to the south; the adrenaline was pumping so fast all I could think of was which one I was going to stick first, then how I would roll, kick and nail the next. It took me several beats to comprehend what Jimmy had said and realize he was right.

I lowered my knife, flipped it over in my hand so I was holding the sharp side and offered it to the nearest of the walking dead.

"Take me to your leader," I said.

CHAPTER 23

"They move pretty well for zombies," I muttered.

The revenants had accepted our knives with little more than a shrug, then bound our hands behind us with golden chains, which made me think they'd been waiting for us. I didn't like that thought one bit.

They looked like real, live people. No rotting parts. No zombie smell. They hadn't said much—though they *could* talk: "Come here." "Hands behind your back." "Move."

"You *sure* about them?" I asked Jimmy as we marched down the asphalt that led out of town, revenants before us, revenants behind us, but no one really close enough to hear us, especially since we'd put our heads together like thirteen-year-old girls at a slumber party and begun to whisper.

"Yeah." He twitched one shoulder, then hissed when the golden chains slid along his wrists and smoke rose from his flesh. "I'm pretty good at sensing the undead. They might not be vampires, but they're definitely the dead come to life."

"So maybe they're just zombies." Had I *actually* used the phrase "just zombies"? "Not some apocalyptic portent."

"Believe me, they're an apocalyptic portent." Jimmy took a slow, deep breath, careful not to rattle his chains, then glanced at the revenants. But none of the walking dead appeared to care if the two of us had a nice long chat. "You've heard about the four horsemen?" I nodded. "They arrive when the first of seven seals is broken."

"Seals on what?"

"In Revelation, they're on a scroll." He scowled at the revenants. "But that scroll represents something else. The first rider comes on a white horse. Some say it's Jesus; most say the opposite."

"The Antichrist."

"Yep. And if the rider appears when a seal is broken and that rider is the Antichrist, what do you think the seal was on?"

"Hell," I answered.

"Give the girl a gold star."

"How did the seal get broken?"

"Hard to say, and it doesn't really matter. What's done is done, and we have to deal with the results."

He was right. No sense crying over spilled demons.

"So the seal broke," I said. "Hell opened; the demons flew free." Now my gaze went to the revenants. "Where do they come in?"

"The first horseman is bent on conquest. Some say peaceful, but who knows?"

"And the second?"

"Red horse, guy with a sword. Makes men kill one another and removes peace from the earth."

"Same guy?"

"I think so."

"To conquer with peace," I said, "you'd need a huge army."

"Walk tall and carry a big stick."

"Exactly. Then to spread war throughout the earth, that army would come in very handy."

"He moves from threatening war," Jimmy said, "to unleashing it."

"Where do you get a huge army when you've been doing crosswords in Tartarus since the beginning of time?" My gaze slid to the revenants, whose footsteps sounded more like goosesteps with every block we walked.

"You raise them from the dead," Jimmy said.

"So many bodies, so little time," I agreed, "with the added plus of their eternal gratitude."

That I'd seen the dead rising as the Phoenix ran over their graves, in her possession a book that contained information that would allow her to control all the demons, was looking less and less like a coincidence. In the "Who Will Be the Antichrist?" sweepstakes, I think we had a winner. Except—

"If she can control the demons, why doesn't she?"

Jimmy didn't answer. When I glanced at him, he was peering into the gloom. I followed his gaze.

The house rose out of a swaying field of moon-tinged grass. Huge, like the revenant had said, the red brick dull with age, the once creamy mortar jaundiced from the elements, the paint around the boarded windows peeling. The front porch listed to the right; the steps creaked threateningly as the revenants followed us inside.

There, what had once been gorgeous hardwood floors were now buckled and uneven, the walls marred by leaks and cracks. A chandelier still hung in the entryway, swaying as the breeze blew in behind us; the crystals rubbed together, the sound so light and lonely it made me nostalgic. For what, I didn't know.

The place smelled moldy—as if it had been flooded, dried out, then flooded again times fifty—and overlying the cool, soft scent of ancient water I caught the sharp, metallic odor of fresh blood.

"I'd like to see my mother," I said. "The Phoenix."

No one seemed surprised by that statement. I guess a simple glance in a mirror explained why. However, the mere mention of her name struck everyone dumb, which didn't bode well for our meeting.

I'd harbored the hope—foolish as it might be— that the Phoenix wasn't as bad as say . . . the woman of smoke. But I had the distinct feeling she was worse. How was I going to convince her that both Jimmy and I were ready to take a walk on the dark side?

"Upstairs." A doughy young man—in both skin tone and body shape—with squinty eyes that screamed of too many hours in front of a computer screen, and messy, mousy hair, shoved me. If I hadn't been super-coordinated I might have taken a nosedive into the banister.

I stumbled and righted myself, considered re-arranging his face and decided I didn't care enough. Jimmy stared at him with narrowed eyes, and the kid actually backed off. Strange considering there were so many of them and only two of us, not to mention the golden chains.

Sure, if we let our vamps free they'd be toast, but considering we were trying to join their club, we weren't going to do that.

Yet.

"You can take off the chains," I said. "We come in peace."

Geek Boy snorted. "Even if you are the daughter of the Phoenix, you aren't getting any special treatment."

"So everyone gets bound with golden chains?"

"Chains, yes. Gold, no."

"But—"

"You think the Phoenix isn't aware of what San-ducci is, that she doesn't know what you've become? She's all-powerful. Or soon will be."

How did she know about us? Did my mother have the same talent as I did? Could she touch people and see their inner thoughts and more? If so, it was going to be damn near impossible to convince her Jimmy and I had changed sides. Not that I'd ever thought it was going to be easy.

The kid had taken a dislike to Sanducci that, from Jimmy's narrowed eyes and tense stance, he appeared to share. In a minute they'd start fighting, bumping chests and snarling, or perhaps they'd pull out their dicks and compare. Sanducci would win. He had the best jewels.

"We were told to keep you chained until you can be tested."

Uh-oh, I thought.

"Tested?" I asked.

Geek Boy smirked, and Sanducci bared his teeth. "You may have passed the first test, but that doesn't mean you're free of the next."

"There was a test?"

"You think we let anyone stroll into town and get close to the Prince who will come?" At last he turned away from Jimmy and came toward me.

"How, exactly, do you keep people out?"

"There's a spell." The kid waved his hand. "Magic shit. Not my department."

Hmm. Was the Phoenix a witch too? Why not? Everyone else was.

"What kind of spell?"

"Only those with an inner darkness get past the borders of this place."

"Explains the buzz at the edge of town," Jimmy murmured.

"And what happens to those without an inner darkness?" I asked.

"Bzzzt!" Geek Boy made a zapping noise and a swift motion with both hands, then rolled his eyes up and stuck his tongue out the side of his mouth.

"Dead?" I clarified

He lifted his head and smiled. I guess we knew now why Ruthie had been so insistent that both Jimmy and I released our demons before coming here.

"You've killed everyone in town?" I asked.

"They didn't stay dead for long." A solid older woman, who, judging from her thick wrists and the muscles in her legs and arms, had been a farmwife, with white hair down to her ass and a weathered face that spoke of decades in the sun, indicated the crowd of revenants. "They're here with us now. Except for those who possessed an inner darkness."

"Nephilim," Jimmy muttered. "They're everywhere."

"Where are *they* now?"

I didn't like not knowing the location of any cursed half demons. Even if we were supposed to be one of them now, Nephilim had no allegiance to their kind. The instant they saw us they'd want to fight just to get the upper hand. Animals behaved like animals even when they were demons.

"They were the first sacrifices," Farmwife answered.

I blinked. "Say what?"

"You'll find out," Geek Boy said.

"I'd rather you told me."

"We can't." Farmwife wrung her big, hard hands. "The Phoenix ordered us not to."

"You always do what she says?"

"We have no choice. She raised us; we're slaves. We'll be the army once the sacrifice is made, and the Prince has come."

As if that explained everything—and it kinda did—Farmwife turned and rejoined the others.

"Where do you think she is?" I murmured, gaze fixed on the army of the living dead.

Jimmy remained silent for so long I didn't think he was going to answer. When I finally managed to drag my eyes from the revenants, I saw a reflection of all my fears cross his face.

"I think she's raising every graveyard between here and Canada."

"Me too," I said. "And the sacrifice?"

He lifted a brow.

Yeah, it was us.

"Go up *now*." Geek Boy pointed to the staircase, then motioned to Farmwife, who sent several of the revenants toward the rear of the house while a few took up guard duty at the front door. "If she comes back and you aren't where she told us you should be—"

"She'll kill you?" Jimmy asked, then glanced at me.

Without even touching him, I knew what he was thinking. If we went upstairs we were toast. We were going to have to break away from them and find another plan.

"I'll stay right here," Jimmy continued, "and save myself the trouble of dusting you."

"No." Geek Boy pulled a long, thin golden stiletto from his pocket. "You'll do what I say or *I'll* dust *you*."

Farmwife gasped. "You mustn't!"

Geek Boy ignored her, placing the tip of the stiletto against Jimmy's chest.

I took a step forward; Farmwife grabbed my chain

and yanked me back. The golden links scraped my wrists and agony shot everywhere.

"Twice to the heart," Geek Boy whispered. Then he tilted his head and slashed the stiletto through the air like d'Artagnan before pointing it at one of Jimmy's narrowed eyes. "Maybe here, or . . ."

He ran the blade along Jimmy's cheek, over his chin and down his neck. Wherever the knife touched, it left a long black line that turned quickly to red. The sound of meat sizzling on a grill filled the room, along with the scent of roasting flesh.

"Stop," I ordered.

The revenant spun toward me. "Shut up. You're next."

"Come on," I urged. "Show me what you got."

I didn't care that my hands were bound, that with my collar on and no Sawyer in sight I was basically a slightly stronger and faster human. What mattered was that I wouldn't die as easily as Jimmy and that the revenant didn't kill him.

"No," Jimmy ordered. "Deal with me. Unless you're chicken."

The revenant rolled his eyes. "Do I look like I'm twelve? That I'd actually care if you thought I was a coward?" He tightened his grip on the stiletto. I tensed, prepared to drag Farmwife along with me as I plowed into the guy like a middle linebacker.

I needn't have worried. The instant Geek Boy came close enough, Sanducci head-butted him in the nose.

The resulting *smack* echoed throughout the house. The pudgy kid landed at my feet, blood spraying from his nostrils like a fountain. I kicked him in the head, then bent my knee and pile-drived onto his chest.

Farmwife got her arm around my neck and started to strangle me. She might not want Geek Boy to kill us, but she wasn't going to let us kill him either. She was strong—stronger than she should be even after lifting hay bales for forty years—but she wasn't me.

I flipped her forward, letting her own weight carry her over my head. She landed on her back with a crack, and then she had enough worries trying to breathe. Luckily, she'd let go of my leash when she fell, or I'd have been dragged off Geek Boy completely— probably dislocating my shoulder in the process—and I wasn't finished with him yet.

My knee did good work, so I stood halfway up, changed my position just a bit, then drove downward again. This time I felt his testicles go crunch. Now who couldn't breathe?

The revenants that had been guarding the door came forward in a rush. The blood flowing from his forehead and down his face impaired Jimmy's vision, but he didn't let that stop him.

He was a dhampir. He could "feel" vampires. But from the way he reacted to the revenants, he could feel them, too. He didn't need to see them. All he had to do was wait until they were close enough, and then he kicked one unerringly in the knee. The guy fell backward into a second while Jimmy twirled and got the third in the throat with his foot. Snap, thud, pop.

The commotion brought others. Revenants appeared at the top of the stairs; they ran in from the rear of the house. Shouts rose from outside.

Blood from Jimmy's forehead had spattered across the front of his brightly tie-dyed *Sesame Street* shirt, but the wound was already partly healed.

Our eyes met. As one we moved closer together; shoulder-to-shoulder we faced the staircase.

"I could try and tear your collar off with my teeth,"

he muttered, chains rattling as he attempted to break them again.

My gaze on the revenants pouring down the stairs, I returned, "I bet it would be more fun if I took *yours* off with *my* teeth."

He choked. "You're so damn—"

I never found out if I was so damn dumb, so damn funny, so damn wonderful, because the front door banged open, slamming against the wall; bits of plaster skittered everywhere. All the revenants froze, wide-eyed, and then they cowered.

Jimmy cursed. I winced. I didn't want to turn and see who could make zombies cringe.

A few of them began to beg. "No, please."

"Wait!"

Then there was a cry, a thunk, then a thunk, thunk, thunk and dust drifted past my nose like confetti. Jimmy looked at me; I looked at him and we turned.

Sawyer was too busy staking revenants to notice either one of us.

CHAPTER 24

My mouth hung open. Dust stuck to my lips, and I snapped them shut, then made spitting sounds, minus the spit, until the particles sailed away.

"Sawyer to the rescue," I murmured.

"You live a very full fantasy life."

"Considering my life, can you blame me?"

Sawyer sawed his way through a few dozen revenants. I'd never seen him so worked up. He appeared truly pissed.

"How did he know we were here?"

I no longer wore the turquoise, which, in light of recent events, was just plain stupid. Except . . . there he was.

Jimmy inched behind me. I glanced over my shoulder with a frown. That wasn't like him. Usually we were shoving each other as the both of us tried to place ourselves in the path of every danger.

Jimmy pressed his crotch to my bound hands. "Take it off," he murmured. "Quick. Before there're more minions to ice than he can handle."

I returned my gaze to Sawyer. His chest covered with dust, his bare feet made tracks in the mess on the floor as, face fierce, he just kept mowing them down.

More minions than he could handle? I didn't think that was going to happen. However—

"Now, Lizzy."

We did need to move along before the Phoenix showed up. Sawyer might be crazy powerful, but who knew what she could do? I'd forced Jimmy to bring back his vampire self; the least I could do was let him use it.

"You can't kill Sawyer," I cautioned, fingers fumbling with the button on Jimmy's jeans, then the zipper.

"I'm sure I can." His voice was low and a bit hoarse.

I paused, zipper halfway down. "I mean it, Jimmy."

He cleared his throat. "I won't be me when I'm like that. I'll kill anything in my way, so keep him out of it."

"Fine." I yanked the zipper the rest of the way down, ignoring Jimmy's sharply indrawn breath. Then I skimmed my fingertips across his belly; the muscles fluttered beneath his skin. His chest was hard and warm against my shoulders; his breath stirred my hair. Memories flickered.

Ruthie's kitchen in the middle of the night. Jimmy comes up behind me in the dark. His arms go around me; he presses his lips to my neck, and my heart tumbles.

The image was so sweet and nostalgic, the feelings that went with it so raw, I couldn't help it, I stroked his stomach, tracing the spike of his hipbone, the dip where it casted inward, the well of his navel and the happy trail that drew me ever lower. I remembered my quip about removing his collar with my teeth. Too bad I didn't have the time.

The clink of my nails when they tapped the metal made me catch my breath. As I wrapped my fingers around it, around him, he leaped, then began to swell.

Too late I understood what a bad idea touching him

had been, because when I tried to remove the cock ring, it was stuck.

"Sanducci," I said in a low voice. "Get a grip."

He leaned closer, and his lips brushed my ear, making me shiver. "I think the problem is that you've got one."

I yanked my hand out of his pants. "Think of England or something. Paint chips. Wallpaper swatches."

"I don't even know what that means."

"Turn it off!" I swatted his swelling erection.

"It's not that simple. This happens whenever you're around."

"I thought you hated me."

"Hate. Love. Doesn't matter to that part of me. You touch him and he's lost."

That we were talking about his dick with a pronoun was almost as weird as why we were talking about it at all.

"Listen, you have to—"

"Too late," he murmured, and I glanced up.

Sawyer was right in front of me. I jumped so high I nearly knocked Jimmy's teeth out when my head thumped his chin. Sawyer grabbed me by the arm and started to drag me toward the door.

"Wait." I tried to dig in, but with revenant dust all over the floor, I only slid along like a water-skier being towed by a powerboat. "Sawyer. Sheesh. Stop."

I couldn't leave. I'd come here for the key, and I didn't have it yet.

I looked back at Jimmy, whose pants were hanging open and his privates peeking out. He hurried after us, sliding along too in the dust strewn across the wooden floor.

Sawyer swung around, fist pulled back to punch Jimmy in the nose, then paused, gaze first lowering to

Jimmy's crotch, then lifting to my face. "What is wrong with you?" he asked.

"What's wrong with you?"

He didn't answer; I hadn't expected him to.

There was something off about him. He was furious. Furious and Sawyer did not go together. Coldly homicidal maybe. Calmly murderous. Serenely dangerous.

Since he was still touching me, I closed my eyes and opened my mind. He shook me so hard my teeth snapped together, and said, "Stop that!"

"You're a great black hole anyway," I muttered.

His gaze narrowed; then he glanced at Jimmy. "Cover yourself, Sanducci."

"I'd be happy to. If you'd just release me from these chains."

With an impatient grunt, Sawyer strode forward. Keeping one hand around my biceps, he used the other to put Jimmy back in his pants. Or at least he tried.

Jimmy twisted, drawing his shoulder away, then slamming it forward, catching Sawyer in the chest and nearly knocking him down. If I hadn't been attached, he would have. As it was, I had to take a couple of quick steps or be dragged along.

"Don't touch me." Jimmy's voice was flat, deadly.

Outside the wind stirred, blowing in through the door, tracing patterns through the dust. I couldn't tell if the distant rhythmic patter was incoming rain, the breeze through the trees or merely the cadence of my own heart.

Sawyer's gray eyes darkened to smoke, and his nostrils flared as he fought to keep himself under control. The air seemed to crackle with fury and power. If they'd been dogs, their hair would have been standing on end. Mine was.

Then Sawyer's gaze lowered, and his lips curved. "A cock ring? The Dagda is my kind of man."

"Since he isn't a man at all," Jimmy snapped, "I can see the resemblance."

"Glass houses," Sawyer murmured.

"Listen," I interrupted. "We don't have time for you two to play 'my dick's bigger than your dick.'"

"It is." Sawyer lifted an eyebrow in my direction. "Isn't it?"

I was so not going *there*.

"We need—" I began, then paused as a singsongy voice from outside called, "Sawwwww-yerrrr!"

He dropped my arm, faced the door. I glanced at Jimmy with a frown, but he was staring at the door too. That distant patter had become a full-blown thud.

Revenants marched in. Brand-new ones from the looks of them. Tiny particles of dirt pinged lightly against the floor, mixing with the dust of their forebears.

"Guess we were right," Jimmy murmured. "Mommy's been raising the dead all over the place."

My chest went tight; I couldn't breathe. My gaze was glued to the doorway as I waited for my first true sight of my mother.

She flew in—not literally, though I guess she could have—shoving aside revenants like the nuisance they were. Every time she touched one they cringed, scrambling as far away as they could get, though stopping just short of the door.

The chandelier's yellow light made her skin glow like gold. Her curly dark hair shone. She'd found better clothes—a bright red sheath, yellow sandals, with turquoise bobbles at her ears, wrists and throat.

I stared at her and felt nothing, remembered the same. How could that be? This woman—loose term,

I know—had given birth to me. Shouldn't there be some connection? But when I saw her I only experienced a sense of the bizarre. That someone could look so much like me yet not like me. That we could share the same blood, yet without the similarity in appearance she could be any other being on the planet.

"My love," she purred, her voice lower than mine, with that thick accent that brought to mind sand dunes and the pyramids of Giza. "What did you do?"

I opened my mouth to answer—who else could be her love?—and Jimmy elbowed me in the ribs. She wasn't looking at me, didn't even appear to have noticed me in the room, which was downright disturbing.

Hey! Long-lost daughter here.

I remained silent as she laid her palm against Sawyer's dust-strewn chest. When she lifted it, she left her handprint in the grit like a brand.

"They disobeyed," he said simply.

"So you killed them all." She licked her lips. "You're so deliciously vicious."

I blinked. I'd just been describing Sawyer with similar contradictory terms. Was that an inherited trait? Or could she read my mind without even touching me? If so, we were all dead.

She drew her fingernail—long, spiky, very Fu Manchu—beneath the mountain lion tattooed on his chest. Rubbing her hand in the blood that welled, she expressed the delight of a child who'd just discovered finger paint, before she pressed her palm to his stomach, leaving behind a more colorful, more gruesome brand.

"Mmm." She tilted her head as if listening to someone, though the room was quiet as the eye of a storm. "More."

She'd cut his neck before my eyes tracked the

movement. Blood spurted, and she stuck both hands beneath the flow, then began to finger paint in earnest, all over Sawyer's body.

Sawyer, who'd been standing still as a rabbit caught in the glare of headlights, grabbed the Phoenix. I figured he'd toss her through the window, smack her against the wall, throw her to the ground and do a rain dance on her head. And we needed her—at least until we had the key.

My mouth formed, *No!* But I never got the word out. It caught in my throat, choked me so badly I couldn't quite breathe, as Sawyer put his hand at the back of her neck. One quick snap and—

Instead he lifted her onto her tiptoes and kissed her more passionately than he'd ever kissed me.

"You see now why I always think it's Sawyer?" Jimmy murmured.

CHAPTER 25

"What the hell?" I demanded, stepping forward.

Jimmy muscled me back with his shoulder. "He's one of them."

I stilled. "A revenant?"

Sawyer didn't look dead, risen or otherwise. He looked like Sawyer. Hotter than hell. Even when he was kissing my . . . I swallowed thickly.

Mother.

"No," Jimmy murmured. "Not a revenant."

And it wasn't until the relief flooded me that I realized I'd been devastated at the thought of Sawyer dying.

Although death just wasn't what it used to be.

"We should have known when they said there was a spell on this place," Jimmy said.

"Just because there's a spell we should automatically think our favorite sorcerer cast it?"

"Not my favorite," Jimmy muttered. "But . . . hell yeah."

I couldn't take my eyes off of Sawyer and the Phoenix. The two of them were really going at it. Kissing, touching, rubbing against each other like cats in a field of catnip. His neck wound had clotted, but the blood all over him, all over her, made them seem like characters in an Anne-Rice-before-she-found-Jesus book. I wanted to glance away, but for some reason I just couldn't.

The Phoenix lifted her mouth from Sawyer's. "Raising the dead makes me so . . ." She leaned forward and ran her crimson tongue around Sawyer's lips as if she were catching the last droplets of an ice-cream cone. "What's the word, lover?"

"Horny," Sawyer said.

"All right," I practically shouted. "I come here to change sides in the war to end all wars, bring along the best general I've got, and you're dry-humping in the front hall?"

"Make it shut up," the Phoenix ordered.

The revenants started forward.

"Oh, sheesh," I said. "Do you really want us to dust them all when you just got done raising them?"

The Phoenix, mouth poised again over Sawyer's, paused as if listening. But not to me. Her eyes went distant, and she nodded once, shook her head, then murmured, "Yes. All right."

I turned my attention to Jimmy, who lifted his eyebrows and twisted his lips, the facial equivalent of a shrug.

The Phoenix let go of Sawyer, but instead of turning to us, she moved into a spare corner and continued to have a nice long talk with herself. Most of it we couldn't hear, because it only existed in her mind; the rest she whispered too softly for even our super-duper batlike senses—until she lost her temper.

"No," she shrieked, the sound rattling the windows, making the revenants freeze, then fall to the floor with their hands over their heads. "I want to play now!"

She lifted her hand. The earth-toned flesh began to glow a dull orange.

"We can play," Sawyer murmured, his gray eyes watching her like a wolf might watch a much bigger wolf. "No need to get—"

Fire suddenly erupted from the fingertips of the Phoenix, hitting the wall and rolling upward to dance across the ceiling.

"Upset," Sawyer finished.

She spun toward me and Jimmy. I leaped in front of him just as he was leaping in front of me. We conked heads, then began to push and shove.

I expected fire to consume us both. We wouldn't die, but being burned is excruciating. I don't recommend it.

When nothing happened, we stopped mid-tussle and shifted our attention to her. The Phoenix stared at me; her lips formed an O of surprise. "It's you," she breathed, and clapped her still-flaming hands against her cheeks.

I waited for the shriek, but instead of being burned, her face merely took on the same orange-yellow glow, making her dark eyes appear surrounded by hellfire.

"Uh, yeah," I managed, moving away from Jimmy.

Skipping forward like a child, this way and that, she sang an off-key tune beneath her breath, then paused halfway between Sawyer and me. At least her hands and her face had stopped glowing. I was starting to think she was nuttier than a Payday candy bar.

"Nefertiti," she whispered.

"I'm Elizabeth," I said slowly. "Or Liz if you like."

She shook her head, scooted closer, and I tensed, thinking she was going to hug me. Instead she slapped me across the face—palm to my left cheek—then she backhanded me on the right one. I stumbled first in one direction and then the other but managed to keep my feet. Without even looking his way, I gave a quick shake of the head to stay Jimmy, but I kept my eyes on the Phoenix.

"Nefertiti," she said again.

"Ooo-kay. I guess you named me Nefertiti."

"It means 'the beautiful one has come,'" Sawyer translated. "She didn't name you. She didn't know about you until she rose from the dead."

The Phoenix scampered over to Sawyer, cuddling up to his side as he draped his arm over her shoulders in a casual gesture that spoke of a long association. Watching them made me want to puke for so many reasons.

I was trying very hard not to dwell on Sawyer's total betrayal. What kind of a leader was I? I hadn't seen this coming. I'd had no inkling at all that Sawyer was anything but loyal.

Oh, sure, Jimmy always said Sawyer had been bought by the federation and what could be bought by one could be easily stolen by another for the right price. But I hadn't believed it. I still didn't.

Sawyer wouldn't change sides for money. He had no use for it. But he did have use for other things. I just wasn't quite sure what they were. It appeared my mother was.

I took a deep breath, trying to calm my pounding heart and my dancing stomach. If I started to think about what could happen if Sawyer's power was against us instead of for us, I really might puke. I had to concentrate on other things, anything, or lose my mind.

"She never knew about me?" I blurted. "I haven't been pregnant"—*praise every saint ever named*—"but I still can't see how anyone could give birth and not be aware of it." I frowned. *Unless* . . . "Did they tell her I was dead?"

That would explain why she'd abandoned me.

"No," Sawyer said shortly.

"I'm a phoenix." My mother moved her hands like the wings of a great bird. "Only when I die is another born."

"I was born when you *died*?"

"How else?"

"How else?" I muttered. "How 'bout how?"

She lowered her hands with a flutter. "I wasn't there." She pointed at Sawyer.

"What would you know about it?" I asked; then as a terrible, nasty thought occurred to me I bent at the waist, afraid I might throw up again.

"Oh, get ahold of yourself," the Phoenix said. "He isn't your father."

It took several minutes to wrestle my stomach and my brain under control. Then I lifted my head. "You're sure?"

"Me?" She put a palm against her chest. Lucky her dress was already red. Her hands still glistened with Sawyer's blood. "No. But he insists such a thing isn't possible."

I turned my gaze to Sawyer's implacable face. "Impossible physically or impossible because you don't want me to puke until I die?"

Something flickered in his too-light eyes, something that made them suddenly appear dark and entirely savage. "Impossible because I would not do—"

The fury overcame him. His hand clenched on Mommy's upper arm so tightly I thought she might break. Instead of wincing, she drew in an ecstatic breath and arched as if in the throes of pleasure.

I coughed. The gag reflex was back.

"I would not do—," he tried again.

"Me?" I offered helpfully, and was rewarded with a growl from so deep in his throat I half-expected his wolf to burst free.

"That," he spit between clenched teeth. "I would not do *that*."

"But you'd do just about anything or anyone else," Jimmy murmured.

Sawyer ignored him, though the flash in his eyes made me think there would be payback later. There always was.

"Elizabeth," Sawyer continued, "you, of all people, should know better."

He'd called me Phoenix in the past. I figured now that would be redundant.

"I don't know what I know anymore," I muttered, my gaze on his hand, still wrapped around my mother's arm as she practically had an orgasm from the exquisite pain.

Freaking nut bag.

I guess Sawyer and I had something in common. Our mothers were on the far side of crazy.

"Does it have a name?" I asked. Two could play the "it" game, and in truth I didn't want to think of her as anything other than sub-human.

She narrowed her eyes. "I am the Phoenix."

I glanced at Sawyer. "Tell me you *didn't* call her Phoenix."

His face was as tight as my own. He understood what I was asking. Had he called us both that? Had he been pretending that I was her?

"No," he said. "Then she was known as Maria."

"Maria," I repeated. "Spanish for Mary."

"It was her name."

I didn't like that one bit. Mary as the mother of

Christ. Maria as the mother of me and, if she had her way, the vessel for the Antichrist.

Names were important. I'd learned that much.

Maria Phoenix, bored with the conversation, tapped Sawyer's hand like a nun with a ruler, and he let her go. Then her dark, mad eyes met mine. "Tomorrow will be time enough for you to prove your allegiance."

Prove? I didn't like the sound of that any more now than when Geek Boy had said "test" before. But when was the last time I'd liked the sound of anything?

I glanced at Jimmy; he appeared as thrilled about this conversation as I was.

"I'm your daughter," I said. "I've been searching for you all my life."

Basically BS, but pretty convincing BS. Didn't all lost kids search for their parents? Or at least all lost kids except for me. Sure, I'd wondered; I'd asked, but I hadn't looked. I'd had Ruthie, and she was all I'd ever really needed.

According to her, I'd been dumped, no record of my birth, my family, anything, until I'd entered the system. Although the more I discovered, the more that seemed like BS too. If that were truly the case—if no one had known anything about my parents—then how had I become Liz *Phoenix*?

"Now that I've found you," I continued, "why wouldn't I want to join you?"

"You were as unaware of me as I was of you until just a few days ago."

"And how did you become aware that you had a daughter?" Jimmy asked.

"How do you think?" Her gaze went to Sawyer.

Jimmy's gaze followed hers, as did mine. Sawyer shrugged. "Someone had to tell her."

"A Judas excuse if ever I heard one," I murmured.

"The federation is losing members by the minute," Sawyer said. "The Nephilim are increasing at the same rate. I saw which way the tide was turning. I like to back a winner."

"Wow, I think Iscariot said that too."

"No more time to talk," the Phoenix snapped. "Take them upstairs."

The revenants clambered to their feet and surrounded us.

"Separate rooms," Sawyer continued. "Leave them bound. If they manage to free their demons . . ." He lifted an eyebrow at me.

"Why would we do that?" I asked. "We came to join you."

Sawyer didn't comment, but I knew he didn't believe me, which could be a problem.

"Whether you did or you didn't," the Phoenix said, "we'll know soon enough."

"Once we prove our loyalty."

The Phoenix just smiled.

We had little choice but to go upstairs with the revenants. At the top I glanced back. Sawyer's eyes were on me, his face expressionless, though his jaw was tighter than I could ever recall seeing it.

Was he being held prisoner somehow? Forced to help the Phoenix by a magic spell? A debt he owed? A promise he'd made?

His right hand, which had been resting on his left biceps, and vice versa, lowered. My gaze followed, lower, lower until a dark, curly head came into view near his waist. He cupped her neck, guiding her forward and back, forward and back. What the—?

I faced forward so fast, agony shot into my brain. I

squeezed my eyes shut, trying to blot out that image, but I doubted I ever would.

My hope, small though it had been that Sawyer was being coerced somehow, faded. I doubted he could be had for the price of a blow job.

No matter how much I hated to admit it, he'd caved. Jimmy and I were on our own.

CHAPTER 26

As ordered, the revenants deposited Jimmy and me in separate rooms. They tied me to the bed. Considering the bumps, bangs and curses from the room that shared a wall with mine, they were doing the same to Jimmy.

I didn't bother to struggle. Sawyer had obviously told Maria all that he knew about us, hence the golden chains. Although if he'd told her everything, wouldn't he have told her that there's no way I'd ever change sides? Of course I'd believed there was no way *he'd* ever change sides either.

The walking dead departed. The thumps and thuds from the other side of the wall continued. I waited until Jimmy settled down, then called, "Sanducci?"

I heard a muffled, "Yeah," in response. If I hadn't had improved hearing, I wouldn't have heard anything, but it was still going to be difficult to carry on any kind of conversation.

My hands were bound to the bedposts with the golden chains, but the revenants had left my feet free. For that I was grateful. If I'd been inclined to sleep, which I wasn't, having my legs strapped down as well as my hands would have made it impossible

I tipped my chin to the ceiling, tilting my neck so I could see the wall behind the bed. Then I was doubly grateful for the loose feet. With my prowess in gymnastics, it was a simple thing to hoist my legs over my head, grasping the bedposts hard at the same time for leverage, then tightening my stomach muscles enough to put some *oomph* behind the move.

My tennies cracked right through the plaster on my side, raining white fragments all over my hair, face and pillow. Though it had hurt, the pain didn't last, and I yanked my feet out of the wall, let my heels touch the mattress, then cranked myself up and did it again. This time, my toes went through to the other side.

"Lizzy." Jimmy sneezed, spit, coughed. Plaster tinkled, a distant tip-tap. "What are you doing?"

His voice was now distinct. I could hear him as if he were right next to me, which technically he was, minus the wall.

Downstairs, no one raised the alarm. They'd obviously expected one of us, probably me, to throw a violent hissy fit. Unless plaster began to rain like hail in the living room or the house came tumbling down, I figured they'd leave us alone.

"Can you hear me now?" I asked, the inflection on the words just like that annoying, bespectacled cell phone hawker on television.

Jimmy laughed once, short and sharp. "Yeah. You got a plan?"

"For what?"

"I don't know. We can't escape or kill them yet. Although I'd really like to do both in reverse order."

"Shh," I hissed.

We were speaking fairly quietly, but still . . . Around here, everyone had supersonic hearing.

"We're alone," he said. "Can't you feel it?"

I closed my eyes and "listened." For us, supernatural entities buzzed like bees; the more demony the demon, the harder the sensation strumming along our skin. I'd been feeling it in the background since we'd gotten to Cairo, so I was surprised I hadn't noticed when it had faded.

Of course that didn't mean Sawyer and the queen of the damned or one of their newly risen slaves couldn't return at any moment.

Then, from what sounded like the second floor but still distant, maybe the rear of the house, came a shout: "Now! We will play now!"

A deep, calm, familiar voice answered, though I couldn't make out the words.

What followed made my skin vibrate. The Phoenix shrieked—fury or passion, I wasn't sure, maybe both. The scream went on so long, my hair ached. Then it lowered—in pitch and volume—lower, lower, lower still, until it became a moan that was definitely sexual. I guess we didn't have to worry about them lounging in the hall eavesdropping on our conversation.

"He does everyone, Lizzy. It's not personal."

"I know," I said too quickly. It had never been personal; it had always been just sex.

"I often wondered why Sawyer hung around," Jimmy mused. "Why he helped us just enough to be considered friendly, but never enough to actually *be* one of us—and never for free."

"What did you conclude?"

"He stayed close so he'd know when it was time to raise the Phoenix and take over the world."

"He wouldn't know that anyway? He *is* Sawyer, remember?"

"Ruthie was the leader of the light. Until she died, we were just marking time."

"You really think Sawyer raised the Phoenix?" I asked.

"He raised Xander."

"He said he could only raise ghosts, not people."

"She's not people."

"I know, but—"

"Lizzy," Jimmy interrupted, voice soft. "Sawyer's said a lot of things."

He had. And I wondered now if any one of them were true.

Another scream erupted from somewhere in the house. Not the Phoenix this time, but I doubted it was Sawyer. I couldn't imagine him screaming in passion or pain. I couldn't imagine him screaming for any reason at all.

Perhaps I'd make it my mission. Before I died, I would definitely hear Sawyer scream.

That decided, I felt much better. I always did once I had a plan.

"What are we going to do?" Jimmy asked.

I wasn't going to tell him what I'd just decided. Not that Jimmy wouldn't be down with it. In fact, he'd probably be so down with the plan, he'd steal it for himself.

"Wing it," I answered.

"I hate winging it."

"You got a better idea?"

His silence was its own response. All we could do was wait—not only because we were a little tied up, har-har, but also because we still didn't have the key.

"You might have to seduce it out of him." Jimmy's murmur drifted on the silver-tinged night, cascading over me like chill water, making me stutter and shiver and gasp.

"Seduce what out of who?" My voice was much louder than it should have been, even if there was no one around who cared to listen.

"The key out of Sawyer, what do you think?"

"He doesn't have it."

"Did he tell you that?"

"No."

"Because even if he did, consider the source."

Silence settled between us again and it went on for a long, long time. Jimmy was right, but there was just one problem.

"I don't think I could seduce anything out of Sawyer."

"Why not?"

"Because to Sawyer sex is—" I broke off. I shouldn't be talking about this with anyone, especially Jimmy.

"A means to an end," Jimmy filled in. "A job. Currency. He's messed up. We all are. But he wants you. He always has."

Sawyer had said as much, and when we were together the sex was incredible. But it was never anything more than that. I never got the feeling that he cared about me any deeper than he'd care about any other protégée who got his engine revved. Perhaps our shared powers, the fact that we could shift into the same animals, gave me a bit of an edge—I was more like him than anyone else on this earth—but I really didn't think our similarities would get me very far with Sawyer. Of course it didn't mean I wasn't going to try.

"Let me get this straight," I began. "You want me to seduce him."

"I didn't say that." Jimmy sighed, sounding tired and old. This job, this world, could wear anyone down. "I said I think you're gonna have to."

I thought I was going to have to, too.

"Lizzy," he began, and paused, interrupted by the distinct click of a door being opened.

A stir in the air, something moved, but no footsteps. How strange.

"What the hell do you want?"

I tilted my head, strained to hear, but got nothing beyond the slight buzz that signaled supernatural energy. No big shock there.

"Hey!" Jimmy said. "Don't."

What followed was sounds of a struggle, one dull thud and then silence.

"Jimmy?" I called.

The only answer was the closing of a door.

I tugged on my bonds, fat lot of good that it did me. I only managed to make my skin burn so badly a cloud of smoke encircled my head, the scent of scalding flesh causing me to choke. I lifted my legs, tried to kick a bigger hole in the wall; I'm not sure why. I wasn't really thinking beyond getting to Jimmy and making sure he was okay.

Then the latch on my door clicked, and I let my legs tumble to the bed, where they bounced once from the force of the fall and lay still.

The hallway was dark; so was the room, no prayer of a silhouette to hint who it was. The air stirred again; something drifted close, no footsteps, just that maddening buzz that said monster.

"What did you do to him?" I demanded.

"Nothing that hasn't been done before," Sawyer answered.

CHAPTER 27

"What," I repeated through clenched teeth, "did you do?"

"Nothing, Phoen . . ." Sawyer paused. I could hear his teeth grinding together. Neither one of us was going to have much left but stubs soon. "Elizabeth," he corrected.

"He'd better not be dead."

"Or what?" Sawyer's voice held the smile so rarely found on his face.

"I'll kill you."

"The threat is getting old. Especially since you have no way to back it up."

"You think I can't do it?"

"I know you can't. You have no idea how to kill a skinwalker."

There was that. No one in the world—except for him—appeared to know how, or if they did, they weren't sharing. Considering Sawyer, his power, his reputation, I didn't blame them.

"Did you come here to show me how?" I asked.

A slight pause reflected his surprise. "You think I came to kill you?"

"Did you kill Jimmy?"

He sighed. "It would be better for you both if I did."

"Mercy killing. That is so . . . not you."

I lost my shoes, then flung out my leg in the direction of the voice, not to kick him—although that would have been an acceptable bonus—but to try to touch him and maybe "see" some of his secrets.

But my foot met air. I'd kicked so hard I nearly shot myself off the bed. Considering I was still chained to it by my arms . . . ouch!

"Relax." His voice now came from the other side, nearer my face. I considered lifting my feet and smashing him the way I'd smashed the wall, but I figured he'd see that coming, if not literally then with whatever tenth sense he'd always had that had kept him alive for so long.

"I don't want to relax."

"You never do," he murmured.

I strained my eyes. He was close enough that I could feel the incredible heat that always rolled off of him in waves, close enough that the breeze through the slightly cracked window no longer overpowered his scent, which was the same as always—the mountains beneath the sun, newborn leaves, a tinge of fire and just a hint of smoke.

However, I still couldn't see him, and I started to wonder if he was really here at all. There were so many things that Sawyer could do that he'd never told me, that I might never know unless he did.

"Touch me," I murmured.

Silence followed my demand. I felt his surprise flare so brightly I almost saw it—fireflies flickering in the depths of the night.

"Touch me," I repeated, lowering my voice to what I hoped was a sexy murmur. I had no idea if it was; I'd never sexy murmured before. "You know that you want to."

"I—uh. What?"

My lips curved. I discovered that I wasn't afraid. If it was my time to die, if Sawyer had been sent to kill me, so be it. One thing I'd learned long ago: When it was your time, it was your time. There was no damn way to stop it.

"Touch me," I repeated. "Now."

"That's not a good idea. I wanted—"

I tried to brush him with my elbow, but the chains rattled and gave me away. Maybe. Since this was Sawyer, he'd have no problem scooting back faster than any movement I made. If he were even in the room in the first place.

"Why are you here?" I asked.

"I don't know."

"You want me to forgive you for changing sides? For fucking my mother? For—" Fury bubbled in my chest, so hot I was half-afraid my skin might start to glow as hers had. "Whatever the hell else you've done?"

I yanked on the chains again, hissed at the pain, threw my legs once more in his direction, and this time I flipped half off the bed, landing hard on my knees, my upper body still attached. I wrenched my back, and my breath caught.

"Nice job," I muttered. Now I ached all over, and I still hadn't managed to brush against Sawyer at all.

"You're going to hurt yourself."

"You think?"

He gave a half laugh that sounded almost like a sob, and I stilled.

"You aren't Sawyer," I said.

I sensed movement in my direction, and since I didn't want to be skewered while lying half on and half off the floor, my back to my attacker, I scrambled and twisted, pushed off with my legs and threw myself onto the bed.

The only way I could detect an approach was a slight shift in the air current, the increase in that scent that was so maddeningly Sawyer's. What creature could imitate his voice, his smell, his very essence? I had no idea.

I waited, tense and ready, until the telltale lifting of the hairs on the arm, the crackle at the back of my neck that shrieked, *Run!* became too strong to ignore. Then I scissor-kicked my legs—bam, bam—right where a face should be.

I didn't hit anything, but I didn't fly off the bed this time either. Only because this time, hands grabbed my calves, shoving me back onto the bed as a heavy, hard, all too familiar body pinned me down.

"Get off!" I shouted. "You're not him."

"What is wrong with you?" Sawyer growled, and when he growled, he actually growled. His beast—which one, I wasn't quite sure—was very close to the surface.

I started to laugh. I couldn't help it. *What was wrong? Let me make a list.*

"I'm captured, chained, and in the morning I have to prove myself to my psychotic nymphomaniac mother, who just happens to be a shape-shifting Egyptian firebird. I'm the leader of the forces of light, but I can't lead. A seer who can't see. Jimmy hates me. I'm a vampire. You're—" My laughter died. "What are you?"

"I'm me."

"Prove it," I said. So he kissed me.

It was good proof. No one kissed like Sawyer.

He tasted of salt and sugar; I liked to lick his teeth. When I did, his tongue flicked out and tickled the base of mine. I felt it all the way to my curling toes.

There were things I did with Sawyer that I'd never done with anyone else. With Sawyer there were no rules, no boundaries. When he kissed me—now and always—every thought disappeared, every memory, every hope and dream, leaving only the burning desire to kiss until kissing wasn't enough, then to get naked, sweat-slicked skin sliding along sweat-slicked skin, plunging within, over and over until at last the burn went away.

A thought meandered through my lust-laden brain. I was supposed to be doing something.

Seduce him.

At least I was right on track.

I arched, wiggling in the hope he might touch me as I'd ordered. I forgot my hands were tied and nearly tore them off at the wrists when I tried to run my palms over his back. Instead, I wrapped my ankles around his, opening my legs so that he lay cradled between. I immediately deduced the seduction was working.

His mouth trailed down my neck; then his breath traced the moisture left behind, and I shivered. My nipples hardened, and he suckled me through my shirt and bra; the sensation of tongue and lips and teeth, along with the friction of the material, made me moan.

The sound snapped me out of the lust coma I'd nearly fallen into. I had to keep my wits from melting along with my body. I needed information.

"Does she have the key?" I asked. Talk about sexy murmur. My voice was so low and hoarse I got excited myself.

"Mmm," Sawyer answered, the sound buzzing along my breast like a vibrator.

Was that mmm, mmm good? Or mmm as in yes?

"She does?"

He lifted his mouth; his face was so close our breath mingled. "You shouldn't have come. I had it under control."

"Had what?" I frowned. "Are you saying you infiltrated ahead of us?"

"That's exactly what I'm saying."

"And I'm supposed to . . . believe you?"

"Why do you think I came here tonight?"

I arched my back, pressing my pelvis into his erection. "The usual reason."

He snorted, his breath a sharp puff of heat against my face. "I've got more sex than I can handle."

"That'll be the day." I had a sudden flash of the Phoenix giving him a blow job in the foyer. "So what was the plan? Fuck her until she told you the truth?"

"It's worked in the past."

Sawyer had whored for the federation before; sometimes I wondered if he did much else.

I should talk. I'd planned on doing the same thing.

"How's it been working on her?"

"Not quite as well," he admitted.

"What have you found out?"

"Nothing."

"If you were still on our side, you'd share what you know."

"I would, if I had anything to share. She's a little leery of trusting me."

"Join the club."

"There's something you should know," he said.

"There's a helluva lot I should know."

His chest lifted and lowered, pushing against me, then flowing away. I was reminded that we were on a bed, body to body, my hands tied above my head. He could do anything he wanted, or at least try. Why did that make my nipples tingle again?

"Get off me," I ordered.

"Not yet."

He rolled to the side, sliding a hand into the pocket

of his jeans. He came up with a key. A few clicks later and my hands were free; the golden chains clattered to the floor.

"I can't leave," I said.

"And I can't let you."

He still lay on top of me. I waited to see where this would lead.

"Do you remember the first time you touched me?" he murmured.

I wasn't exactly sure what he meant. I'd touched him when I was fifteen, but as little and as gingerly as possible. He'd tried to teach me so much, and I hadn't been able to understand most of it. Then I hadn't known what he was, what I was. I'd only known that he frightened me.

When I'd returned ten years later I was Ruthie's heir. I could hear her voice on the wind revealing the names of the supernatural creatures that walked through our world.

She'd whispered, "Skinwalker," and I'd touched him, then seen the aeons of his life. Or at least what he'd wanted me to see.

Not long after that I'd touched him in the night, become a part of him and him of me, and discovered a way to channel my power, to control and increase it.

"Which first time?" I asked.

"When I let you see my mate."

Ah. He'd lived as a wolf, mated as one, loved and then lost her. The devastation I'd seen . . . It was one of the most human behaviors I'd ever witnessed in Sawyer, and he hadn't even been human at the time.

"I remember," I murmured. "You loved her very much."

He didn't answer.

"I'm sure you had a good reason."

"For loving her?"

"For killing her."

"I didn't kill her." His voice was so calm, so reasonable. You'd never know I'd just accused him of killing the only wolf he'd ever loved.

"Then—?"

"How did I get my magic?"

"Yes."

He stood abruptly, and I tensed. Sawyer might sound calm, but that didn't mean he was. He could easily reach over and break my neck just to shut me up for the few seconds it would take to heal.

Instead, he sat again, hip brushing mine, the scent of his skin washing over me and making me remember all the first times that had come before. I had to resist the urge to press my face to his flat, hard belly and taste.

"Touch me," he whispered. "Touch me and see."

CHAPTER 28

I kept my fingers clenched. He'd hidden his past from me before, shown me only what he wanted me to know. Now he was inviting me in, and I wasn't sure I wanted to go. Knowing Sawyer, the blast of his past might just short-circuit my brain.

"I can make you," he said.

I was so tired of being pushed around, threatened into doing things I didn't want to, ordered by angels and demons and ghosts to kill that, fuck this, save everyone. I was supposed to be the boss of this side of the Apocalypse, but you'd never know it.

"Break my fingers," I said tightly, "crack my wrist, force me any way that you like. You're the one who taught me to block the view. If I don't want to see, Sawyer, I won't."

"You keep on believing that."

Then he was touching me, his dark clever fingers gentle yet sure, cupping my breast, thumb stroking the nipple back to a tingling peak. He ran his other palm over my ribs, tracing each and every one before inching beneath the waistband of my jeans, then the lacy strip of my panties, and stroking me where I was still wet from before.

I couldn't help it; my legs fell open, my breath

coming fast and hard, as my hands splayed wide, fingers reaching for . . . him.

"Touch me," he whispered again.

I sat up, then slowly placed my palm on his stomach where there were no tattoos. I didn't want the distraction of the beasts when they called.

His skin was smooth, the muscles stone-hard; I flexed my fingers, drawing my nails along the plane, and he caught his breath, tightening the muscles even further. Closing my eyes, I reached with my mind, caught just a flicker before it was gone, so I dipped my thumb into his navel and gently scored the rim.

Bam. Flash. Light. Dark. I thought I saw his hogan, but—

"I can't be sure."

"You know what we have to do."

I opened my eyes; his were right in front of me— silvery gray surrounded by a thin thread of black. So familiar yet so cool and distant. I had been as close to this man physically as I'd been to almost no one else, yet I hardly knew him at all.

"Just tell me," I said.

He kissed me instead. I caught where this was headed. We'd been there before. The only way to truly open—for me and for him—was to give ourselves over to the power of our magic. For Sawyer, his magic was based in sex, and now mine was too.

So be it, I thought.

I pulled him onto the bed, running my fingers all over his back, chest and arms, getting flashes of wolf, cougar, shark, interspersed with the silhouette of a bird in the sky—at night, dawn, noon.

He yanked off my shirt, nearly ripped my bra in two, filled his palms with my breasts and lifted them to his mouth. His hands were so hard, yet clever and true. He teased my nipples with tongue and teeth, then worked his way downward, tracing my belly, tickling my navel as I'd tickled his. My pants fell on top of the golden chains as he meandered lower still.

I tried to focus, to see into the darkness of his mind, but his breath stirred the curls between my legs, hot, almost scalding, and I moaned, my fingers tangling in his hair, my thumb rubbing over the spike of his cheek-bone, then tracing the curve of his ear. Hard and soft, so many contrasts in just one man.

His tongue flicked over me—once, twice—then he suckled, rolling me in his mouth. I tried to buck away.

"No, we should—"

I grasped at his shoulders, tried to pull him up and over, then inside, but it was like trying to move a mountain. He slipped his hands beneath me, grasping and lifting me, tilting me so he could feast.

My arms flopped limply to my sides as my legs first opened, and then, when he began to flick his tongue back and forth, back and forth, harder and faster, clamped around his shoulders and tightened.

He must have felt me swell, the bud of my clitoris going tight against his tongue in that instant before I came, because then he did rear up and over me, plunging within before going completely still.

"Wait," he whispered. "Just . . . wait."

I was on the verge, in that place where everything in the world narrows to the circle of body on body, body in body, body surrounding body. The very air seemed to pause; silence engulfed us. There *was* only us.

At last he moved, drawing himself against me so I could feel every inch of the slide. I was so wet, so swollen, so ready that when he grew and jerked and spurted, it only took me a millisecond to erupt.

I might have screamed if he hadn't put his hand over my lips; as it was, I bit him. The taste of his flesh in my mouth, the salt of his skin, the promise of blood, made me come harder, and I clenched around him so tightly he froze, holding himself motionless as if he didn't want this ever to end.

Eventually it did. Someone had to move, and that someone was him. He rolled to the side, then stared at the ceiling too.

"That was supposed to open me," I said. "Or maybe you?"

"Mmm."

"I'm not getting much of a news flash."

"Wait," he murmured.

"Sawyer, if you did me just to . . . do me, I'm going to—"

Suddenly, he rolled back on top of me, toe-to-toe, hip-to-hip, chest-to-chest. He pressed his forehead to mine, his eyes widened, the whites blazing like lightning through a clear midnight sky. The bed rattled; the windows did a thrumming dance.

He groped for my hands, drew them next to my head and then pressed down with his own, palm-to-palm.

I was drawn into the past with such force the breeze stirred my hair. In one-quarter of my mind I knew I was still on that bed in Cairo, but the other three-quarters was full of him.

He's laughing, teeth bright white against the bronze of his skin, and he looks younger, but not because of any difference in his face, or his eyes or his stance. Perhaps it is just that he's happy.

Have I ever seen Sawyer happy? I don't think so, and I have to wonder why. Sure, our lives aren't fit for a Disney movie, but there should be a little joy some-where; otherwise, really, what's the point?

The terrain surrounding him is both familiar and new—the Southwest from the shade of the dirt, the shape of the rock formations, the incredible blues and golds, reds and pinks and oranges of the sky at dusk, or is it dawn? Miles and miles and miles of desert, distant mountains, but not a road, a telephone pole or the hint of a house anywhere at all.

Sawyer lifts his face to the sun. He is naked. The colors of the sky cascade over him, tracing his skin like a rainbow. His tattoos writhe wherever the light hits.

He doesn't have as many tattoos as he does now. The wolf stalks across his biceps; the tiger strolls along his thigh; the snake twists lazily between his legs. Then light sizzles so brightly nothing can be seen but white, and when it fades a tiger stands where Sawyer had been.

The wild cat continues to stare upward; a shadow cants across his face, and he watches the great bird sail overhead, then trots after, loping along with tiger grace, so beautiful, so deadly and strong.

Thunder rumbles, and the earth shakes. Dust rises on the horizon. Something is coming. Yet still the ti-ger follows the black V in the sky that is the bird.

A long, low, moving dark cloud appears; the thun-der becomes the pounding of hooves. A hundred, no, a thousand, buffalo race toward the single tiger in their path.

They don't appear afraid of the huge cat that does not belong. Perhaps they've never seen one and there-fore don't know enough to be afraid.

Before the herd tramples him, the tiger veers off, loping around them, hunkering down, tail twitching as he waits. His gray-green eyes remain focused on the whirl of brown stampeding past like props in an old-time western. He springs, straight up and onto the back of a huge bull with massive hooked horns and a shaggy, matted ruff.

The buffalo stops, snorts, bucks. The others gallop around them, managing not to turn both the bull and the tiger on his back into dust.

Sawyer sinks his claws into the beast's hide for leverage, then leans over and tears out his throat.

I wait for the buffalo to stumble, perhaps throw Sawyer to the ground where he'll be trampled by the stragglers. Blood will spray everywhere, and if the animal is lucky, he might be able to gore the tiger once, even twice, before he dies. Obviously none of this will kill Sawyer—in reality he is still alive and right next to me—but it will be bloody and ugly and painful.

Instead, the buffalo bursts into ashes, disintegrating beneath Sawyer like an imploding Vegas casino. Sawyer lands on all fours, and as he races away gray particles swirl off his coat like mist.

The sun, which had been rising, not setting, now blazes with fury from a crystal-blue sky. When the bird circles back, diving toward the earth like a missile, it is easy to see what kind of bird it is.

Peacock-bright feathers mixed with red and gold, a huge wingspan. Definitely not a bird found in America. Technically not a bird found in nature.

The Phoenix dips close to the ground, shifting in a flare like a sunburst so that when my mother's feet meet the earth they have toes.

She is naked. If I were actually *in* the desert I'd turn away. Who wants to see their mother like that? But this is merely a memory, and not even my own.

Lifting her face to the sun, she breathes in as if its rays are liquid gold, then runs her fingers along Sawyer's ruff. "I told you he'd be here."

The tiger shimmers beneath her hand and becomes a man, naked, gleaming, exquisite. "You did." He looks down at her; she is much shorter than me, and his gaze is softer than I've ever seen it. "And as always you were right."

She tilts her head as if someone has called her name, the move birdlike; then her gaze lifts to the sky, focusing fiercely on the sun. Her eyes flare, yellow, then orange, the black pupil forming the shape of a bison.

"There's another," she intones.

"Show me," Sawyer says.

The Phoenix lifts her arms, and they become wings that carry her into the sky. A flash of light and Sawyer is again a tiger loping after the bird, and I tumble back into my body, still trapped beneath Sawyer's on the bed in Cairo.

"She was a seer," I whispered. "Like me."

CHAPTER 29

"Yes," Sawyer agreed.

His eyes were now closed; his forehead remained pressed to mine. I couldn't hear any emotion behind that single word, couldn't see any reaction in that granite face.

"And you were her DK."

He stayed silent and still, our bodies aligned, our hands making a gesture of prayer against the bed.

The memory explained a lot. The connection between a seer and a DK is strong—a bond of secrecy and trust. Was that why Sawyer had come back to her when she'd risen? Had he been unable to stop himself?

"What happened?" I asked. "When did things go wrong? Why? How?"

Sawyer's fingers threaded between my own, clenching so that our palms rode ever closer. The room receded as I returned to the past.

The scenes flash quickly, images like photographs tumbling from an album and cascading across the ground.

The flare of her eyes, yellow to orange, the shifting of her pupil to reflect what she saw, creatures that populated legends all dying by his hand. Time passes;

together they fight, always together. He is as gifted at killing as she is at seeing what needs to be killed. Nothing can stop them.

Until it does.

"Where have you been?" Sawyer asks.

The shadow of Mount Taylor casts over them, purple against a dusky pink sky. Sawyer's place looks almost the same as the last time I saw it. Perhaps the hogan is less weathered, the outside of the house less faded.

Time in the West is hard to determine. If the house hadn't been there, the year could be B.C. for all I knew. The Navajo arrived on this continent back when Moses was still bobbing in the bulrushes, although they didn't migrate south until much later.

I had no idea when the Phoenix had decided to come from Egypt or why. Maybe she'd had a falling-out with Cleopatra. I guess it didn't really matter.

"I've been busy," she says.

"People are dying, Maria. We're supposed to stop that."

She lifts her chin. "We can't save everyone."

"We're supposed to try."

"You're the local killer." She waves her hand. "Kill."

The difference between the woman she'd once been and this one is marked. They'd been a team and now . . . they aren't.

"I need you to tell me where and what they are," Sawyer says. "I can't see them the way that you do."

"Then I guess you'll have to wait until I see something."

She turns, and he snatches her arm. "I've watched you, Maria. Talking to someone who isn't there."

"You're wrong." She pulls out of his grasp, shifts shape and flies away.

He lets her go, watching as she becomes smaller and smaller, fading quickly into the burgeoning night.

The scene changes. Sawyer still stands in the yard, but now a tan station wagon bumps up the drive. I recognize the vehicle, though it's a lot less rickety than the day I rode in it.

The woman inside is Lucinda. She's Navajo, a seer. She's also dead, which gives me a strange, dizzy sense of being in two worlds, which I am.

Her face is as sun-bronzed as when I met her, but less lined, her hair black and long, without any silver threads. The hands that I'd once likened to monkey's paws—shriveled, bony and dark—are just dark.

Her ebony eyes refuse to meet Sawyer's. She's as scared of him now as when she dropped me off at his mailbox, then hauled ass before he ever came out the door.

Sawyer is a skinwalker, to the Navajo, *adishgash*. A witch. They believe he hurts others for his own selfish reasons, and I suddenly understand why. He's been out killing what they believe are people, or in some cases harmless, helpless animals. That those he killed are actually half demons bent on the destruction of the human race is not something those half demons go around sharing.

And Sawyer, being Sawyer, has probably gone along doing his job however he can do it, never worrying about how things look, never caring. In truth, he's probably fed his legend by allowing people to see him kill, allowing them to see the bodies burst into ashes and disappear. The more others fear him, the less likely they are to come around and try to kill him.

Lucinda keeps her gaze fixed on her feet. "There has been an attempt on the life of the leader of the light."

In Cairo I jerked, and Sawyer's muscles bulged as he pressed my hands, my head, my body, back down. "Shhh," he murmured. "It's in the past."

I hadn't been worried about me. Hell, attempts on my life came along as often as breakfast. But Ruthie—

If the leader then had even been Ruthie.

"You've been summoned," Lucinda continues.

"Why me?"

She glances up, then quickly back down. "You're the best we have. You won't stop until the traitor is dead."

Sawyer lifts one shoulder, tilts his head, then twists his mouth in an expression that very clearly says, *Got that right*, before he begins to strip. Since, as usual, he isn't wearing a shirt, shoes or even underwear, it doesn't take much. He hooks his thumbs in his loose tan trousers and drops them to the ground.

Lucinda chokes, then runs for the station wagon. What is wrong with the woman? Scary badass or not, why refuse a free peek? Sawyer obviously doesn't care. I doubt she'll view a finer male specimen this side of paradise.

The sun glints off Sawyer's skin, smooth and bronze, the ink of his tattoos seeming to sparkle and shimmer and shift. He traces a finger along his neck and lightning flashes from a clear sky as he becomes an eagle.

The beat of his wings is drowned out by the roar of Lucinda's engine, then the spraying of gravel beneath her tires as she reverses direction and leaves Sawyer's now-deserted homestead behind.

Night falls as the eagle catches the scent of Lake Michigan. The Bradley Clock looms out of the jumble of low-slung industrial buildings. He veers off before he reaches it, clinging to the tree line as he coasts over block after block of fifties-style ranch houses, zeroing in on the only two-story in the area.

It's late. He purposely took his time, planning to arrive after midnight. There are eagles in Wisconsin, but not many and most live much farther north. None would soar into a suburb and land in a backyard.

He stands on the grass and tilts his snowy white head, black gaze on the windows. Every single one is dark.

Human intelligence, bird body, sometimes it's a hassle. No thumbs to open the door even if it wasn't locked. He could burst through a window, but which one?

He lifts his beak to the just-rising moon; his call is shrill and loud. No one who hears it will ever confuse that shriek with the chirp of a twirpy city bird.

"No need for all that racket." A voice drifts free of the smoky tendrils that surround the house. "I'm right here."

A much younger Ruthie steps into the frail moonlight—forties maybe—her dark skin unlined, her Afro still tight and short, but pitch-black, without a single strand of gray. Her breasts don't sag; her legs aren't veined, her hands not yet gnarled with arthritis.

I've never seen her like this, not in a photo or any dream or vision. To me she's always been Ruthie— my only mother. Soft heart, bony hips, firm but gentle hand. But seeing her young has me wondering for the first time why she never married, although maybe she did. Maybe he died; maybe he left her. Being a seer isn't for sissies. Being the leader of the light leaves precious little to spare for anyone else but those in the federation and those just begging to die by it.

Her thin arm is framed by a charcoal-gray housedress, which only makes her appear even thinner, as its voluminous folds fall around her skinny body like a tent. That arm is wrapped in a stark white bandage; a tiny dot of blood has leaked through.

"Careful, or some nosy neighbor might call the DNR with a wild tale of an eagle in my yard. Been enough stories 'bout strange goin's-on. Don't need any more."

That voice. I want to crawl out of Sawyer's memory and right into her lap. When she'd died I'd been devastated, but having her pop into my dreams, flit through my head, speak to me even if it was to announce impending death by Nephilim had made her seem less gone.

Exchanging Ruthie for a whispering, whining demon had been like losing her all over again. Every time I saw her in my memories or the memories of others, or heard her voice coming out of Luther's mouth, I wanted to weep, and I was not the weeping kind.

"There's somethin' I need done." Ruthie lays her dark hand on Sawyer's head, and he fluffs his feathers, preening. "I'd do it myself, but I got kids here can't be left. Besides." Her bony shoulder shifts beneath her sagging dress. "I'm the leader now. No more fieldwork for me."

Those were the days. Since the battle is *now* it's fieldwork for everybody. Although . . .

Ruthie was a seer. What in hell was she ever doing in the field? Funny how some answers only bring more questions.

"Someone came to kill me." Ruthie glances at the dark house, and silvery moonlight spills across her face. Is that a shadow or the hint of a bruise along her jaw? "Tried to bring about Doomsday." Her dark eyes narrow. "We ain't ready for that yet. Someone knows where I live, what I am, and that can't be. Only way to make it *not* be is for them to no longer be." She lowers her gaze to the eagle's. "Understand?"

Sawyer dips his head, waddles back and forth, back and forth on taloned feet.

"This ain't gonna be easy." Ruthie sighs, long and sad and deep. "It never is."

She reaches into her housedress and pulls out a feather. Even in the moonlight, which seeps color from everything, making the backyard appear like a scene from 1940s film noir, the plumage is radiant.

Sawyer makes a different sound—caw, screech— an unearthly howl of shock and pain.

"Hush now," Ruthie whispers, and lets the feather go. "Just hush."

The feather coasts downward, a bright red slash canting to and fro, coming to rest half on Sawyer's bird feet and half against the thick carpet of ebony grass.

He lifts his beak. Gray eyes meet black.

"You know what you have to do," Ruthie says.

Sawyer picks up the feather and heads back to New Mexico, to the Glittering World, the Dinetah, where he can walk as both man and beast. He feels stronger there, in the shadow of that mountain where he first changed.

He waits, still and silent, the light from the fire flickering across his naked skin as he stares at that red feather night after day after night.

I appreciate his confusion and pain. There is right and there is wrong and attempting to kill the conduit to God . . .

So wrong.

That Sawyer's seer, the one he trusts most on this earth to guide him, has obviously gone to the dark side . . . Well, it takes some getting used to.

Not that he isn't going to kill her when she shows up. He has to. The only question is how. As far as he knows, there is only one Phoenix, which makes legends on how to kill them nearly as rare as they are.

He pulls out his ancient book, pages through it over and over. There are beings of fire and smoke. Hell, his mother is one. He's tried to kill her every way he's heard and read and learned, but he's never had any luck.

He snaps the book shut. Lack of oxygen, dousing with water, covering with earth. The evil bitch has survived all of them. She has more magic than he does, and she probably always will.

The Phoenix is a shape-shifter. He can try silver; he can fight her as one of his beasts, and if that doesn't work, he'll just strangle her, drown her and bury her alive, one after the other, until something does.

At last the sound of great wings fills the sky, and the Phoenix appears, circling lower and lower until she lands on her feet in the yard.

Sawyer doesn't waste any time. What would be the point? Words will only be lies; a touch will be an even bigger one.

He crosses the short distance between them as if he's missed her so much, he can't bear to be apart one more second. If he didn't know the truth, he'd never notice the quick tensing of her body, the way she forces herself to relax, to smile, to let him draw her close and lean over, mouth hovering just above hers.

He lays his hand on her throat and she purrs; then he puts the other there and she frowns. As her eyes snap open, he squeezes, quick before she becomes a bird.

She's strong; he's stronger. Her hands pull on his, but they are like buzzing flies, annoying but no real trouble. Even when they begin to glow and his flesh begins to burn, he keeps up the pressure. He'll heal soon enough.

But strangulation works no better on the Phoenix than it did on the woman of smoke. Even when the

Phoenix has no breath, she doesn't die, and eventually he releases her with a shove.

She falls to the ground, hands on her neck, taking great gulps of air. Her gaze, focused on him, is full of horror, as if *he's* lost his mind instead of her.

Sawyer touches his eagle, shifts, then dives beak first, talons outstretched. Before the light fades from his change, she is a bird as well.

The battle rages. Neither one of them can win. Blood and feathers fly until the ground beneath them looks like a farmyard after a rooster fight.

This is getting them nowhere, so Sawyer flits up the mountain, leading her farther from the ground, closer to the summit and to a place he's shared with no one else.

Below them the sun sparkles off the crystal mountain lake. He slams into her with all he has and takes her with him toward the water.

They hit the surface so hard it knocks the air out of them both. He holds her beneath as she struggles and kicks. The water begins to churn, to smoke and bubble; the chill turns to a caldron in minutes. The scent of boiling meat fills the air.

One second he is holding down a phoenix, brilliant feathers made even more so by the reflection of the sun on the water. The next he is holding down a woman, naked and slick; her dark hair mixes with the blood streaming from the deep cuts his talons are making in her skin.

She stares straight at him, and the confusion, the pain and the misery are so real—as if she doesn't know why he is doing this—he nearly lets her go. For a second he thinks, *I should have asked her*, and then suddenly—

She stops fighting. Her eyes cloud over, and the life

leaves her body like the air sifting from a tire. In the distance thunder rumbles, and somewhere lightning flashes. But the sky is completely clear.

Sawyer shifts, eagle to man, and drags Maria to the banks of the lake. Her face holds the eternal expression: *Why?*

He begins to wonder himself.

Reaching out to touch her, his hand trembles, and he yanks it back. Fury shoots through him, and thunder shakes the ground. He throws back his head; storm clouds race toward him as if he's called them home, and he knows in a flash of understanding as bright as the lightning that slams into the earth all around them just what he has done.

CHAPTER 30

"You loved her," I whispered, my voice full of both awe and horror.

Sawyer continued to press his forehead, his body, against mine, though he did stop crunching our hands together. "So it would appear."

"You didn't know."

"No?" He rolled off me and sat on the side of the bed, scrubbing at his hair as if he'd just woken up.

"Sawyer." I put my hand on his shoulder, felt the shimmer of the shark and yanked it back.

"Perhaps I did know. Perhaps I wanted the power that killing love would bring me. My mother had it. Why shouldn't I?"

"You're not her. You're *nothing* like her."

He stood and walked to the window, staring out at the night. "Soon, Elizabeth, you'll think differently."

I sat up then, his tone, his words, making my skin prickle. "What are you talking about?"

He produced a cigarette from nowhere, literally since he was naked, and then a match the same way. "You'll see." He took a drag, let the smoke trail out his nose in a slow, curling stream. "We're all going to have to choose."

"I have."

"No." Another drag. "But you will. Make sure it's the right choice."

"Gibberish," I muttered. "I need help, answers, *something*, and he gives me gibberish."

Sawyer glanced over his shoulder. "You can't trust me. Sanducci is right about that."

"You came here tonight to—" I stopped, confused. "Why did you come here?"

He let his gaze wander over me from the top of my short, dark hair down to my rapidly cooling toes, then lifted a brow.

"Ew. You just did my mother."

He shrugged.

"There's something you're not telling me."

Sawyer turned calmly back to the window and didn't answer.

I clenched and unclenched my fingers, dazzled by the thought of beating it out of him. As if I could, but right now it was so appealing to try.

"Certain things you have to figure out for yourself," he continued. "Certain choices must be made from . . ."—he took a final drag of the cigarette and tossed it out the window—"the heart."

"Gibberish," I muttered again.

"Take it or leave it."

He was trying to tell me something. So why didn't he just tell me? Maybe he couldn't.

I crossed the floor. "What happened after she died?"

He didn't answer, so I laid my hand on his back, careful to avoid any legs, heads or tails, and wonder of wonders, he continued to let me see.

Lightning rains all around them, slamming into the ground, leaving behind scorched earth and the scent of ozone. The rain pounds down, drenching them, though they are already drenched. Sawyer lifts his hands to the sky, in anguish, in fury, and the lightning . . .

Strikes him.

His outline sizzles, neon white and blue. He shape-shifts; a man reaching upward hunches into a great ta-rantula. When the light fades, a new tattoo traces one forearm. Again he reaches; again the lightning an-swers. Man to shark, leaving behind the likeness on his shoulder. Several more times the lightning flashes and when it fades a new tattoo is in place.

When at last he drops his hands, then sinks to his knees in what is now mud, every tattoo he had when I first met him is stenciled into his skin, and he's be-come the sorcerer he never wanted to be.

The storm wanes as he loses consciousness, the thunder dies, the rain slows to a drizzle, then stops completely, burned away by the return of the sun, leaving two bodies on the muddy banks of the moun-tain lake—one breathing, one not.

When Sawyer awakens, he rolls away, unable to bear looking at her. He's dreamed of her death, of holding her beneath the water until her life drains away, even as more power than he's ever imagined flows into him. He is haunted by the glittering dazzle of the magic, tempted by all the possibilities that are now his. He doesn't want this power, but there's no giving it back.

He shifts into a wolf and runs. Then he runs and runs and runs. He hunts; he kills; he doesn't come back for months. By then her body is gone. He tries not to think of her ever again, but he does. Every time he sees—

Sawyer turned, grabbing my wrist and holding my hand away from his skin. "Enough," he said.

I stared into his face. Had he thought of her every

time he'd seen me? Had he felt her skin every time he'd touched mine?

Sawyer had loved Maria Phoenix. Did he still, even though the woman who'd risen from the grave was a far cry from the woman who'd gone into it? Which side was he truly trying to infiltrate? Hers or ours? I might never know. He certainly wasn't going to tell me.

"You didn't need me to bring the storm, did you?" I tugged on my wrist; he didn't let me go. "You could always do it by yourself."

"Not always," he murmured, and released me.

"How did she end up buried in Cairo?"

"Your guess is as good as mine." Sawyer crossed to the bed and found his trousers.

"You were good; she went bad," I said. "It wasn't your fault."

He stood there, holding his pants in one hand as if he weren't sure what to do with them.

"Jimmy thinks you hung around, doing just enough to be considered one of us so you'd be ready to join her when she rose."

"Sanducci thinks a lot of things." Sawyer shrugged one shoulder, the muscles rippling like water beneath. "He's often right."

"You had to do it," I said. "She tried to kill Ruthie."

"Did she?"

"What?" The word erupted, too loud, too high.

"Perhaps Ruthie merely needed a sorcerer, and she needed one fast."

"You think she played you?"

"She isn't above it. Ruthie's played us all; she's played you."

"It's a far cry from making me think Sanducci didn't love me to having you kill someone."

"Not that far."

"Your morals are skewed."

"Pot. Kettle," he murmured.

I let that slide. "Ruthie had the feather."

"So?"

"And a wound."

He snorted.

"You seriously think she stuck herself with a knife and bled, then lied about it as she ordered you to kill the woman you loved just so you would become the great and powerful Sawyer?"

He let out a long, low, sad breath. "Maybe."

"You've been listening to the evil voices in your head."

His gaze narrowed. "What evil voices?"

Whoops. That was me.

"I'm just saying—where in hell do you get this stuff?"

He glanced at the door, then back.

"Her?" I asked. "She's insane, or haven't you noticed?"

"Waking up in a grave and having to dig your way out will do that."

I was pretty sure the Phoenix had been crazy long before she'd clawed her way out from under, but that was beside the point at the moment. At the moment I had a bigger, better point that needed clarifying.

"Did you raise her?"

"I told you I couldn't raise the dead."

"And then you raised Xander."

"Ghosts are different."

I wasn't sure if I believed him, so I reached for his arm, and he growled at me.

"All right." I lowered my hand. "Let's move on to another question. If you didn't raise her, who did?"

"Whoever buried her?"

"Hmm." Hadn't thought of that. Typically one question just led to another. "How did I get here?"

"You just appeared in town, or so they say."

"Not here." I resisted the urge to stomp my foot. "I mean on earth. When she died I rose, or that's what—"

"She said."

"It isn't true?"

"I don't know."

"You were there when she died. You didn't hear a baby crying."

"No." His lips tightened. "But I ran and then—"

"Then *what*?"

"She was gone."

"Which doesn't explain how I was born, and how you can be so damn sure you're not my father."

"I'm *not*."

"Because incest is on your very short, nearly nonexistent list of no-nos."

He flicked his hand, a careless movement that belied the fury behind it, and I slammed into the wall just hard enough to knock the wind out of me but not hard enough to really hurt.

"I know I'm not your father, Elizabeth, because I did not choose to be."

"You may have rattled my brains that time. I thought you said you didn't choose to be my father and so you weren't."

"That's right."

"Are you aware how procreation works?"

"I'm not like other men."

"You're not even a man at all."

His hand twitched; I tensed in expectation of being thrown out the window. Why I had the sudden and undeniable urge to poke Sawyer with the proverbial stick I couldn't quite say.

"I'm a skinwalker." He relaxed his fingers until they hung limply at his sides. "Both witch and shape-shifter, by definition a *man* with magic. Because of what I am, I have certain abilities."

"Which I now have too."

He cast me a sharp glance. "Not all of them. Not yet."

"Right." Hadn't murdered someone I loved. *Yet.*

"One of my abilities is to choose when I make a child."

"And you haven't chosen."

"I did not choose to make you," he said.

"Technically, you *did* choose to make me." I lifted my hand when he would have argued. "You chose to kill the Phoenix, which in turn caused me to be born."

"But you're not my child."

"Thank God."

He frowned. "I'd be a good father."

"Now you're just freaking me out." I retrieved my clothes and put them on. "Do I even have a father?"

"Everyone has a father."

"Every human," I muttered. "Maybe the Phoenix just dropped me like an egg. She is a bird after all."

"You have a point."

"Fabulous. I was hatched."

His lips curved. "I doubt that."

"But you don't know for sure."

"No," he admitted. "But I do know where you were found."

I'd been putting my shoes back on—the better to kick someone with—and my head snapped up. "Where?"

"Cairo."

CHAPTER 31

"The plot thickens," I said.

"You remember being sent to Ruthie's?"

"Of course. I was twelve. I remember pretty much everything," *in excruciating detail*, "from about three on."

"You didn't pop up on the radar until then or the federation would have snatched you long before they did."

"Bummer for me."

I had not had a good experience in foster care—until Ruthie. Being strange, knowing things you shouldn't, getting yourself noticed—the-three-strikes-and-you're-out-on-the-street plan for foster kids.

"There was nothing in the files about what you could do," Sawyer continued.

"No?" I wasn't surprised. Most people didn't understand why I made them uncomfortable, just that I did.

Oh, sure, when I was little I didn't at first realize that touching someone, then seeing things in their head was something few others could do, and I talked about it, which got me sent to another home, and then another. But no one with half a brain would say, *Take this kid back; she reads minds.* So I was labeled a smartmouth, even before I was; add to that disrespectful, ungrateful, crazy with a side order of thief, slut and addict as I got older, and you had the recipe for what I soon became.

A runaway.

I did better on the streets. Being able to "read" people told me what kind of people they were, and that kept me out of harm's way more than most street kids. Worse things happened to me in places where I should have been safe.

"So what tipped off the federation when I was twelve?"

"You know there are members everywhere?"

"Cops, nurses, government workers. I'll assume that we've got a few plants in Social Services too."

"More than a few. That's how we find a lot of our recruits."

Since becoming leader of the light I'd learned that children with special abilities were dumped more often than most. Maybe one of their parents had been a Nephilim slumming on the human side and wound up dead; then the remaining parent was unable to deal with a very strange kid. Or maybe both parents wound up dead and the aunts, uncles, grandparents couldn't handle it either. Or maybe, as happened to Luther, Nephilim killed both parents for no reason that anyone could fathom and the kid was "hidden" in the system until the federation found them and took them into the fold.

"You'd been bounced back enough times," Sawyer continued, "that someone got suspicious and forwarded your file to Ruthie. Once she took a peek, she made certain you were brought directly to her."

"I thought there was nothing in my file about what I could do."

"There wasn't."

"Then what was so damn special about me?"

"Your name, for one."

I'd always thought some social worker got creative,

or that I'd first been found in Phoenix. But I no longer believed that.

"You were left on a doorstep in Cairo with a note that said you were Elizabeth Phoenix."

"Interesting."

"Very. There were no Phoenixes in the area, and every other family by that name did not lay claim to you."

"So I went into the system."

Sawyer spread his hands. "In your file there was a photograph. Ruthie took one look and sent for me. I came to Milwaukee as a wolf."

"The first sight of me must have rattled your cage."

"So to speak," he murmured. Then he took a deep breath, in and out. "You smelled like her too."

"Why don't I remember this? I know teenagers are oblivious, but being smelled by a wolf should be pretty unforgettable, especially in Milwaukee."

Sawyer passed his hand, palm up, through the air, and wind swirled through the room, making the curtains sway to and fro, whipping the covers off the bed, ruffling my hair and his. Then he turned his palm downward, and the wind died.

"Magic has its uses," he said. "I came in the night; I slipped in and slipped out. No one saw me but Ruthie."

"Weren't you worried? My mother bought a ticket to the dark-side ball. Pledged her soul, sold it; hell, maybe she even sold mine."

I frowned. That would be bad.

"She couldn't sell what she never knew existed. She was dead when you were born."

"There is just something so wrong about that statement."

"Would you have preferred that she raised you?"

I thought about the woman I'd seen in Sawyer's head—the early years. She might not have been so bad.

Then I remembered the psycho downstairs. Perhaps the foster homes *had* been the lesser of two evils. At least there'd been Ruthie. Although lately, Ruthie was scaring me.

"You told me once that you knew no more about my parents than I did."

"I lied," Sawyer said simply.

"Ask a stupid question," I muttered. "So why should I believe what you're telling me now?"

"I didn't tell you. You saw it for yourself."

"For all I know you're perfectly capable of making me see whatever you want me to."

"I can't."

"But you lie."

His gaze flicked to the door again, and I spun just as it opened. The Phoenix stood there with a knowing smile, fingers wrapped around Jimmy's forearm.

There wasn't a mark on him, though I had to assume there had been. Sawyer had knocked him out—jaw, forehead—Jimmy had no doubt sported a bruise that had already faded. He did appear hungover and pretty pissed off. I couldn't blame him.

His lip curled as he glanced first at me, then at Sawyer. "Jesus, Lizzy, have some pride. He's Satan's pool boy."

I opened my mouth to explain, then thought better of it. Sawyer had showed me a lot last night. Probably not a good idea to let the Phoenix know that. Jimmy could just live with it. We all did what—and sometimes who—we had to do.

"I know he's been doing you for the past few months."

The Phoenix leaned over and lowered her voice. "But that was his job. He loves me. The only reason he was ever interested in you was so he could pretend I was back. Now I am."

I glanced at Sawyer, but his face was as inscrutable as always. Maybe she was right. Maybe Sawyer had only been with me because I looked like her. Maybe that was why he'd insisted on showing me the past. So I'd understand whatever he might do in the future.

"He's yours," I said. "Not a problem."

"I know you hear the voice like I do."

She changed topics so fast it took me a few beats to catch up. "What?"

"The voice in your head. Who do you think that is?"

"My demon."

"Sweetie." She made a tsking sound. "The voice isn't your demon. It's *the* demon. Samyaza."

"No," I said, too quickly and too loudly, "it's the vampire inside of me."

I glanced at Jimmy, who was staring at me with an expression I didn't like, and that was saying a lot considering the disgust that had so recently been there. Instead his gaze had become predatory. I suddenly knew what it felt like to be the next Nephilim on his to-do list.

"Right?" I whispered, and Jimmy shook his head.

"Fuck me," I muttered.

"That seems to be everyone's favorite pastime," Jimmy said.

I narrowed my eyes and thought about slugging him.

"We both hear the voice," the Phoenix continued.

"How do you know what I hear?"

"Samyaza told me."

Of course he did.

"Why don't we just call him Satan and be done with it?" I snapped.

"Satan. Samyaza. Abaddon. Whatever," the Phoenix agreed.

"I thought Satan, upon being released, would possess the one who released him," I said.

"He would have. Except you tore the head off the woman of smoke, then tossed her body to the four winds."

"Ah, the good old days."

The Phoenix smiled. "And don't think I don't appreciate it."

"Here's a question—how did the woman of smoke open the gate?"

"From what I've read, the opening of Tartarus is a process—there are a lot of little things that put cracks in the door. For instance, Doomsday being set in motion. Imbalance between the forces of darkness and light."

I felt rather than saw Jimmy wince. Though it wasn't truly his fault, he still blamed himself for the deaths of so many seers and DKs.

"What else?"

"Moral decline. Hatred. Racism. Concern for others grows cold." She waved her hand. "Blah, blah, blah. Once there's a fissure, the Benandanti descends. If she wins, the door slams closed. If she loses—"

I glanced at Sawyer. We'd met the Benandanti—a crone who'd turned young overnight after she'd helped make Sawyer's curse more manageable. For a price. I'd been sorry to hear that she'd died defending the door, even sorrier now that I knew her losing the battle had opened it.

"If the Benandanti's death opened Tartarus, where does the woman of smoke come in?"

"Oh, the Benandanti's death didn't open it," the Phoenix said.

I wanted to smack myself, or her, in the head. "What *did*?"

"Sacrifice."

"Of what?"

"I'm not sure. There was blood and death. A life freely given."

"Damn," I muttered. Who had the woman of smoke killed so she could become ruler of the world and all the demons in it?

"So the door to hell cracked when Ruthie died, the state of the world made the opening bigger, the Benandanti lost, the woman of smoke sacrificed"—I spread my hands—"someone, the demons flew free, I killed her before Satan got there, and now he's looking for a host. Does that cover it?"

"Yes," the Phoenix agreed.

"What would have happened if *you'd* managed to kill Ruthie all those years ago?"

"Same thing. Except there wouldn't have been any you to interfere."

"Why'd you change sides?" I asked.

Her lips curved. "Why did you?"

"I like to back a winner."

"Like daughter, like mother. He promised me the world; who was I to turn it away?"

"But you screwed up. Ruthie lived and the man you loved killed you."

"All I had to do was try. If I failed, we knew I could rise again."

"Aren't you a little pissed about the woman of smoke? What if she'd managed to steal your demon king? You'd still be six feet under."

"No." She shook her head as if I were incredibly

stupid. "Samyaza promised to raise me when he was released. Either I'd be the Prince or I'd be his right hand. I would definitely not be left beneath."

I wanted to point out that the Prince she was talking about was the Prince of *Lies*. But since he'd actually kept his promise, I figured the point was moot.

"What's Satan waiting for? You're back; he's free; let the possession party begin."

"Not that simple. Since I didn't actually release him, I have to prove I'm worthy. I must command all the demons of the pit."

Guess we'd been on the right track.

"How you gonna manage that?" I asked.

"By a sacrifice of the innocent and the damned."

I cast a quick glance at Jimmy. That did *not* sound good.

He lifted his eyebrows, tilted his head—a shrug without the shrug. Sawyer refused to look at me. He knew something, but if he was going to tell me, he already would have.

I returned my gaze to hers. "How does that work exactly?"

"Samyaza said the one I needed would come to me here. So I've sacrificed every being that has managed to enter this town, but I'm still me." She lifted her hands to her head and pulled at her hair, yanking out several strands. "And Samyaza just keeps whispering."

Her voice, when she spoke again, reminded me of Danny Torrance in *The Shining*. Redrum! Redrum!

"Find him," she chanted in that creepy-crawly voice. "Find him."

The Phoenix was channeling crazy again. I guess if my demon—or *the* demon—never shut up I might start to lose it too.

"Him?" I asked.

She breathed in and out, then slowly lowered her arms. The tendrils of hair she'd yanked out stuck to her sweaty palms. "Or her." Her voice had returned to normal, thank God. "But I think I've found the answer."

"What's that?"

"Seize them," she said.

CHAPTER 32

Revenants, which must have been slinking around in the hall waiting for her signal—two words stolen from a late-night movie—crowded into the room. They snatched both Jimmy and Sawyer, then dragged the two men out.

I tensed, waiting for more to march in and grab me. But they didn't. "What's going on?"

"Choices must be made," the Phoenix said.

"I chose you."

"Now you get to prove it." The Phoenix walked out, leaving me behind.

Holy hell. This was going to be bad.

I hurried after, catching up as she reached the ground floor. The house was empty. Tracks in the dust left from last night traced a path to the wide-open front door.

The sun was full up, the sky clear and bright. There was no mistaking Jimmy and Sawyer being trussed like twin Joan of Arcs to a pair of electrical poles at the right edge of the yard. I expected to find a pile of wood at their feet, but there was nothing.

The Phoenix strode through the door, and I was forced to catch up again. She stopped several feet from the men, looked back and forth between them. Jimmy struggled even though they'd bound him with

gold hand, foot, waist and throat. Sawyer had been
bound too, but he didn't bother to fight. Which made
me really nervous. He'd only give up if there were no
way out.

"Choose." The Phoenix flapped her hand in their
direction.

I got a chill, even though the sun was already hot
and there wasn't a prayer of a breeze.

"Choose what?" I asked, knowing the answer was
not going to be one I wanted to hear.

"Which one dies first," she answered, as if I was
incredibly dim.

And I was.

"What? No. They're on our side. Especially him." I
jerked my thumb at Sawyer. "He does whatever the
hell you ask. I'd *keep* him."

"Fine." She put out her hand, and one of the revenants slapped a golden knife into the center. She began to walk toward Jimmy.

"Whoa! Hey! I didn't choose."

Stall, I thought. It was all I *could* think.

"No?" She paused and turned back. "Then do."

"But why? They have incredible powers. You'll
command them in your army."

Over my dead body, but I had to keep stalling.

"I won't have an army; I'll command nothing but
revenants while someone else becomes the Prince, if
I don't make the sacrifice."

"You think one of them is the innocent and the
damned?"

"Yes."

"And if they're not?"

She shrugged. "I'll keep on killing until I find one."

Well, when you're crazy, you're crazy. What could
I say?

"Choose," she ordered again. "If you truly came to join me, you'll do whatever I ask."

"My test," I murmured.

"Take it or die."

I considered the threat. Maybe that would be the best bet. Killing me wasn't as easy as it appeared.

"Okay," I said. "I choose me."

"No!" Jimmy shouted, at the same time Sawyer said softly but somehow just as forcefully, "No."

"Ignore them." I fingered my collar. "I'm definitely damned."

"But probably not too innocent." The Phoenix smirked.

"And they are?"

She crossed the dry grass and kissed Sawyer. It took a while. I didn't want to watch, but I couldn't seem to stop myself. When she lifted her mouth from his she said, "He once was the most innocent of innocents. Until his mother made him into this."

I winced. So did Sawyer.

The Phoenix cruised on to Jimmy, kissed him too. He tried to avoid it, but the chain around his neck wouldn't let him move very far. When she lifted her mouth, there was blood on both their lips. "I heard what you did to him."

I glanced at Sawyer, who refused to meet my eyes. Had he told her every damn thing?

"He was innocent until you seduced him into making you a monster." She glanced over her shoulder. "I'm impressed. Hutzpa like that I can use."

"I'm so glad you approve." My voice was dry, but I managed to make myself smile, even as I wondered just how she planned to kill Sawyer. Had he told her that secret too? If so, I wasn't safe either. If not . . . we might just have a way out.

I filed that thought. If I had to, I could choose Sawyer, buy some time. He wouldn't die and maybe . . .

What? The cavalry would show up? Highly doubtful, since the cavalry was me.

"Which will it be?" The Phoenix came toward me twirling the golden knife. "If you choose wisely, the other one lives."

Because if I chose the one who fulfilled the requirements in the key, she'd be the Antichrist and there'd be no need to kill anyone else—at least right now. Talk about pressure.

"Let me think." I moved past her, headed for Sawyer.

"Search her," she ordered. A revenant came forward and pawed me like a seventeen-year-old with his first prom date.

He stepped back. "Clean."

"No one kills around here but me," the Phoenix said. Guess she was worried I'd steal Samyaza. No thanks.

"Five minutes," the Phoenix continued. "I've waited long enough."

I didn't even glance at her as she walked away. I had no idea what to do. I could only hope that the boys did.

I approached Sawyer first. He was closest.

He'd said I couldn't trust him, and he was probably right, but I had to hope that having her treat him like any other sacrifice in town might have shifted his loyalties a bit.

His gaze met mine. "Shhh," he breathed.

That was promising.

I laid my body against his, put my lips to his neck, then slid them up to his ear. "Does she know how to kill you?"

"Yes."

I cursed.

"Hold on," he murmured. "Remember when I said there are certain things that only happen if I let them?"

I leaned back, stared into his eyes, but as usual I saw nothing I could hold on to in their smoky depths. "Are you saying what I think you're saying?"

"If you're thinking that I must choose to die in order to die, then yes, that's what I'm saying."

"Seriously?"

His mouth twisted—half smile, half grimace. "It's what the old ones sang when I was a boy."

"Back when Noah was a pup," I muttered.

The Navajo passed down their legends in songs and stories. Year after year, century after century, the elders sang around the fires and the next generation learned the traditions.

"Nothing that's ever been tried has actually killed me," he continued, "so I'm inclined to believe the legends are true."

"You've never wanted to die?"

Those eyes that had only a second ago been unreadable became anything but. "I didn't say that."

How could I ask such a question after meeting his mother? Or after seeing his pain at the loss of his wolf mate, or his agony upon killing Maria?

"Yet you're still here," I murmured.

"I've always had things to do, people who needed me."

I laid my head on his chest. "So I can choose you," I said. "She'll try to kill you, but you won't die."

"Even if I did, my blood wouldn't bring her what she wants. I'm too damned to be innocent, Elizabeth."

I lifted my head, gazed into his eyes. "Aren't we all?"

His lips curved. "You need to think this through. When I don't die, she'll turn right around and kill Sanducci. You can't let that happen."

"Damn skippy," I muttered.

"You have to kill him first."

"What?" I straightened with a jerk, then tried to back up so fast I stumbled. "No."

"Listen to me," Sawyer began.

A mumble started among the revenants—unease combined with excitement. Sawyer looked into the sky and cursed.

I figured the Phoenix had lost patience and was flying toward us, ready to take the decision out of my hands. Though what would be the fun in that? Didn't she look forward to the agony and pain that would inevitably follow whatever choice I made like any evil thing should?

Maybe that was what she was after. Could she be staging this stupid "choose who dies" tableau so that once I did, and I lost my will to live, she could kill me too? Wouldn't put it past her.

My hands clenched into fists as I turned. Until that moment I hadn't known I planned to fight. I was supposed to be changing sides, doing whatever it took to steal the damned key, even if it meant sacrificing one or both of these men. If I didn't, more people would die than just them.

However, the Phoenix wasn't the one sailing out of the sky to land softly on the ground.

"Summer?" My fingers uncurled from my palms. "What in hell are you doing here?"

CHAPTER 33

I'd forgotten about the fairy. I'd had a few things on my mind. Seeing her turn up right in the middle of the chaos . . . I wasn't sure what to think.

"Where've you been?" Jimmy asked.

"I—uh—" Summer put her hands behind her back, thrusting out her perky breasts as her tiny white teeth bit her perfect pink lip. "Well, you see—"

"She's been hanging around here." The Phoenix spoke from the porch steps, where she sat paging through a book.

Hello.

The tome appeared very old, very familiar. I could see the star and the lions on the cover. I had to resist the urge to run across the yard, snatch it and—

What? Stand there while she murdered me, or at least tried?

I was going to have to kill her to get it. I'd known that all along.

I glanced at Jimmy, but he couldn't seem to take his eyes off of Summer.

She looked the same as she always did. Impossibly pretty in her fringed white halter top, cowboy hat and boots. Did she ever wear anything else? Why bother when that looked so good?

"*Why* have you been hanging around here?" I asked, unease bubbling in my belly.

"Go ahead," the Phoenix said, continuing to absently page through the key. "Tell them that you work for me."

Summer narrowed her cornflower-blue eyes. "Not yet."

"What is she saying?" Jimmy's voice shook.

I cast him a quick glance. He was pale beneath the olive tone of his skin, his dark eyes hollow.

"And you said *I* broke him," I muttered.

"You did." The fairy transferred her glare to me. "So I had to fix him."

"He's fine."

"He doesn't look fine."

Summer and I moved closer as we argued until we were almost nose-to-nose. Or nose-to-throat, considering she was the size and weight of a ten-year-old.

"My patience is waning," the Phoenix interrupted. "I need a decision."

Summer spun on her booted heel. "Jimmy isn't available for your sick games."

The Phoenix glanced up from the book with a smirk. "And why is that?"

Summer hesitated. "You know why."

"Because you sold your soul to protect him?"

"Yeah." The fairy sighed. "That's why."

My eyes widened. I glanced at Sawyer, whose expression gave nothing away—had he known or hadn't he?—then Jimmy, whose expression revealed all. He hadn't known, and he was as horrified by the revelation as I was.

I shoved Summer in the back. "You've been on their side all along?"

She stumbled forward several steps before whirling, hands clenched into fists as mine had been. "No!"

"Are you aware what selling your soul means?"

"More than you are."

"I'd have to agree. Because I'd never do it."

"I know you wouldn't," she shouted. "You don't love him like I do."

"Summer," Jimmy whispered. "Why?"

All the fight went out of her. Her shoulders slumped; her hands went limp. She closed her eyes and took several breaths before facing him. "I can see the future. I knew what would happen if I didn't. You'd die."

"That's going to happen anyway."

"No. I made a deal."

"You didn't make a deal with me," the Phoenix said.

"I made it with your boss."

"He isn't my boss yet. He won't be my boss until I find the right sacrifice. Once I do, then I'll be bound by his agreements. Until then, kiss my ass."

Wow, she really was my mother.

Summer didn't waste time arguing with a crazy person; she shot her hands out, spewing fairy dust like water from a fire hose.

All right, I thought. *We are in business now. We might just get out of here alive.*

Then the sparkly stream seemed to hit a wall a few inches in front of the Phoenix, and it ricocheted, streaking back in our direction, coating both Summer and me in enchanted silver dew.

The dust had no effect on me; it rarely did. Fairy magic doesn't work on those on an errand of mercy, which was pretty much the story of my life. However, Summer got knocked on her ass.

She tumbled into me, cursing. Between the swear words, I caught "charm" and "rowan." The Phoenix had come prepared to repel fairy magic.

I reached out to steady Summer. As soon as my palms grasped her arms I saw everything.

Summer arrives at the lake in her light blue '57 Chevy Impala. She gets out, appearing exactly the same then as she does now. Tight jeans, boots, cowboy hat. The only difference is a fringed western shirt instead of her usual halter top.

The lake is deserted. Sawyer is gone; the body of Maria lies where he left it. Summer loads the Phoenix into the trunk and heads east.

The Impala's headlights wash over the *Welcome to Cairo* sign. Summer drives straight to the cemetery and in the shadow of the moon digs a grave, then tosses in the Phoenix and fills it back up. She shoots fairy dust across the damp, dark earth and new grass sprouts; then Summer turns and goes back to the car.

Before she's taken five steps, fire erupts on the grave, flaring high and bright, painting the silver-tinged night red and orange and gold. She keeps walking, ignoring the flames. She has her hand on the Impala when the thin wail splits the night.

Her head hangs between her shoulders; her fingers clench on the handle, but she doesn't jump in and drive away. Instead she returns to the grave.

The new grass is french-fried. The place smells like a bonfire. In the center of the blackened earth a naked baby squalls and kicks. A girl, with a cap of dark hair and burnished skin. When Summer's shadow falls over her, she opens her bright blue eyes and screams even louder.

"I am born," I whispered.

And Summer slugged me in the gut.

I let go of her arm. "You—" Cough. Cough. Breathe. "Moved the body."

"The only way to be resurrected was to be truly dead," the Phoenix said from her perch on the porch.

"You *were* dead." If she hadn't been, Sawyer wouldn't be the sorcerer we all knew and feared and I wouldn't be here.

"Yes and no."

Why couldn't anything ever just be yes *or* no? Good or evil. Black or white. Lately everything was one big glob of gray.

The Phoenix set the key aside as if it were no more important that the latest *New York Times* bestselling beach read. My fingers fairly itched to snatch it, but I had to bide my time. First I'd kill her; then I'd grab it.

"You know how a fire seems to die," she explained, "but deep down the embers still glow, and the only way to be sure is to kick dirt over it?" I nodded. "Same principle. I'm a phoenix. The only way for that last spark of life to go out was for me to be buried in the earth of my homeland."

"This isn't really Egypt."

She picked up the book again—was she taunting me with that thing?—and shrugged. "Names have power. A little grave, a little magic, and it was obviously good enough."

"Obviously," I agreed, gaze on Summer, who'd crept closer to Jimmy, though she didn't get too close. He was still looking at her as if she was Satan's handmaiden, which apparently she was.

"You dropped me on a doorstep," I accused.

"Would you have preferred I left you to die on the ground?"

Considering certain memories of my youth ... maybe.

"Why didn't you take me directly to Ruthie?"

"You were the daughter of a traitor," Summer said. "Your mother tried to kill the light."

I jerked a thumb at Sawyer. "So did his."

"By then he was a big boy. He didn't need anyone to protect him."

"You were *protecting* me?" My voice was aghast. "You really do need a dictionary." I thought of the note that had been left along with me. "Why 'Elizabeth Phoenix'?"

" 'Phoenix' so we could find you later."

"And 'Elizabeth'?"

"I liked it."

"You say you sold your soul for Sanducci, but he wasn't even born when this happened."

Her dewy blue eyes met mine. "The future was bright with him. I dreamed of him when I slept. When I woke, my chest ached for missing him. I saw how it would be when I lost him. I couldn't let that happen."

"So you dialed Satan's hotline and volunteered your immortal soul?" Call me crazy, but that wasn't love; it was obsession.

"Samyaza found me," she said.

Ruthie had told me that Satan had been pulling strings on earth since he'd been thrown into the pit. All he needed was a willing conduit, and there were plenty. We had one right here.

"I just had to bury the Phoenix, and Jimmy's life would be spared. It seemed so easy."

"It's all fun and games until the Apocalypse shows up," I muttered.

"He'd be dead by now if it wasn't for me," she snapped.

"Well, we'll never really know that for sure, will we?"

Summer lifted her chin. "I do."

"How did the key end up in there with her?"

"Wasn't me," Summer said.

"Time's up." The Phoenix crossed the yard; the key lay discarded on the top porch step. "Choose now, or I'll choose for you."

"You can't choose Jimmy," Summer blurted.

I narrowed my gaze on the pastel perfection of her face. "How about we kill you?"

"No!" Jimmy shouted, and I turned to him in surprise.

"I'm sorry. Did you actually say no to killing the soul-selling fairy?"

"Lizzy." His face was tormented. "You can't."

I could, but that wasn't the point. That he was so bent out of shape about it seemed to be. Since when did Sanducci care? Sure, he'd slept with her. A lot. But he hadn't loved her. He'd loved me.

Except he didn't anymore.

Why Jimmy loving Summer mattered I couldn't quite say. I had bigger issues at hand.

"Choose!" the Phoenix screamed, and her hands began to glow.

"Shit," Summer muttered. "I think we're gonna need a bigger phoenix."

I actually laughed. Nerves? Panic? End of the world fever? Probably all three.

"Elizabeth." Sawyer's gray eyes seemed to glow as silver as the lightning that had flashed from the sky on the night he'd killed my mother. "Listen to the fairy. Think. And remember."

My laughter died as I stared at Sawyer, and all the little pieces clicked into place.

Lightning.

I looked at Jimmy.

Love.

I returned my gaze to Summer.

A bigger phoenix.

And I knew what I had to do.

"I choose Jimmy," I said.

"No!" Summer shrieked, and lunged for me.

The Phoenix backhanded her; the fairy flew several yards and lay still. My mother walked across the grass and stared at the still form. Then she lifted her foot over Summer's head. Before she brought it down, I turned and hurried toward Jimmy.

I could tell by the way he stared at me that he'd added all the parts and come up with the same solution.

I kissed him, quick and hard. No time for anything more. "I *do* love you."

"I guess we're gonna find out."

I reached for my collar, casting a quick glance at Sawyer, who nodded, grim-faced, so I opened the catch. The necklace tumbled to the ground and someone gasped.

I stilled as the change flowed over me, relishing the flare of strength and power, the knowledge that anyone with a brain should be afraid. They should be very afraid.

In this form life was magnified—color and sound and scent. Every whisper, every movement, from the revenants crashed in my ears like waves breaking on a rocky beach.

Sanducci's eyes glistened onyx, his hair blue-black night, his skin—

"Ahh." I rubbed against him.

The sun sparkled off his skin, and he smelled like . . .

"Lunch."

The vein in his neck pulsed as it called my name. Ba-*bump*. Liz-*zy*. Ba-*bump*. Liz-*zy*.

"Do it," Jimmy growled.

"Happy to."

When I was a vampire, the urge to kill was impossible to deny. Hand in hand with that urge went another, that of an alpha wolf drawn to destroy any other alpha in the vicinity. I felt myself pulled toward Jimmy like the tide.

My fangs lengthened, the sensation itchy. The only thing that would soothe it was blood; the only way to end the buzzing in my brain was death.

But how to kill a dhampir. It wasn't easy. Twice in the same way. Two stakes to the heart. Two golden bullets—kill shots in the exact same place.

I had no weapon but myself. I wanted to drain him, but how did I do that twice? Only one way to find out.

I reached for his head.

"No!"

The word swirled around me, along with a cool, twinkling mist. My arms fell to my sides. I was no longer on an errand of mercy; in this form I didn't even know what that meant. I still wanted to kill Sanducci, but because of the fairy dust I couldn't.

I guess Summer wasn't dead. I'd fix that later.

My fangs still itched; my throat was parched; my stomach cramped in agony. But there was another powerful being very nearby.

I turned toward Sawyer.

"Lizzy, no," Jimmy said. "That won't help. You have to kill *me*."

"Can't," I muttered, drawn across the grass toward the dazzling scent of blood and man and magic that was Sawyer. "And I'm *not* Lizzy."

Jimmy began to curse and fight his bonds in earnest.

Out of the corner of my eye I saw fairy dust flying like cat fur in a catfight as Summer splashed the army of revenants.

"Grab her," she ordered, and they went after the Phoenix like fury.

She fried them of course, but it took her some time. Which allowed me to reach Sawyer.

His face was so sad. I tilted my head. Sadder than I'd ever seen it. His pulse did not beat my name; his pulse barely beat at all.

"You chose him," Sawyer said.

"Liz loves him. Always has, always will."

"I know." In his voice lay despair, and I breathed it in like nectar.

"So sad," I murmured. "I like it."

I pressed my hand to his chest, felt his heart beating beneath.

"One thing before I go," he said.

"Be quick." I was focused on the steady thump-thump against my palm. I wanted to feel that on the outside instead of the inside. I wanted to taste a heart as it stopped beating. I thought I probably could.

"I chose to leave a child behind." My eyes flicked to his. "You must protect that gift of faith."

"Whatever," I said, and tore out his heart.

CHAPTER 34

I never found out if a heart could continue to beat on the outside of a body, because as soon as Sawyer died the power slammed into me like a truck.

In the distance thunder rumbled; I smelled rain on the wind. My hair crackled. The lightning danced nearby, and I wanted it.

Come to me.

The words were both in my head and in the roll of the thunder. Demonic laughter swelled; the whispers commenced, and I slammed the door. I was too fascinated with the magic to listen.

The Phoenix shrieked her rage, but there was nothing she could do. The fury of the storm was mine; I would command the lightning. Right now, as the newborn power flowed through me, I thought I could command just about anything.

I faced her. She was still fighting revenants, but she was mowing them down pretty fast. Summer had run to Jimmy, of course. But I didn't care about them now; all I cared about was her.

"Bigger phoenix," I growled, and called down the storm.

Bolts of lightning slammed into the ground at my feet. The earth trembled beneath my wrath. Blue light shimmered; I had to close my eyes as the lightning hit me. The sizzle and burn, the flare of electricity, made my teeth hum. The back of my neck blazed, and I knew that I could fly.

Dark clouds shrouded the sun, turning the air so cold my breath became smoke. Dust swirled by on the wind, and the rain began to fall like tears.

"You bitch!" The Phoenix stalked across the yard and slapped me in the face. The more I got to know her, the happier I was about foster care. "I told you I was the only one who got to kill around here. Daughter or not, you die."

"Good luck with that," I said.

"You forget. I'm still the Phoenix." She poked me hard in the chest. "And you're not."

Then she turned and headed for the porch. I assumed she'd read something in the key that she thought might kill me.

"Wrong," I said, and clasped a hand to the phoenix tattoo imprinted on the back of my neck only moments before by the lightning.

Shifting as a vampire. God, it was great. The flash of light so much flashier, the bone-deep chill delicious when followed by the flare of welcome heat.

I fluffed my wings. The colors dazzled—scarlet and neon orange, daffodil against sapphire. I opened my beak and called out. The Phoenix froze as suddenly she understood.

Slowly she turned, lip curled like a rabid dog. "You *loved* him?"

Yeah, it was news to me too.

She shot fire in my direction, but I could fly, and I zoomed straight up, then dived back down, headed right for her. Except she'd already shifted, admirably fast, and we met a dozen feet off the ground.

Our clash was the thunder, the slash of fire new lightning. My wings sizzled, and I called on the rain to put them out. Before I circled back to hit her again, I'd grown new ones, and so had she.

The battle was epic—flames and blood across the sky. Feathers flew everywhere, like a rainbow tumbling to the earth in a thousand oval pieces.

We could do this for days—hurt and then heal, die and be reborn—but the simple fact remained that I was the bigger phoenix. I was more than just a firebird; I was a vampire and a shifter and now a sorcerer too; the depth of my power stunned even me.

So I called on the storm; I brought the lightning, and then I hit her with everything at once—fire and electricity, wind and magic.

Her outline flared white. The silhouette against the stormy sky made me think of a cartoon X-ray. *ZZZAAAPP!*

Then the light went out. For a single instant she hung there, no longer brightly colored, but black as coal dust.

Slowly the cinders began to drip away, falling toward the ground like silver-edged snowflakes. Before they could pile into a drift and—who knows?—maybe regenerate, restore, renew, arise, I hit them with a gale-force wind and sent her in a thousand different parts to a hundred different places.

Resurrect that, I thought.

I sailed downward, and the dust of the revenants blew past me like a sandstorm. I ignored them, all my intentions centered on the two beings left alive in the yard.

Summer had released Jimmy. They stood close, but not touching, staring up at me. As I neared, the fairy stepped in front of Jimmy, but he shoved her back.

I imagined myself as myself, and the change reversed—a bright flash, the heat gave way to a certain chill, and I touched down with five toes instead of three.

Naked, but I didn't care. Vampires don't care about much. Pure evil can be so liberating.

I still wanted to suck Jimmy dry—he practically glittered with power—and it occurred to me that if I killed the fairy, I could.

I crossed the short distance between us. Summer flew upward without benefit of wings, a graceful leap-frog, over Jimmy's head, to land between him and me.

Idiot. I couldn't touch him until she was dead, and she'd just made it so much easier.

I grabbed her by the throat, lifted her off the ground, glanced around for something to kill her with. I didn't have to look far. An old bird feeder atop a steel bar listed crookedly at the side of the house. I dragged her in that direction by her shiny blond hair.

I should have known that something was wrong when Jimmy let me have her. He didn't jump on my back; he didn't yank off his cock ring and try to kill me. And I say *try*, because killing me just wasn't going to happen—unless I chose to die.

Talk about liberating.

I reached the bird feeder, yanked it out with one hand, while I held Summer with the other. A quick shake and the wooden container on the top flew into the side of the house and burst into smithereens. I considered shaking Summer the same way, just for the hell of it. Could I rattle her brains? I kind of thought so.

But I wanted to open Sanducci's neck, let the blood run free, touch it, drink of it and discover how long it would take him to die. Unless he tasted so good I decided to keep him alive forever. The possibilities were endless once this annoying Tinkerbell takeoff was gone.

I needed cold steel, but the post in my hand remained warm from the sun that had shone down before I'd called the storm. I closed my eyes, and an icy wind stirred my hair. Seconds later hail pinged against the ground. I waited until my fingers cramped from the cold, until the metal became foggy with frost; then I lifted the post and prepared to ram it down her throat.

The light began to flicker and I paused, tilting my head upward. The sun came out from behind the storm clouds, but the shapes flying in front of it made the rays go dark-light, dark-light.

I'd seen this once before. When the Grigori had flown free of Tartarus they had made patterns across the full white moon. Now, they were returning at their master's call—at my call—making the same shadows across the brilliant flare of the sun.

Command them.

I glanced at Sawyer, still hanging on the pole, heartless. I guess he hadn't been too damned to be innocent after all.

I dropped the fairy, and she crumpled to the ground; then I tossed the steel through the front window of the house. The resulting crash of glass made me laugh, and the laughter was that of the demon inside.

"Kill her," I ordered, and the Grigori—chaos spirits that glimmered like misshapen bats and crows and vultures—swooped down.

That's it, the familiar voice crooned. *Command them and you are the Prince; then all you have to do is let me in. No more pain, no more fear, no more death. Anything you've ever wanted will be yours.*

Sounded reasonable to me. I opened my mouth to agree, and the catch on my collar clicked closed. Like air running out of a punctured balloon, the evil flowed away, leaving behind only a whisper.

"Call them off." Jimmy grabbed my elbow so hard my bones seemed to grate together. "Now, before they kill her."

The dark, whirling cloud of evil spirits had gathered above the fairy. The way they slithered and danced, the scent of them—burned rubber garnished with rotten eggs—their voices, part screech, part insane murmur, repelled me.

"Stop," I ordered, and they did.

Feel the power. Wouldn't you like more? Wouldn't you like it all?

The Grigori began to murmur again, their voices just like his, promising impossible things, guaranteeing all. I fell to the ground, covered my ears with my hands, but I could still hear, because the voice inside of me had only gotten louder.

The temptation was overwhelming. No more pain. No more fear. No more death.

Let me in. Let me in. Let me in.

The words pulsed to the beat of my heart. I thought I might go mad if they didn't stop. So I sat up, and I shouted to the sky, "Go to hell!"

And they did.

CHAPTER 35

The Grigori were pulled shrieking from the earth, their voices inhuman with fury, their screams full of pain. I watched, stunned, as the flickering shadows lengthened, seeming to cling to the rays of the sun. My ears ached; my skin prickled with gooseflesh, my muscles so tense they threatened to cramp. Then, the Grigori were gone, their howls fading along with their misshapen black bodies, as the sun brightened.

The silence after so much noise was overwhelming. I sat on the ground stunned as everything I'd said and done rushed in; the scents and sights, the words and the feelings, the temptations I'd accepted and rejected, bombarded me.

I waited for Jimmy to touch me, to whisper that everything was all right, that I'd had to do all that I'd done. Instead, he stepped around me and went to the fairy.

"You okay?" He touched her shoulder, took *her* into his arms as she cried.

I was so shocked I just stared at the two of them, blinking in the sudden sunlight—the storm had disappeared as if it had never even been—expecting the scene before me to fade, a hallucination, a vision, anything but the truth, except it didn't.

Neither did the one behind them, a scene that would haunt me for the rest of my days.

"Oh, God," I whispered. "Sawyer's dead."

I didn't want to touch him, wasn't sure what I'd see. But I couldn't leave him hanging there like some kind of sacrifice.

"Jesus," I muttered, and dragged myself to my feet as all that had happened became clear.

Sawyer had been the sacrifice that allowed me to command the demons. He'd been wrong. He wasn't too damned to be innocent. Perhaps he was just damned enough. At any rate, his death had allowed me to send the Grigori and, from the welcome silence in my brain, Satan back to Tartarus.

Because the only way Sawyer could die was if he wanted to and therefore he'd given his life freely. A sacrifice.

Jimmy and Summer didn't move, didn't speak, didn't offer to help. I had to stop looking at them, or I might do something I'd regret.

I stumbled across the dusty ground. Sawyer's head hung limp. The gaping hole in his chest had not healed; the blood that washed over his tattooed skin had just begun to dry.

His heart lay at his feet where I'd dropped it when the magic took me. A strange thought trickled through my numb brain. What if I put it back?

I was a sorcerer. I could command a storm, control lightning. I could raise a ghost. Hell, I'd just sent demons back to hell. Maybe if I combined every power I had, I could raise him like I'd killed her.

Bending, I scooped up the gory organ. Dirt and grass and dust clung to it. I didn't bother to wash them away. If I could raise Sawyer from the dead, a little grit wouldn't hurt him.

I pressed the heart back into his chest; the squishing sound nearly undid me. Someone was whimpering and so I crooned, "Shh. Shh," as if talking to a frightened child. But I was just talking to myself.

My hand shook. My fingers were as cold as ice atop a lake, his skin the chill water beneath. I patted his chest, uncertain what to do next. Call the storm? Cast a spell? I couldn't remember how to do one and didn't know how to do the other.

I was in shock; I knew that, but I couldn't seem to stop myself from touching his face, calling his name. Then I was slapping him, begging him, and at last Jimmy came.

"Lizzy." He grabbed one arm, Summer the other. I flipped my hands upward, but only Summer flew away. Jimmy was unaffected, the fairy dust spell still intact.

"Take it off," Jimmy ordered Summer, his voice low and flat. He was angry, but I wasn't sure why.

"Sh-she'll hurt you."

"Do it," he said. "Now."

Strange, but he sounded mad. At her.

"Hit me," Jimmy whispered into my hair. "It might help. It usually does."

I reached for Sawyer again, and this time when Jimmy took my arm I punched him. My fist met his rock-hard gut, and then I was crying, even though I never cried. There was no point. But again, I couldn't seem to stop myself.

The crying didn't last, but the buzzing sense of unreality did. I kept expecting Sawyer to lift his head and demand to be released; then he'd annoy me, piss off Jimmy, scare Summer, and everything would be back the way it should be.

But, regardless of what I'd just accomplished, nothing was ever going to be as it should be again. I knew that.

I stared over Jimmy's shoulder as he patted my back, stiffly, as if he didn't want to hold me, to help me, but he didn't have much choice.

My gaze was drawn to Sawyer's tattoos. They no longer sparkled and danced; they were just ink, growing darker as his skin began to pale.

I inched out of Jimmy's arms, and he breathed a sigh of relief. But when I reached again for Sawyer, Jimmy snatched my wrist before I could touch him.

"Take your hand off me before I break every finger you've got." I met his eyes, and he lifted his arms, palms face out as he surrendered.

I moved closer to Sawyer's body and rubbed my thumb, then my fingers, then my whole hand against the wolf on his biceps. I didn't see a single shimmer, didn't feel a breath of air, nor a hint of the phantom chill. I began to panic, frantically patting the tiger, the tarantula, the crocodile. None of them worked. Why would they? The power lay in Sawyer, not the ink.

There had to be a way to fix this. Maybe a spell. Hey—

"The key."

That had been the mission all along. Find the key, send the Grigori back to hell. The spells in that book were ancient and obviously very powerful. There had to be something in there about raising the dead.

My clothes appeared in front of me, clutched in Jimmy's hand. I'd forgotten I was naked. I had to be pretty out of it to forget that.

Yanking them on, I glanced at Summer, who hovered a few feet away chewing her nails, eyes on Jimmy. For an instant I felt sorry for her. If I'd seen this future, would I have agreed to anything to make it go away? I had no idea.

I hurried toward the porch, then walked up the steps to the place where I'd last seen the key.

It wasn't there.

I turned right, then left, then all the way around. "You saw her with the book, didn't you?"

Jimmy joined me, gaze becoming as frantic as mine. "What the *fuck*!"

"The Phoenix was reading it."

"Then she put it down right there." Jimmy pointed to the same place I'd expected to find the thing.

The three of us began to hunt all over the porch, in the bushes, the grass, everywhere. Once that was done, by unspoken consensus we went inside and searched the house, top to bottom. I touched everything, tried to see something, got a whole lot of nothing.

"This sucks!" I clenched my hands, frustrated, furious, and thunder rumbled in the west. I wanted to kill someone. My gaze moved to Summer, and Jimmy stepped between us.

"Not yet," he said.

Summer's eyes widened and, if possible, her already pale skin got paler. She'd never believed that Jimmy would kill her if he had to—she certainly wouldn't kill him—but I think she was starting to catch a clue.

"Why not?" I asked.

"She did it for me," Jimmy said softly.

"She's a traitor. You know I can't let her live."

"You let me live."

"You seriously think it's the same thing? She knew what she was doing. She chose to sell her soul."

"For me," he repeated.

"And that excuses it? How many people died because she listened to Satan whispering? If the Phoenix had never been raised, Sawyer might still be alive."

Someone else would probably be dead, but I wasn't exactly rational at the moment.

"So you're going to punish Summer because she knows what love means?"

"No, I'm going to kill her because she's a whiny, traitorous bitch. And just what in hell does 'love mean'?"

"It means you'll do anything, even die, even sell your soul, for someone else."

"And you're saying I wouldn't?"

Jimmy threw up his hands. "You were going to kill me!"

"You told me to."

"It had to be done."

"Hey, I chose you because I *loved* you," I said.

"You loved him too, obviously."

"Lucky him." My voice broke. Why were we arguing? Because it felt good. It felt like nothing had changed, even though everything had.

"Summer would do anything for me," Jimmy continued. "You'd do anything for the world."

"Which is why I'm the leader of the light and she's not." I took a deep breath. "You do realize that I managed to send the Grigori and their leader back to Tartarus? This wasn't a total loss."

"Unfortunately, someone stole the *Key of Solomon*, which contains the directions for letting them right back out again."

I frowned. "First they have to kill me."

"They can get in line," Jimmy muttered.

I knew he was just blowing off steam, but still—

I turned toward the door; so did Jimmy. One glance outside and we froze.

Sawyer was gone.

CHAPTER 36

We couldn't find a trace of Sawyer or the *Key of Solomon*. Believe me, we looked.

No footprints. Not a single ash at the base of the telephone pole.

"He stole the key," Jimmy accused.

"He was a little dead to be stealing anything."

"He was a little dead to be walking away too, but there you go." Jimmy threw his hands out in the direction of the empty pole.

"He was still here when the thing disappeared."

"You sure about that?"

I hadn't glanced in Sawyer's direction once we went to retrieve the book from the porch. Why bother? He wasn't going anywhere.

"If he wanted the key he could have taken it before we even showed up," I pointed out.

"You're going to have to raise him," Summer said.

Both Jimmy and I turned to her, and she shrugged. "Aren't you?"

"Yeah." I sighed. "But we'll have to go back to New Mexico first."

"What the hell for?" Jimmy demanded.

"I'll need a part of him. Hair, nails, spit. Okay with you?"

If Jimmy had been an animal, he would have

snarled. As it was, he just kicked the dirt and walked away.

Summer had left the Impala off the highway a few miles from Cairo. She hadn't had any problem getting into town either, and I wasn't surprised. Selling your soul to the Devil must create one hell of an inner darkness.

Once she'd retrieved the vehicle, we piled in and headed west. I didn't even ask to drive. I just wasn't up to it. The last time I'd gone on a road trip in this car I'd been with Sawyer, and I couldn't stop thinking about it.

Luther waited in front of the hogan. As we got out, Ruthie's voice greeted us. "Been waitin' on you."

"Sawyer," I began.

"I know."

"He's with you?"

Jimmy snorted. "You think Sawyer's in heaven?"

My eyes met Ruthie's, and she shook her head.

I went into the house, reemerging with Sawyer's toothbrush, which I tossed on the ground, then drew a circle around it.

"Stand back," I said; then I raised a storm.

I brought the rain, the clouds, the thunder and the lightning. I did everything the way that Sawyer had— almost. But after the earth moved and the blue-white light flashed, all that lay in the circle was the damn toothbrush.

"Sanducci," I ordered, "get over here."

He frowned, but he started forward; then Summer grabbed his arm. "Sex increases her power."

He stiffened and looked me in the eye. "No."

"Don't make me come and get you."

"Lizbeth," Ruthie said softly. "That won't help."

My breath hitched. I gritted my teeth until they ached. "What will?"

"You need to learn how to manage your powers."

"That's going to be a little hard, since I had to kill the one who knows that info in order to get them."

"Did you think fighting for the light would be easy?" Ruthie asked. "It would be simpler to fight for the darkness, to give in to the evil that lives in everyone. But it's the fighting of that evil, the triumphing over it, that gives us our strength. When we win, we'll win because we *chose* right over wrong, because we believed in it and in ourselves."

"I just . . ." I trailed off. I wasn't sure what I'd meant to say.

"Everything happens for a reason, child." Ruthie's voice—Luther's face softened. "Quit bein' so hard on yourself. You did what you set out to do, didn't you?"

I sighed. "Yeah."

I'd saved the world, at least from this threat, but there'd be more.

"We're going to have to find us another skinwalker."

"There's another?"

"How you think Sawyer got his first tattoos?"

I *hadn't* thought of it. But obviously, since he hadn't been a sorcerer until he'd killed my mother, someone had given them to him.

"It's gonna take me a little time to track one down," Ruthie continued. "You three get back to work. The Grigori have increased the Nephilim tenfold. There are more of them and less of us."

"What about her?" I jerked my thumb at the fairy.

"Jimmy will keep an eye on her."

I scowled. "She's a soulless traitor."

"She still has her soul and will until Samyaza takes form. Until then, we need her."

I glared at Summer; she did the same right back.

"If Sanducci's keeping an eye on her, who am I working with?" I asked.

"Me," Luther said.

Jimmy and Summer went to her Irish cottage on the other side of the mountain. I called and checked in with Megan. She was fine and still had no clue that Quinn was anything other than a slightly klutzy bartender. She wasn't catching a hint of his adoration either. Poor guy.

I went to bed early. I hadn't slept since we'd left Cairo. Every time I closed my eyes, I saw Sawyer. Tonight was no different. As soon as I drifted off, there he was.

I chose to leave a child behind.

I sat straight up in bed, heart pounding so loudly I couldn't hear anything else. What had he meant?

My hand drifted to my stomach, which was rolling and pitching enough to make me sick. "Nah."

I was on the pill. Had been for years. However, I doubted something as flimsy as 98 percent effectiveness would stop Sawyer's magic sperm.

Now my heart really started pounding. Which is why it took me a few seconds to hear the knocking at my door.

I tumbled out of bed, stumbled across the floor. Luther stood in the hallway, looking as tired as I felt.

He tapped his head. "We gotta go."

"We?"

"Take my word for it, you're gonna need me."

The Grigori might be confined, but the Nephilim were still here. Not much had changed except there were more of them, less of us. Until we managed to even things out, DKs and seers were going to be interchangeable. Luther and I would go out together and so would Jimmy and Summer, as well as a host of others I hadn't met yet.

I might be the leader of the light, but there was a lot I didn't know. What had happened to Sawyer? Who had stolen the *Key of Solomon*? Would we win or would they? Who would live and who would die?

"We need to get going." Luther shuffled his big feet, then glanced uneasily over his shoulder. "It's chaos out there."

Well, there was one thing I *did* know. One thing of which I was completely, utterly certain.

"Chaos bites," I said, and then I followed him into the night.

Read on for an excerpt from the next book
by Lori Handeland

Chaos Bites

Coming soon from St. Martin's Paperbacks

Being the leader of the supernatural forces of good isn't as cool as it sounds. For one thing, I had to put the world first. So everything else was second, third, four hundred and fifty-ninth. And we're talking about important things like love, friendship, family. Which was how I ended up killing the man I loved.

Again.

Oh, I didn't kill him twice. I killed two separate men. One didn't stay dead, the other . . . I'm not so sure.

Yes, I'm in love with two different guys. It was news to me, too. Add to that the beginning of the end of the world and you've got chaos. As anyone who's ever experienced it can tell you—chaos bites.

Since the night my foster mother died in my arms, leaving me in charge of the Apocalypse, chaos had been, for me, standard operating procedure.

Several weeks after I'd killed him, Sawyer invaded my dreams. He was a Navajo skinwalker—both witch and shape-shifter, a sorcerer of incredible power. Unfortunately, his power hadn't kept him from dying. Considering that he'd wanted to, I doubted anything could have. I still felt guilty. Tearing out a guy's heart with your bare hand can do that.

The dream was a sex dream. With Sawyer they usually were. He was a catalyst telepath—he brought out the supernatural abilities of others through sex. Something about opening yourself to yourself, the universe, the magical possibilities within—yada-yada, blah, blah, blah.

I'd never understood what he did or how. Not that it didn't work. One night with Sawyer and I'd had more power than I knew what to do with.

In my dream I lay in my bed, in my apartment in Friedenburg, a northern suburb of Milwaukee. Sawyer lay behind me. His hand cupped my hip; he spooned himself around me. Since we were nearly the same height, his breath brushed my neck, his hair—long and black and silky—cascaded over my skin. I covered his hand with mine and began to turn.

Our legs tangled, his tightened, along with his fingers at my hip. "Don't," he ordered, his voice forever deep and commanding.

"But—"

He nipped lightly at the curve of my neck, and I gasped—both surprise and arousal. I knew this was a dream, but my body was responding as if it weren't.

He felt so real—sleek, hard muscles rippling beneath smooth hot skin. Sawyer had had an exquisite form; living for centuries had given him plenty of time to work on every muscle group for several decades each, honing every inch to a state designed to make women drool. He'd have been perfect if not for the tattoos that wound all over him.

To shift, most skinwalkers used a robe adorned with the likeness of their spirit animal. For Sawyer, his skin was his robe, and upon it he'd inscribed the likenesses of many beasts of prey. Sometimes, in the firelight, those tattoos seemed to dance.

"Why are you here?" I asked.

"Why do you think?" He arched, pressing his erection against me. I couldn't help it, I arched, too. Sure, it had only been a few weeks. But I missed him. I was going to miss him for the rest of my life.

Without Sawyer, the forces of good—aka the federation—were in deep shit. Certainly I was powerful, and would no doubt get even more so, but I'd been thrown into this without any training. I was like a magical bull in a very full china shop, thrashing around breaking things, breaking people. So far I'd been able to keep those who followed me from getting completely wiped out, but only because I'd had help.

From Sawyer.

"It's a long trip from hell for a booty call," I murmured.

His tongue tickled my neck in the same place he'd so recently nipped. "I'm not in hell."

"Where are you?"

He slid his hand from my hip to my breast. "Where does it feel like I am?" He rubbed a thumb over my nipple, and the sensation made me tingle all over.

"I know you're not here," I said. "You'll never be here again."

I was proud I'd kept my voice from breaking, even though it had wanted to. I couldn't show weakness, even to him.

Sawyer didn't speak, just kept sliding his thumb over and back, over and back, then he sighed and stopped. I bit my lip to keep myself from begging him to start.

His lithe, clever fingers brushed over the chain that hung from my neck, then captured the turquoise strung onto it. "You're wearing this again?"

Sawyer had given me the necklace years ago. I'd taken it off only recently. When he'd died, I'd put the turquoise back on. It was all I had left of him.

I hoped.

"I—" I paused, uncertain what to say. I didn't want him to know how badly I missed him. How I rubbed the smooth stone at least a dozen times a day and remembered.

"I'm glad," he said softly. "It brought me to you."

In the beginning I'd thought the necklace just jewelry, but it had turned out to be magic, marking me as Sawyer's, saving my life on occasion and allowing him to know where I was whenever he wanted to.

He let the turquoise fall back between my breasts. "Do you remember the last thing I said to you?"

I stiffened so fast I conked the back of my head against his nose. The resultant thunk and his hiss sounded pretty real to me, as did the dull throbbing in my skull that followed.

"Phoenix," Sawyer snapped. "Do you—"

" 'Protect that gift of faith'," I repeated.

He ran his palm over my shoulder. "Yes."

"What does that *mean*?"

"You'll see."

I closed my eyes, drew in a deep breath. Right before he'd said those words, Sawyer had said a few others. Words that had kept me up nights almost as much as his death had.

I chose to leave a child behind.

I blotted out the memory of what had come after those statements with what had come not long before. He'd crept into the room where I was chained to a bed, a prisoner of my own mother, a woman I'd thought long dead. She'd been a winner. Five minutes in her company and I no longer regretted being an orphan.

The situation had been dire, yet he'd seduced me. I hadn't wondered why until he was gone. My hand went to my still-flat stomach. Had he left a child behind in me?

"Sawyer," I began. I had so many questions. I didn't get to ask any of them.

"You need to wake up now."

"Wait, I—"

"Phoenix," he said, then more softly, "Elizabeth."

Most people called me Liz, but Sawyer never had.

"There's someone here."

In the next instant I scrambled toward consciousness, and as I did, the sound of his voice, the weight of his hand, and the warmth of his body began to fade.

"Someone or some*thing*?" I asked.

"Both," he answered, and then he was gone.

My eyes snapped open, my hand already reaching for the silver knife beneath my pillow.

The world wasn't what it seemed. Beneath the façades of many humans lurked half demons bent on our destruction. They're known as the Nephilim, the offspring of the fallen angels and the daughters of men.

They've been here since the beginning, glimpsed more often in times past when wolf men and women of smoke were commonplace and gave rise to the legends we now see most often on the screen at the Multiplex. Unless you're me, and then they show up in your apartment.

My fingers wrapped around the hilt of the knife even as I stilled, waiting for the slight buzz that signaled evil creepy thing to wash over me. But it didn't.

I sat on the edge of the mattress, eyes narrowing, ears straining, then I took a deep breath, and my skin prickled. The bed smelled of Sawyer—snow on the mountain, leaves on the wind, fire and smoke and heat.

"Dream my ass," I muttered.

Downstairs, outside, there was a soft thud, then the scrape of something hard against the pavement. A shoe? A toe? A claw?

As I crossed the room, I could have sworn fur brushed my thigh. I glanced down but saw nothing but the flutter of the loose cotton shorts I'd worn to bed along with a worn and faded Milwaukee Brewers T-shirt.

An odd cry drew me to the window, where I kept to the side and out of sight. New moon and the sky was dark, the stars pale this close to the city. The single streetlight in Friedenburg revealed nothing but empty sidewalks and dark storefronts. Which meant nothing. Nephilim rarely used the front door. They didn't have to.

Uneasy, I glanced up, but found only shadows on the rooftops. Of course those shadows could become anything.

"Psst. Kid."

I kicked the cot shoved against the wall in the corner. My apartment was an efficiency located above a knickknack shop. I owned the building, rented out the first floor, and was considering renting out the second. I was rarely in town these days. The only reason I was here now was that I'd promised my best friend I'd attend her daughter's ninth birthday party. I owed Megan so much, the least I could do was show up when she begged me to.

"Luther!" I nudged the cot again. I didn't want to touch him if I didn't have to.

I was psychometric. Had been since birth I assumed, since I couldn't remember a time that I wasn't able to touch people and see where they'd been, what they'd done. In the case of the Nephilim, I could see what they truly were. Or at least I could until recently. Now I had Luther for that.

"Wha—? Huh?" Luther rubbed at his face. His kinky golden-brown hair stuck out from his smooth brown skin even more than usual.

"Getting any bad guy vibes?" I asked.

I'll give the kid credit; he woke right up. "No," he said slowly, head tilted, hazel eyes narrowed.

"You sleep pretty deep." From what I heard, most kids did, though Luther would say he was no longer a kid but a man.

He swore he was eighteen, but I had my doubts. Tall and gangly, Luther's feet and hands were huge. Many Nephilim had believed Luther's awkward appearance meant he was slow and clumsy. However, Luther moved as quickly and gracefully as the lion he could become.

The kid was a breed—the offspring of a Nephilim and a human. Being part demon gave him supernatural powers. Being less demon than human meant he could choose to fight on the side of good. A lot of breeds did.

"I'd hear Ruthie if she had somethin' to say. Wouldn't matter if I was sleeping or not."

Ruthie Kane, my foster mother, had been the former leader of the light. Now I was. In the beginning, she'd spoken to me on the wind, in dreams, or in visions, to let me know what flavor of evil lay behind a Nephilim's human face. Now she spoke through Luther. I had demon issues.

"There's something out there," I said.

Luther's silver knife appeared in his hand as quickly as mine had. Silver kills most shifters, and if it doesn't, it will at least slow them down.

"Ruthie talking to you again?" Luther was already making his way toward the door that led to the back stairs.

"No." I paused to retrieve my gun and Luther's from the nightstand—if a silver knife works well, a silver bullet works even better—then I hurried to catch up.

We tossed our knives on the kitchen table. The kid reached for the door, but I shouldered in front of him. Luther was a rookie. Not that I was much better. I'd been on the job less than four months. Still I was the leader, which meant I got to go through the door first.

In the past, a seer—someone with the psychic ability to recognize a Nephilim in human form—worked with several DKs, or demon killers. However, that arrangement had gone to hell when the Nephilim infiltrated the federation and wiped out three-quarters of the group. Now the remaining members pretty much did whatever they could. Seers became DKs, DKs became seers, and everyone killed anything that got in their way.

"If Ruthie still isn't talking, then how do you know something's out there?" Luther asked reasonably.

I wasn't going to tell him that I'd had a dream visit from the dead. Not that such news would be a shock. Luther got visits from the dead every damn day. I just didn't want to share right now. Right now I wanted to know what was out there, and then I wanted to kill it.

I crept down the stairs, silent on bare feet. Luther was even quieter. He'd been born part lion. He couldn't help it.

A door led into the parking lot behind the building. I opened it but didn't step out. Instead I listened; Luther sniffed the air, then our eyes met, and together we nodded. Empty as far as we could tell.

"Don't shoot anyone I'll have to dispose of later," I cautioned, a variation of *don't shoot until you see the whites of their eyes*, or in federation-speak, *don't kill a human by mistake*.

Nephilim disintegrated into ashes when executed

in just the right way, eliminating impossible-to-answer questions and the annoying necessity of bloody body removal. People were another story.

Luther's only answer to my caution was a typical teenage sneer combined with an irritated eye roll. I didn't have to touch him to know his thoughts.

As if.

We stepped outside. No one shot us, not that a bullet would do much damage. Supernatural creatures, even those like Luther and me—more human than not—healed pretty much anything but one thing common only to them. Which meant the killer had to know what that single thing was.

I indicated with a tilt of my chin that Luther should go around the building to the left, while I went to the right. We'd meet back here, then together check out the dark gully at the far end of the lot where the Milwaukee River gurgled merrily past.

My gaze was pulled in that direction. There could be something hiding there—several somethings. Although the lack of a warning from Ruthie made me think that whatever I'd heard had probably been human. Not that a human couldn't be a huge pain in the ass. They usually were. And anyone sneaking around in the dark just had to be.

As I slid along the side of the building, back to the wall, I caught movement near the river and spun in that direction, gun outstretched. For an instant I could have sworn I saw something slinking low to the ground, a black, four-legged . . .

I blinked, and the shadow was just a shadow, perhaps a log with four branches, perhaps the reflection of a distant streetlight off the river. There were also foxes in Friedenburg, a few coyotes too and dogs galore. But that had looked like a wolf.

"Sawyer?" I whispered. My only answer was the sharp wail of the wind.

I lifted my face to the night, waiting for the air to cool my skin. Instead, humid heat pressed against me; there wasn't even a hint of a breeze. Not the wind then, but definitely a wail.

Shit. Luther.

I sprinted toward the front of the building. Though every instinct I had shrieked for me to skid around the corner, gun blazing, I paused and checked the street first. Charging into the open was a good way to get my head blown off. I didn't think even that would kill me, but it would take a helluva long time to heal. By then, Luther could be dead.

There was also the added concern of my possible pregnancy. I didn't *want* to be pregnant, could think of little I wanted less than that, except maybe slow, tortuous death by Nephilim, but what was, was. If I carried Sawyer's child, he, she, or it was all that was left of his magic, beyond what he'd given to me. I had to protect his gift. I'd promised.

Four AM on a Friday morning and Main Street was deserted. Friedenburg boasted its share of taverns—this was Wisconsin, after all—but they'd closed on time, and everyone had skittered home.

Not a sign of Luther. Hell.

"Kid?" I didn't want to shout, but pretty soon I would have to.

I hurried along the front of the knickknack shop, so intent on the next corner I nearly missed what rested in the shrouded alcove of the doorway. I'd already scooted past when what I'd seen registered. I stopped and took several steps backward.

On the top step sat a blanket-shrouded basket. Despite the lack of light in the alcove, and the lack of color to the blanket—either black or navy blue—I still detected movement beneath.

The back of my neck prickled, and I had to fight not to slap at an imaginary mosquito. I dared not touch that area unless I meant to. Sawyer wasn't the only one with tattoos, nor the ability to use them.

Had someone brought me a basket of poisonous snakes, tarantulas, or Gila monsters? Maybe something new like a land shark, a water-free jelly fish, a teenie-tiny vampire. Believe me, I'd seen stranger things.

The wail I'd heard before came again—from the basket. I leaned over and caught the end of the blanket with the barrel of my Glock, then lifted. What I saw inside made my heart beat faster than any vampire ever had. I let the blanket fall back into place and nearly tripped over my own feet in my haste to move away.

"Fan-damn-tastic," I muttered.

Someone had left me a baby.